THE JERUSALEM CREED

ERNEST DEMPSEY

D1191070

Prologue
Jerusalem
598 B.C.

Chaos raged through the streets of the ancient walled city. Women ran with tear-filled faces through the dusty alleyways and thoroughfares, hauling screaming children with them. Able-bodied men were issued swords to help defend the walls, some lucky enough to also receive a shield. Supplies were limited, so many were only equipped with farm tools as weapons. Even some of the older men were ushered to the walls to defend the city, despite their confused and bewildered complaints.

Their king, a noncommittal man by the name of Jehoiakim, had pledged allegiance to Babylon after the pagan king Nebuchadnezzar II had defeated Pharaoh Neco at the Battle of Carchemish several years before. When the Babylonian king failed in his attempt to invade Egypt, Jehoiakim had flip-flopped back to an alliance with Egypt once more.

The high priest, an old man named Tovar, had warned against making an allegiance with any pagan kings, telling Jehoiakim that God had forbidden any such alliance.

Now, their city and its people were paying the price for the king's disobedience. Nebuchadnezzar had laid siege to Jerusalem, the last stronghold of the Jewish nation. Now, after several weeks of strangling the city, his armies were raining down on the walls from the surrounding hills.

Tovar stared up into the late afternoon sky from his quarters at the temple. The blazing sun seemed to provide no warmth, even though the day itself was as hot as he could remember for that time of year. He knew the Babylonian tactics, perhaps better than Jehoiakim himself. This attack would be the first of several waves. They would withdraw to reinforce themselves, strengthen their numbers, and then return at first light when the Israelites were in a slumber of false security.

He felt the presence of someone on the balcony with him, and he turned around. His two assistants stood in the doorway with pained looks on their faces. Both were in their early twenties and outstanding scholars of the Scriptures. If their nation were to live on, one of them would make an excellent high priest someday. Tovar knew, however, that day would never come.

"Master," the one on the left, a dark-haired man with thick eyebrows named Lamesh, spoke first. "The Babylonians are attacking. We must get you to safety at once."

The other one had slightly lighter hair. With his youthful face, he still looked to be in his teens. He went by the name Daniel, and he had shown great promise as an adviser to the high priest, and the king. He'd been taken as a hostage during Nebuchadnezzar's first campaign against Israel, one that had ended much more peacefully than this one would. When he spoke, it was with a calm demeanor.

"Master Tovar, Lamesh is right. You must get to safety. The Babylonian king will not be as kind as he was seven years ago when he came here."

Lamesh nodded in agreement.

A woman screamed from down below. Tovar glanced over the balcony wall to the street and saw her spinning around in the mass hysteria, her dark-blue robes twirling in the dust. She was screaming a name, probably that of her child who had been lost in the madness.

He returned his gaze to the two young men. "My days have been long. I have seen more sadness and grief come to our people than I ever cared to. I fear it will only grow worse after this night passes."

"Which is why we must get you safe passage into the mountains. There is talk of a stronghold where you will be protected from the sword of Nebuchadnezzar." Lamesh meant well, but he was wrong. Any rebel outpost would soon be laid to waste, just like the capital.

"I have a far more important mission for the two of you," Tovar said, his eyes narrowing as he looked from one to the other. Their faces skewed with concern, but they listened respectfully. "Follow me."

With a quickness they'd never seen from their high priest, Tovar swooshed by the two of them, his white robes and ephod flowing dramatically behind him. The two followed, uncertain where he was taking them, but with the knowledge that they were not to question, merely obey, whatever his orders might be.

He led the way through the white stone halls, past enormous marble columns and flaming sconces that kept the interior illuminated. High above the hall, cedar timbers blocked out the sun, providing a perpetually cool temperature within the temple walls. Guards were stationed at various points of entry to protect the sacred center of worship.

They reached the end of the massive corridor and turned right, heading past the dormitories and behind the main courtyard toward Tovar's personal quarters. Even as his pace quickened, the high priest gazed upon the majesty of the temple's interior for fear that it might be the last time his eyes beheld it in this state. It had withstood hundreds of years of war, famine, pestilence, and political unrest. The work King Solomon had done would soon be gone. Nothing could stop that now.

Inside, the sounds of pandemonium had quieted; only a few muffled prayers could be heard coming from the priestly cells as they passed by open doorways.

At the end of the narrow passage, they reached a gilded door. Tovar twisted the circular latch and pushed it open. The two younger men stopped short of the threshold, daring not enter into the high priest's quarters. It was forbidden for anyone other than him to do so.

He motioned for them to follow, but they hesitated.

"We are not permitted, master," Daniel said respectfully.

Tovar, a few feet inside his suite, motioned again with his hand. His face expressed kindness but firm resolve. "Our laws will soon be at an end, young Daniel. Breaking them now will bring you no punishment from me, or our feeble king."

Lamesh and Daniel looked at each other, still uncertain whether or not they should obey their master's order, then reluctantly stepped into the suite.

The room was much larger than the other dormitory cells in the temple. Vibrant blue curtains hung next to the windows. A cedar bureau sat against the wall near a closet, the home to Tovar's priestly vestments. A much smaller chest, made from pure gold, sat against the wall on the other side of the bed. Prayers were engraved on it in Hebrew. Atop the lid was a golden sculpture of an angel. Once again, the sounds of panic drifted to their ears from outside. In spite of the lavish apartment, the bed was simple: made from beech wood and covered with plain white sheets and pillows.

Tovar moved swiftly over to the golden chest and removed the lid, carefully placing it on the floor next to two of the claw-shaped legs. The two younger men watched with wide eyes as Tovar removed an item they had seen many times on the chest of the priest's ephod. He reverently set the object on the foot of the bed and returned to the chest, hurriedly grabbing a small goatskin bag cinched at the top with a leather strap. He set it down next to the other object and put the lid back on the chest.

"Master, what are you doing? It isn't time for you to go into the Holy Place?" His associate echoed Daniel's look of concern.

"I am not going there, Daniel." He stood erect and faced his apprentices. "My friends, my loyal servants, I have a final request for you that is of the highest order." The two listened closely, taking in every word as if each was the last drop of water in a drying desert oasis. "Tomorrow morning, Nebuchadnezzar will take this city. When he does, the first two places he will send his men will be the palace and the temple. They will steal and loot everything they perceive to be of value. Daniel, you have spent the last seven years in the service of the Babylonian king. You know this to be true."

Daniel nodded but said nothing. He had become a trusted adviser to Nebuchadnezzar, though his true loyalty would always be to the one true God of Israel. It was why he'd requested that the king allow him one last visit to the temple before the second attack came in the morning. He too knew that the first attack on the city walls was merely preliminary. The carnage that would come with the morning would be swift and merciless.

Tovar looked down at the two objects on the bed. "We must not allow these to be taken by the Babylonians. If they were to fall into the hands of our enemies, I fear that Israel will never be able to rise from the ashes. Nebuchadnezzar would be unstoppable, from the far reaches of Asia all the way to the foreign lands to the west. No army could ever stand in his way."

His grim words hung in the air and reverberated off the marble walls.

He turned his attention to the older apprentice. "Lamesh, you have served me since you were just a boy. You have always done as I asked and have been loyal to the one true God of our people. What I ask you to do now, both of you, could get you killed. But I must ask: Will you serve your high priest and your God one last time?"

Lamesh nodded without reservation. Daniel did as well.

Tovar swallowed hard. "I wish there was another way. I truly do. If I were younger..." His thought trailed off. "Lamesh, you must take the Hoshen with you. Wear it under your robe. Take it far from here to a place not yet touched by the empire of Babylon. I have the fastest horse from the royal stable ready for you. Go through the southern gate where Nebuchadnezzar's presence is weakest. Ride hard through the night, keep to the tree lines, and you should be safe."

"Daniel, the king will be expecting you to return from your diplomatic mission. Carry this bag with you. It is imperative that Nebuchadnezzar never knows its contents. If the stones in that bag are ever reunited with the breastplate by the forces of evil, all will be lost."

Daniel's gaze lowered to the pouch that the high priest had placed in his hand. There was barely any weight to it, but he knew that inside, the fate of the nation, perhaps the world, rested in the balance. He looked back up at Tovar, his eyes full of question. "Master, keeping it so close to the king could be very risky. Should I not ride far to the west and hide it there?"

Tovar's eyes filled with peaceful determination. His kind expression instantly relaxed the two younger men. "Nebuchadnezzar knows about the Hoshen, and the two stones. You both must understand something, something only the high priest knows."

They waited breathlessly to hear what their rabbi had to say.

The old man took a breath and let his eyes wander around the room as if trying to find the right words. "These relics are not the first of their kind. The Babylonians have their own. They call them the Tablets of Destiny. Nebuchadnezzar's tablets, however, are useless. His pagan priests tell him things as if the tablets are answering their questions, but the king is no fool. He knows that there is no power in those false relics. But he has heard of these." Tovar pointed at the breastplate and then the pouch in Daniel's hand. "Nebuchadnezzar knows that our relics are blessed by the one true God, and that with these there is very real power. After he sacks the temple and finds that these holy objects have been removed, he will search far and wide for them. So we must hide them in the only places he will never look. One of those places is right in front of him, in the pockets of someone he trusts."

It suddenly made sense to the two assistants. The plan was perfect, and Tovar was right. The king would never in a million years think to check the people in his own court.

"What about me, master?" Lamesh asked. "Where should I go?"

The old priest put his hand out and pressed his palm into the young man's shoulder. He stared into his apprentice's eyes with calm, blue orbs. Something about Tovar's eyes was soothing, reassuring. "Your task is equally as dangerous, though should you succeed, your danger will come to an end as soon as you are relieved of the Hoshen."

"Relieved?"

Tovar nodded. There was something in his expression that almost seemed mischievous. "There is a new religion in the lands to the east. Rather than serving gods and idols, they look to purify themselves through deep, inner reflection. By doing this, they believe they can attain heaven, or a place they call Nirvana. They are a peaceful religion, and their priests and monks believe in the preservation of life. You are to take the Hoshen to a monastery in the east. It stands where the impassible mountains meet a sacred valley."

He reached into his robes and withdrew a scroll. It was tiny, only six inches in length and maybe one in diameter.

"This will tell you how to get there," the high priest said as he placed it in Lamesh's hand.

The young man looked down at it and back up into Tovar's face. "These priests to the east, they will protect it?"

"Yes, my Son. They have a deep respect for all religions and the things those religions hold sacred. They will keep the Hoshen hidden, and safe. To the outside world, it will be lost for thousands of years."

Lamesh nodded. "Then I will ride swiftly."

Tovar grinned approvingly, but his satisfaction only lasted a few seconds. A new sound flooded in with the chaotic noises from the streets and wall. A low, heavy thud came every five or so seconds. All three of the men knew what it was. The Babylonians were hammering the gate with their battering ram.

"It will not break today," Tovar said, more hopeful than certain. "But you must hurry. When night falls, you both leave."

Two hours went by, and the high priest was proved correct. The gate did not break that day. As predicted, the Babylonians retired to their tents for the night. Sounds of jubilation rose up from the walled city like a plume of joyful smoke into the heavens. As darkness set in, one star after another appeared in the endless black sky until there were millions of them twinkling overhead. A few fires burned in their pots along the wall's ramparts, the orange flames recklessly licking the night air in the occasional cool breeze.

Outside the royal stables, Lamesh and Daniel readied the horses Tovar had arranged. The ponies were small and milk chocolate brown in color, likely a breed that came from the eastern lands. They slung saddles over the animals' backs and fastened the buckles. They both knew it was highly unlikely that they would ever meet again. For the first few minutes, neither said anything. Finally, having packed his satchel and made sure the pouch in his pocket was secure, Daniel spoke up.

"Ride safely," he said, putting his hand out to the other.

Lamesh turned around and clasped Daniel's forearm. "You as well, Brother. I do not envy your task. You must always keep vigilant. In a few days, my burden will be lifted."

Daniel smiled and looked down at the ground. "I will survive it. The king has found favor in me and my friends. It can only be the will of God that makes it so and preserves us in the enemy's house."

"I pray it is His will that we survive the night," Lamesh grinned. His eyes drifted off to nowhere in particular.

"Well," Daniel said. "It's time. Good luck."

He stepped into the strap on the horse's left flank and swung his leg over the saddle.

Lamesh copied the maneuver. "You as well." He took off at a slow trot and picked up speed, staying just below a gallop as he weaved his way through the vacant streets. Daniel clicked his tongue, and the horse turned left and headed in the opposite direction.

Thirty minutes later, Daniel left the walls of Jerusalem and let his mount run a little more freely as the animal sprinted into the valley and up to the ensuing hills. The wind smelled good as it washed over him, whipping his robes, belt, and headpiece. He wondered how Lamesh was faring. He'd already be beyond the city walls as well, streaking toward the east and whatever dangers it posed.

He slowed his horse as he approached the Babylonian front lines. Even though he was an emissary of the king and one of his most trusted advisors, Daniel knew that he wasn't a favorite among many. Some of the pagan king's priests detested Daniel because he'd been able to interpret the king's dreams when the others could not. For a Jew to rise to power so quickly in Babylon was something that caused quite a stir. That stir could easily spill to a well-bribed archer on the front lines. It would be easy to say that he fired his arrow

Daniel drew in a slow breath and after a few seconds of thought, shook his head. "The king will never surrender, your excellence. You will have to break through the gates first. When you do, he will crumble in your hands like a dry piece of dirt. Then you will have peace in the land of Israel."

The king nodded, appreciative of the information. He waved for the women to leave the room, as well as his interior guards. The latter glanced at each other questioningly, wondering if they should leave their king alone or not. "Go," he ordered more firmly, wiping away any doubts they had.

When the last person left the room, Daniel stood alone with the most powerful man in the world. Nebuchadnezzar stood up and towered over the younger man. In spite of his physical prowess, it was Daniel's presence that dominated the tent.

"Belteshazzar, were you able to see anything of interest in the temple?" The king put his hand on Daniel's shoulder, staring through his eyes.

"There are many treasures and holy items in the temple, my liege. As your friend, I advise you not to take things that have been consecrated by the one true God. However, I understand you feel that you should because of Jehoiakim's betrayal."

Nebuchadnezzar considered the words carefully. "I am sorry, my young friend, but your people must be punished. If other people see I am weak with yours, there will be uprisings everywhere. My justice will be swiftly dealt."

Daniel could tell that wasn't the only thing the king wanted to know. He waited for a moment, but the king obviously expected his adviser to give up the goods.

"There is no sign of the objects you seek, sire. They have been removed from the temple. You will not find the stones or the breastplate in Jerusalem." Daniel didn't lie, but he didn't exactly tell the whole truth.

Nebuchadnezzar studied his eyes for what seemed like ten minutes. When he spoke, there was malice in his tone. It was sterile, lifeless.

"We will keep looking. If your high priest tried to hide them, it will only be a matter of time. For now, return to your tent. We attack the city at dawn. You will watch the battle from the hill with me."

Daniel blinked rapidly and then nodded. The king had no idea that within a few inches, and behind a garb of linen, was half of the treasure he so desperately sought. "Yes, your majesty."

1
Atlanta, Georgia

Sean's eyes wearily opened like slow, automatic window blinds; the room filled with blurry points of light. As his vision began to steady, he saw that he was lying on the tile of his kitchen floor. Most of the lights were out except for a row of three hanging bulbs in silver, conical casing over the kitchen island.

The back of his head throbbed like a slow-pounding heartbeat. He winced as he reached for the back of his skull to check the source of the pain. Underneath his thick blond hair, his head was significantly swollen, but when he examined his fingers, he was relieved to find no blood.

He tried to push himself up from the floor, but his body was overwhelmed with fatigue, and his muscles protested in response to his mind's command. He slumped back down on the floor for a moment. It almost felt comfortable, if it weren't for the cold surface against his strong cheek.

His brain struggled in the fog. What happened? Why was he on the floor? Why was he so tired? And why did his head hurt?

He directed his eyes to the nearby island. Two wooden stools, stained a dark brown, were tucked in under the countertop. The lights above it dangled like fireflies whose tails remained on. He must have passed out and hit his head. That had to be it. But what would have caused him to faint? And why would he feel so absolutely exhausted?

Sean pushed his body up again and over onto his side. He stayed in good shape, working out several times a week. Most recently he'd taken up interval training and working out in short circuits in the weight room. Now, though, his body felt like it had a skyscraper strapped to it. The room spun around, but he grabbed ahold of one of the stool's lower rungs and kept his balance. Somehow, he managed to struggle up to a sitting position and leaned against the side of the kitchen island. He drew in long, deep breaths as if he'd just sprinted a hundred yards. As he sucked in air through his lungs, he smelled something foreign. The years of training and work for the government took root again, as they'd done for him time and time again, instantly heightening his senses.

He looked around and saw that the room had been splattered with an orange gelatinous substance. His eyes wandered across the space until they came to a stop on a little cardboard box sitting against the wall. It was smaller than a box for a pair of earrings, a tiny wire protruding from the top.

His mind snapped to full alert. It was a bomb.

He grabbed the lip of the island countertop and pulled himself up, his legs wobbling like a newborn foal. They quickly regained their balance and strength. Instinctively, he made a move toward the box, but a little red LED light on the top flashed once. In the next instant, the bomb erupted in a bright, yellow-and-orange flash. Sean jumped back, expecting a bigger concussion blast or some shrapnel. He quickly discovered that the device was not meant for that. It was an incendiary explosive designed to ignite combustibles.

The bomb's flames touched the orange goo, and fire ripped through the entire kitchen in mere seconds, encircling Sean and quickly spreading toward him. Black and gray smoke swirled around, rising into the air to gather at the ceiling before rapidly sinking downward; Sean's kitchen was now more like an upside-down bathtub filling with dirty water.

He was standing in the middle of an eight-foot circle of burning death. If he tried to jump through, he would land in the middle of the flames, the fire so intense that his clothes and skin would be fried instantly.

He shielded his face from the searing heat for a second and thought hard. Suddenly, Sean remembered what he kept stored inside the kitchen island. Salvation was right behind him, but the doors were on the other side near the sink, and that area was already engulfed.

The flames crept closer, encroaching into his circle of safety every second. He grabbed one of the stools and swung it back. He brought it forward, smashing the seat into the back of the island cabinet. The stool's solid construction held, but the back of the island gave way a little. Sean repeated the move, this time almost completely removing the cabinet's back panel. Another quick strike knocked it free, and he could see the object he needed just inside.

He reached in, grabbed the red fire extinguisher with his right hand, and yanked it out. That end of the kitchen opened up into a three-sided eating space, with a six-person dark wooden dining table. There was no way Sean could make it back through the house and out one of the doors. From his vantage point, he could see the fire had already spread into the next room and was probably on a rampage through his entire home.

His only chance for escape was out one of the windows. Aiming the nozzle at the flames closest to the dining room windows, he pulled the safety pin and squeezed the clasp trigger.

A cloudy white jet burst out of the extinguisher. Sean moved the nozzle side to side to clear a path wide enough for him to walk through without getting burned. He kept low to keep from inhaling the smoke and to make sure he smothered the flames close to the floor. The napalm-like substance sizzled as he muted the heat source, and he pressed to the back of the kitchen across the now-blackened tile. Behind him, the path he'd cleared started to reignite. He would have only seconds before he was standing in a lake of fire.

A foot from the closest window, the extinguisher gave the last of its life-saving cloud. Sean took the metal cylinder and smashed through the window that was framed on both sides by white-hot flames. The wood and glass gave way, already weakened by the heat, and shattered outward into the tall junipers that surrounded the home. He leaped through the opening, still jagged with broken glass and splintered wood.

A piece of stray glass cut the side of his forearm as he flew through, but he landed safely in the folds of the evergreen bush. His lungs flooded with the fresh evening air. The clean oxygen hit his lungs, and he coughed, his body realizing how much smoke he'd actually inhaled. He made himself get up again and move as quickly as possible away from the inferno. His legs started moving on their own, taking him down and around to the lower side of the house where the garage was located almost underground. He stopped at the far left of six garage doors where a keypad was imbedded in the wall. He keyed in four numbers and hit enter.

He snatched a set of keys from a board containing more than twenty key chains, all with different keys attached. He grabbed a helmet from a workbench and strapped it on as he hurried over to his Triumph T100 special edition cafe racer. He had faster bikes, but top-end speed wasn't what he was looking for. The current situation required a little more maneuverability and agility on the tight streets of North Atlanta.

Sean hopped on the bike and slid the key into the oddly placed ignition near the front forks. He turned the switch and hit the button that started up the throaty motor. His right hand twisted the throttle as he released the clutch, and the bike lurched forward, shooting out of the garage. He wound his way down the path in the back that led to the secret entrance to his property. In a side mirror, he saw the flames lashing out of his first- and second-story windows. The dark smoke looked paler against the hazy black backdrop of the sky.

He reached the rear gate and hit the remote he'd affixed to the handlebars of all his bikes. The gate slowly rolled open, allowing him to keep rolling through it and out onto the street beyond. He stopped by the sidewalk as the gate automatically closed. Tall shrubs and hedges rolled on a track with the gate, effectively concealing it as an entryway and giving it the appearance of just another piece of the fence surrounding the property.

Sean gazed up at the top of the hill. His home continued to billow smoke into the air. The familiar sound of sirens blared in the distance. His alarm would have gone off, alerting the local authorities of the blaze. By the time they arrived, there would be nothing left. Truthfully, he didn't keep many sentimental things in his home except for his motorcycles. A small piece of him said a silent prayer that the bikes would be okay. But he didn't linger on that thought.

His mind shifted to the aching bump on the back of his head. Someone had drugged him. The memory started coming back to him. There'd been a knock at the door, which was strange because he hadn't rung anyone through the main gate. When he looked through the window to see who was there, secretly hoping Adriana had surprised him with a visit, someone had wrapped their arms around him from behind and shoved a rag into his face.

Chloroform was old school. It was rare to even see the stuff anymore, but sometimes the best techniques were the old ones. In the struggle, something or someone had hit him in the back of the head. He remembered trying to fight off the faceless arms and hands when everything suddenly went black.

He wasn't entirely sure, but it seemed as if he'd heard voices speaking Arabic. Or was it Farsi?

Sean winced as the pulsing pain continued through his skull.

Arabic? Why would they be speaking Arabic?

He processed the question and twisted the throttle again. Images of what had transpired in his house flooded Sean's mind. His brain recalled one particular image from his fight against the unseen foe. On the inside of the attacker's wrist was a tattoo, a triangle with a dot in the center. He'd never seen one like it before. If he ever saw it again, his plan was to make sure the person the wrist was attached to didn't survive the second encounter.

He steered the motorcycle around a row of cars and at the next stoplight made a left, driving away from his burning home. There was nothing he could do; it would be destroyed. Sean wasn't concerned about that. He was more worried about what the men who'd come after him were going to do next. The bike cut around the protruding manhole covers and sped down the road toward Virginia Highlands.

There could be only one explanation for the sudden attempt on his life. Someone knew about the project he and Tommy were about to undertake. And if whoever *they* were, were willing to kill him, there was no doubt in Sean's mind that they would go after Tommy next. He hammered down on the accelerator and zoomed through a yellow light just as it turned red. The wind whooshed through the cracks of his full-face helmet, causing a whistling sound he'd grown accustomed to over the years.

If he made most of the lights, his friend's home was less than twenty minutes away. Sean wasn't sure whether or not that would be enough time, but he had to try. Better to be wrong and early than right and late.

2
Virginia Highlands, Atlanta

Sean's Triumph screamed the last mile down the quiet borough street. He was fortunate most of the bar hoppers had settled on a location, leaving the roads relatively vacant of pedestrian traffic. The last thing he wanted was to run over someone crossing the road. Fortunately, he'd not had any close encounters and had been free to speed around the slower vehicular traffic as needed. The one police officer he'd seen had been at a stoplight, which luckily Sean had been forced to obey due to the line of three cars in front of him.

He whipped the black British motorcycle into Tommy's driveway just as he saw a familiar yellowish flash from the living room. Keeping his helmet on, he rushed to the front door and tried the doorknob. The door swung open easily. Sean glanced at the doorframe where it had been splintered from forced entry. He'd run out of his house so quickly to get to his motorcycle, Sean hadn't even considered grabbing one of his spare firearms from the garage. He kept a small arsenal of weapons in a locker there. Now, as he stepped into Tommy's house, he wished he'd thought of it.

No time for regrets now. The tiny incendiary device ignited the putrid gel, and Tommy's living room sparked into flames in an instant. His eyes scanned the room, trying to find his friend. He was nowhere to be seen. Quickly, Sean moved into the hallway that joined with the kitchen and a small breakfast nook in the back. Tommy wasn't there either. He turned and hurried down the hall to the master bedroom as the flames ran after him along walls, doused in the orange substance.

He kicked open the door and slammed it behind to cut off the fire. That would only keep the blaze at bay for so long. Sean looked around the room and found his friend lying prostrate on the bed off to the side near a window.

"Tommy!" Sean shouted at his friend as he stepped closer to the bed. He could see the same handiwork on the back of his skull that he'd been dealt. A little patch of dried blood mixed with his friend's curly, dark hair.

Sean reached down and shook his friend. "Tommy. Wake up. We gotta get out of here."

Tommy grumbled something incoherent, still clearly unconscious from the drugs and the blow to the head. Picture frames cracked in the hall just outside the door, and Sean knew he only had seconds to get the two of them out.

His eyes surveyed the room, and he saw that the walls and hardwood floor had been doused in the flammable gel.

"Not good," he said to himself.

He couldn't wait any longer. Sean moved back over to the bed and kneeled down. Grabbing one of Tommy's arms and the back of his corresponding leg, he hefted his friend's limp, two-hundred-pound frame over his shoulders. Then he remembered the hallway would be a tunnel of flaming doom.

"Man, you are going to need to drop a few pounds," Sean grunted, knowing his friend couldn't hear him.

He set Tommy back down for a second and grabbed a baseball bat that was sitting on the floor, propped up against the side of a chestnut dresser. Sean gripped it with both hands and moved to the backyard-facing window. He bashed the glass, shattering it into hundreds of pieces and sending it flying outward. He continued to chop away at the window frame until there was nothing left that resembled what it had once been. Thankfully, the window sill was only two feet from the floor, so heaving his friend through the opening wouldn't be as bad as if it were a four-foot-high window.

Something exploded in another part of the house, shaking the entire structure violently. Sean figured it was a gas line, but he had no intention of investigating or sticking around. He grabbed Tommy again and hefted him over his shoulders. His friend was bigger than he was, but he managed. All those nights he spent at the gym were worth their weight in gold at the moment. He staggered over to the window and lowered his friend out, feet first. Holding Tommy around the neck and pinning him to the exterior wall so he wouldn't fall down, Sean straddled the window sill and climbed down.

Once his feet touched the thick pine mulch below the window, he grabbed Tommy under the armpits and dragged him out into the yard, all the way to the back fence to get as far from the house as possible.

As he backed away, Sean could see the scope of the damage being done to the home.

Enormous flames roiled out of the windows. The outer edges of the roof were entirely consumed. Black smoke, like he'd seen at his own home, poured into the night air. Even two hundred feet away, Sean could still feel the searing heat of the flames.

There was another explosion, and the bedroom they'd just escaped erupted in flames. The door must have given way. Once it did, the free oxygen inside was sucked into the fire and gave it an extra breath of life. In a matter of seconds, the blaze flared out of the window Sean had broken.

Once again, the sound of sirens in the distance filled the air. Twice in one night. Any doubts that lingered in Sean's mind about what was going on were completely eradicated. Someone was trying to kill them. But why?

His thoughts raced as he smacked his friend gently on the cheek. Tommy started to rouse and jerked at the sudden contact to his face. His eyelids lifted like upward flowing molasses, and he rolled around uncontrollably for a few seconds. The words coming out of his mouth were incoherent at first.

"Sean?" The name came out loud and blubbery, like a drunk who'd fallen off a barstool and smashed his lip.

"I'm here, buddy. Everything's okay." He held his friend still for a minute until Tommy's eyes started to focus.

"What's going on? Is that my house?"

Sean hesitated to answer, but he was going to find out eventually. "Yeah."

"What the...?" Tommy grabbed the back of his head, reminding Sean of the thumping pain still pounding away at his own skull.

First order of business would be locating some ibuprofen. Sean leaned back against the wooden fence and eased his head against it, taking in a few slow breaths.

"Is my house on fire?" Tommy asked, staring in drug-fogged confusion.

Sean moved his head up and down in an overly deliberate nodding motion.

"Why is my house on fire?"

"If it makes you feel better, so is mine." He tilted his head and stared over his shoulder at his friend.

"How did we end up in the backyard?"

"I pulled you out of your house."

Tommy's eyebrows lowered. That didn't seem right. "I'm way bigger than you. How'd you get me out?"

"Leverage."

He seemed to accept the answer and tried to stand up. The fire trucks were getting closer. Tommy wavered for a moment and then plopped back down onto the ground. Sean used the fence to help him get on his feet and then offered a hand to his friend, who still struggled to find his balance.

Sean braced him and started walking around the side of house that had the most clearance between the burning walls and the fenced perimeter.

"Where are we going?" Tommy asked. "I think I want to sit down again."

"Nope. We need to get out of here."

More bewilderment washed over Tommy's face. "What do you mean? Shouldn't we wait until the police arrive?"

Ordinarily, that would be the correct thing to do. In this case, however, Sean had a bad feeling. Something in his gut said they needed to disappear, and fast. The two staggered into the front yard, and Sean was relieved to see his motorcycle virtually untouched by the blaze. He'd purposely left it far enough from the house just in case something like this happened.

"I'm not riding on the back of that," Tommy blurted out.

"Well, you're in no condition to drive it. It's the only way right now."

Tommy's head went back and forth in a dramatic, drunken motion. "Where are we going? And why not wait for the firemen and the cops?"

"We need to get to the IAA building. I'm not sure, but I have a feeling that whoever just tried to kill us might come back. It would be better for us to not stick around."

Tommy seemed to accept the answer and swung his leg over the back of the bike. The only problem was he was facing the wrong direction.

"Other way, buddy," Sean said, still helping him.

When he got his friend turned around, Sean hopped on and slid the helmet over his short, messy blond hair. The key was still in the ignition, so all he had to do was hit the button. The Triumph revved to life.

"Do I get a helmet too?" Tommy asked, his speech still fairly slurry.

"Not this time. But I'll keep one around for you in the future. Just hold on tight."

Sean sped out of the driveway and down the street just as a giant red fire truck appeared over the hill. A few seconds later, they passed a police car on the same trajectory.

Tommy and Sean had been the best of friends since early on in life. They attended the same high school and kept in contact through college. When Tommy's parents died suddenly, the Wyatts took him in for a short time. While he appreciated their help, Tommy's mind and heart were torn apart. He struggled with his emotions for years, even through college. Things changed when he disappeared for a year. He'd told Sean not to try and find him, that it was something he needed to do, something about finding his life's purpose.

One night, while sitting at a bar in Istanbul, Tommy realized what it was he needed to do. Two days later, he was back in the United States working on the idea that would become his legacy, an agency that served the world by recovering ancient artifacts.

Somewhere in that year abroad, Tommy learned how to fight, though Sean never asked him about it. He'd become a brawler, able to defend himself in a pinch, though still clumsy at times. The two had found themselves back-to-back in more than a few situations. Now, awkwardly, they were back to front.

Sean chuckled at the irony.

The cool evening air sprayed over their skin as Sean steered the motorcycle down the tree-lined streets. One of the things he liked most about Atlanta was how there were still so many trees in spite of the massive city's population. Tourists had commented on how different it was from cities in the West where all you could see were vast metropolitan areas filled with hundreds of miles of streetlights and homes stretching in all directions. Atlanta wasn't like that because of the hilly terrain and the fact that the populace preferred to keep nature a more prominent feature.

He thought about this as he twisted the accelerator and sped out of the highlands and into midtown. Posh coffee shops, boutiques, sushi bars, and trendy hangouts blurred by. Sean pointed the single headlight at downtown. His friend kept his arms around him, more tightly than Sean would have liked, but he'd rather Tommy be safe than sorry, especially given his condition.

At the next intersection, the light went yellow and then red, forcing Sean to hit the brakes and bring the bike to a stop. The light was at a four-way stop. A late night cafe was open on the corner a few feet from them. Three gorgeous young women, probably in their midtwenties, stared at the awkward couple on the motorcycle. Tommy, without a helmet, looked especially uncomfortable.

He smiled and nodded at the girls. "It's not what it looks like," he tried to explain. The few minutes of fresh air on the bike had seemingly sobered him up. That or being seen riding bitch on the back of a bike with another guy.

Sean twisted his head to the girls, who were giggling in short summer dresses as they sipped their drinks. He flipped up his visor and said, "Yes, it is." He patted Tommy on the leg to emphasize the statement.

Just then the light turned green, and he hit the gas again before Tommy could try to defend himself.

"Thanks, man!" he shouted over the swooshing wind and throaty engine. "Now they think I'm into dudes."

"So? You're never going to see them again."

"You don't know that! I could bump into them somewhere."

Sean laughed and spoke over his shoulder. "Yeah but now if you go back to that place you'll look like a creep."

"Yeah, thanks for that. I love that cafe."

Sean yelled over the noise. "You're too old for them anyway."

He weaved around a slow-moving minivan and into the left lane that had just opened up as the road widened on its way into downtown.

"Too old? Those girls were, at most, ten years younger."

Sean thought about it for a second. "Yeah, I guess you're right. My fault. If I see them again, I'll be sure to tell them you and I are no longer an item." He squeezed the throttle harder, increasing their speed, zooming past the Jimmy Carter Center.

3
Dubai, UAE

A bluish-gray haze hung in the room. Through the fog of cigar smoke, the sandstone walls and columns appeared to be something out of a thousand-year-old palace. It may as well have been. To say that the mansion's owner was wealthy would be a vast understatement, like saying the surface of the sun was warm. Mamoud Al Najaar puffed on his cigar as he watched the half-naked women dance in front of him. The doors to the balcony behind them were wide open, and the Persian Gulf beyond provided a unique and expensive backdrop to the view before him.

Another scantily clad woman fanned him as he watched the show. He occasionally took a sip of tea from the silver cup on a table to the right of his Corinthian leather chair. Six feet away, his friend and bodyguard, Sharouf Al Nasir, watched with restrained pleasure.

Mamoud smiled a toothy, perverse grin as the women moved in synchronized rhythm. Their hands flashed back and forth, gripping red silken scarves. The thin, lightweight fabric trailed around behind their bodies, occasionally grazing their bronzed skin.

He'd grown up in the deserts of Syria, a child of privilege and high tastes. When his father sold their familial lands to the oil companies, the money ensured their lifestyle would be one the sheikhs of old would have envied, and without all the worries of drilling, refining, and exporting.

When his father died, Mamoud inherited everything. He was one of two children, but his younger brother had died years before. Mamoud hadn't understood why his brother joined the insurgency in Iraq, or why he had thought it a good idea to go head to head with an entire platoon of American soldiers.

As children, their father had taught them that the only way to defeat the West was to learn everything they could about Western culture: its people, its way of life, and its weaknesses.

He'd been trained to fight by some of the best martial arts teachers money could buy and still kept up an intense sparring regimen with his bodyguards to make sure he never got rusty. His expertise in Jujitsu and Isshin-Ryu was unrivaled throughout the Middle East.

Mamoud went to school in Great Britain. Not just any school either. He attended the most expensive private prep schools and university. He was steeped in the ways of capitalism, freedom of thought and expression, and in their religious and atheistic learning. The more he learned about those things, the greater his hatred of the West grew. His father had encouraged him to bide his time, to be patient. When the moment was right, he would know what to do with the resources he'd been given.

Know thine enemy. The quote went through his mind even as he watched the women entangle each other with the scarves, drawing each other seductively close before releasing and going to opposite corners of the room in their constant expand-and-contract dance.

Life, Mamoud had learned, was a dance much like the one his girls were performing. It was a lesson, like so many others, that he'd learned from his father. There was a rhythm, a beat, a melody, a moment of intensity, and then a release.

When the music stopped, he looked at the two girls as they panted for breath, their stomachs and chests heaving for air. They never stopped smiling in spite of the arduous workout. They knew better than to displease Mamoud. His reputation for being cruel and exacting had stretched across the sprawling city of Dubai. No one crossed him. And if there was such a foolish, ignorant soul, their mistake would be short lived, but their pain would not.

He stood up from his throne-like chair and began clapping slowly, the cigar hanging from his lips just past the V-shaped soul patch of hair above his finely trimmed beard. Dark eyes underneath waves of thick black hair pierced through the girls as he stepped deliberately toward them.

"Impressive, ladies," he said, beckoning them closer to him with open arms.

The girls obeyed and slid their hands around his back in a sultry fashion, snaking them under his armpits and around his waist.

"I want you both to go wait for me in the master bedroom," he said pointedly, taking out the cigar and pointing toward a lavishly decorated master bedroom through a set of ornately carved double doors. The bedroom was off to the right and featured a white marble balcony providing almost the exact same view as the sitting room. "Feel free to lose those clothes, but keep the scarves. We may need those."

While Mamoud had been indoctrinated in the conservative, fundamentalist ways of Islam, there were a few things he didn't take to heart. One was the way that many believed women should remain covered. Another was the principle of chastity. Despite his hatred for the West, these two things seeped their way into his life without much protest on his part. The carnal temptations, he found, were the best. No one dared call him a hypocrite.

The girls giggled, bowed, and hurried off to the bedroom.

When they'd bounded beyond the threshold and started removing the few pieces of clothing they had left, Mamoud motioned for one of his guards to close the doors, apparently wanting secrecy.

He called his right hand, Sharouf, over with a flick of four fingers.

Sharouf obeyed and was by his boss's side in an instant.

Mamoud put his arm around the man's shoulders and walked with him out to the balcony. When they reached the white stone, their eyes narrowed, trying to squint out the bright afternoon sun.

Four stories below, several other members of Mamoud's harem lay topless by the pool. It was what he required of them. His property was closely guarded by an array of palm trees and thick brush, all bounded by a high sandstone wall that stretched to the edge of the beach. The only way in or out of the white sands was through a gate that always remained locked.

The two men stared out at the scene beyond the walls. Turquoise water was intermittently interrupted by the soft, rolling waves of white foam. To the right and to the left of the private property, tourists and Dubai's elite frolicked in the sea while others lounged in mesh beach chairs.

Mamoud wasn't thinking about any of that, though. His mind was thousands of miles away. "Is it done?"

"My men said that Wyatt and his friend are both dead."

"How?"

Sharouf never turned to face his employer, even though Mamoud tilted his head slightly to look indirectly at him. "They were burned to death. My men used a substance that's similar to napalm but far more difficult to put out. It also spreads twice as fast. The targets were drugged, and their homes set on fire around them. All that is left are charred, unrecognizable corpses."

Mamoud drew in a long breath and then put the cigar back between his lips. He took a few puffs, letting the smoke escape his mouth and drift away, disappearing instantly in the sea breeze.

"You are certain?"

"You doubt my methods?"

Mamoud was taken aback by the insolence, but he quickly regained his composure, knowing his man meant nothing by it. He was right to say it. Sharouf's methods were good. Better than good.

"No, my old friend. I simply seek to remove all doubt."

Sharouf turned his head and peered through Mamoud's soul. "They are dead. I am sure of it. But my men will linger in the area until the local authorities confirm the deaths. If that is what you wish."

Mamoud acknowledged it with a dramatic nod. "That will be fine, yes. And I do not doubt your methods." He felt compelled to reiterate his previous statement. "You are the best at what you do, as are your men. That's why I pay them."

He put his hands on the white stone rail and leaned forward, staring out at the scenery. A few miles away, the enormous sail-shaped Burj Al Arab sat precariously in the bay, a strange and miraculous structure that had been built on man-made land. The financial investment that went into creating the opulent hotel had been staggering. It was the first of its kind, a hotel built in the water where no land previously existed. Now, tourists and wealthy visitors flocked to the place. The cheapest room available cost thousands of dollars a night. At one point, the helicopter pad had been converted into a tennis court as a ridiculous publicity stunt. Roger Federer and Andre Agassi had been brought in to play a friendly little game atop the dangerously high area.

Off toward the center of town, the massive Burj Khalifa building towered above all the other tall skyscrapers in the city. It loomed against the skyline like a giant, making all others bow before it.

"Is there anyone else who might know about the artifact?" Mamoud returned his attention to the conversation.

"From what we can tell, Wyatt and his friend were the only other two who knew about it. We haven't seen any correspondence relating to information on your operation."

"Good." He pulled in another puff of smoke from the cigar and released it between his lips. "Has he made any progress?"

Mamoud didn't need to mention the man by name. Sharouf knew exactly whom he was talking about. The man was the reason all of this had been set in motion, and was why they were talking on the balcony overlooking the Persian Gulf right now.

"He is working day and night to decipher the tablet. He claims that it could take weeks to unlock the meaning of the symbols."

"Weeks?"

For the first time in their conversation, Sharouf appeared apologetic. "It is a very complex code. The man says it could take a few weeks, but the truth is that he may never be able to solve it. Whoever designed that tablet didn't want *anyone* solving it."

"If they didn't want anyone to solve it, why leave it there to begin with?" Mamoud shot down the theory immediately. He shook his head as he spoke. "No, this tablet is the key to victory for us. It is the lone clue to finding the

Jews' secret. Once we have it in our possession, no one will be able to stop us."

Sharouf considered his employer's words. In his heart, he hoped the man was right. Doubts lingered, though. "He believes it is what you think it is?"

"He is one of the foremost experts on the subject. His life has been dedicated to research and study in hopes of finding those two artifacts. It is what led him to the grave he was excavating when he discovered the tablet. He has set things in motion. Now we must coerce him to continue for our benefit."

"And if he delays or outright refuses?"

"He won't. He's too afraid of death."

"But what if he does?"

"Then convince him."

Sharouf gazed into Mamoud's eyes, studying the cold, merciless orbs. He knew what his boss meant. He'd done his fair share of convincing in the few years he'd been in Mamoud's employ. For all of his money and life of ease, Mamoud was ruthless. Sharouf had seen him do his own dirty work many times in the past. He was unafraid of being the trigger man when the time called for it. A specific instance from eight months ago popped into his head. He'd watched Mamoud butcher one of his guards for fraternizing with one of the girls from his harem.

No one was to touch his possessions. The only one even allowed to look and halfway enjoy the stable full of women was Sharouf, and he remained cautious about it.

When Sharouf spoke again, it was with clinical certainty. "I will make sure he cooperates."

4
Atlanta

Sean peered through the huge window's blinds. He surveyed the parking lot, making sure no one was coming or going.

It was late at night, technically early morning, and the only cars in the lot belonged to Tommy's research team he affectionately referred to as *the kids*. Tara Watson and Alex Simms spent more time at the IAA labs than they did at home; at least that was the joke around the offices of the International Archaeological Agency. The two twentysomethings loved their work, and when Tommy had called them after the fire at his home to see if they were still around the lab, he wasn't the least bit surprised to find they were still busily working the night away.

While the motorcycle ride to IAA headquarters had been awkward, it was at least fast, taking Sean and Tommy less than twenty minutes to reach the secure building. It wasn't until they were inside, safely behind locked doors and a slew of security measures, that they began to relax. That respite was tempered by the fact that someone had tried to kill both of them earlier, and questions remained as to why.

Sean backed away from the three-inch-thick glass and let go of the blinds. "Still no signs of anyone that might have followed us." His report was barely acknowledged by Tommy, who was deep into a stack of papers he'd printed earlier.

Tara and Alex were at separate computer stations nearby, working across from each other at an open table. They preferred to operate like that in case they needed to bounce ideas off each other.

Both of them had been working on Tommy's newest project for the entirety of the day, and for the last couple of days, which caused him concern for their safety. Fortunately, they each had an empty office that doubled as dorm rooms in case they ever wanted to stay at the labs overnight. That happened more than he'd anticipated. Tommy was lucky to have such dedicated researchers. Once they started on something, both Tara and Alex had trouble walking away from it until the job was done.

Such was the research they were doing at the moment.

Tommy had received an email from a friend in Israel by the name of Nehem Ben Asher. Nehem was a colleague, a student of ancient Israeli history by profession. He'd been working in the field of archaeology for nearly three decades and was considered one of the foremost experts on the late kingdoms of Judah and Israel. One of his preferred areas of study was the many prophets of the old kingdoms. His knowledge of the Biblical prophets was greater than most historians on the planet. Tommy had often wondered what his friend's fascination was with that particular area of Israeli history. He attributed it to the man growing up in that culture, and likely to religious teachings as a boy. After all, a researcher had to pick a niche. Prophetic history was Nehem's.

The correspondence from Nehem had been somewhat of a surprise. Tommy hadn't spoken to the man in almost a year, and even then it had been only a short phone call about a question Tommy had regarding a translation of Old Hebrew. There'd been few pleasantries exchanged between the two other than the usual chitchat. Both men's time was highly valuable, especially Nehem's, so when they talked, Tommy didn't like to beat around the bush too much.

Tommy sat at his computer station, off to the side at a different worktable from the kids. He was shuffling through the papers, trying to make sense of what he was seeing. They'd been at it for the better part of two hours now. Sean had been given a desk of his own but was still being brought up to speed with what the other three were trying to do.

A few days ago, Nehem sent Tommy an email containing images of a peculiar object, the likes of which the latter had never come across. It was a stone tablet in the shape of a wide rectangle, almost a square. Cut into the surface were twelve smaller sections, each a rectangle as well. Above the grid were two additional sections, separate from the others. What was most perplexing, though, were the symbols at the bottom of the tablet. The symbols were the reason Nehem requested Tommy's assistance. He claimed that he'd been unable to decipher them, and as he knew Tommy had software that Nehem did not have access to, he hoped his old friend could lend a hand and save him some time. The last words in Nehem's email had been cryptic, though. *"They're coming."*

The line had frozen Tommy and sent chills up his spine. When he tried to reach out by phone to clarify the task Nehem had requested of him, there'd been no answer. Tommy replied to the email, but still nothing. It was as if Nehem had disappeared as soon as he sent the message.

The man's lack of availability could have been attributed to him being in the field, working on another dig site. There were times when Tommy had been on a dig and didn't have cell service other than his sat phone. If that was the case, he completely understood. Nonetheless, he found it odd that Nehem would make the request and then vanish like that. He should have expected Tommy to reach out with questions.

That reasoning caused Tommy to worry. Coupled with the recent events surrounding his and Sean's homes, there was little room left for doubt. Nehem might have been the victim of an abduction, or worse. The question was why. And that question was the reason the four of them were working to unravel the meaning of the symbols on the tablet.

Maybe it was a huge conclusion to jump to, but given the circumstances, it was the only explanation they had.

Sean sat back down at his temporary desk and flipped through the copies Tommy had given him. The symbols were different from any hieroglyphs he'd ever seen. Some of them were repetitive, which he and the others took to mean they stood for letters.

The computer screen flashed quickly in front of Tara, bouncing light off her black-framed glasses as she took another sip of her second cup of coffee. Her blonde, curly hair looked almost yellowish in the dimly lit lab. Tommy suggested keeping the lights low to make it look like no one was there, just in case they'd been followed.

Across from Tara, Alex clicked his computer mouse busily, letting the software do its thing by running an analysis of the different possibilities the symbols could represent. The computers had been running for the last couple of days, pretty much nonstop. Even with the incredible power and speed of the latest technology, deciphering something so vague and ancient could take a long time.

Their two computers beeped simultaneously, and the screens froze in place. The noise caused both Tommy and Sean to peer up from having their noses in paperwork.

Tara clicked the screen a few times, zooming in on something. "I think we've got it," she exclaimed. She wasn't typically the excitable type, not like Alex, but when it came to deciphering codes, it was her guilty pleasure.

Tommy and Sean popped out of their seats and hurried over to the two wide computer screens. IAA had provided nothing but the best as far as technology went, and Tommy made sure that everything was updated on a yearly basis. Their processors were some of the fastest in the world, and the monitors were state of the art.

The two stood over Tara's shoulders and stared at the screen that proclaimed a match had been found.

"I'm not sure what this means," she said, clarifying her earlier statement. "The translation is either gibberish, incomplete, or is some kind of riddle."

Sean peered at the lines and read them silently to himself.

"One to the north, into the belly of the beast. May it rest with him forever. One to the east, may it find safe harbor in the high tower of the seekers of light."

A pall fell across the room. The only sound came from the exposed air ducts near the ceiling, twenty feet above, as cool air poured from the vents.

"One to the north and one to the east?" Alex asked. "What could that possibly mean? And what is the *it* it mentions?"

History wasn't necessarily his strong point, nor was figuring out the meaning of ancient texts. In translation and technology, there were few better than he and Tara. Riddles, it seemed, weren't his strong suit.

"Where was this tablet found?" Sean asked in response to the younger man's question. He directed it at Tommy.

Tommy pulled out his phone and scrolled down the screen until he came to the email from Nehem. He read through some sentences and then said, "Looks like he was working an excavation of some important person's tomb; in the valley just outside of Jerusalem."

"Important person? Like a governor or a king?"

"No," Tommy shook his head. "Seems that Nehem believes he discovered the tomb of a

Hebrew high priest. The tablet in these images was found with the priest's remains."

"I don't suppose he sent you any dating they might have done with the body." Sean looked hopeful, but he was realistic. If Nehem had just discovered the grave, it was unlikely he'd had time to date it.

"No. But according to the email, Nehem believes it to be the tomb of a high priest named Tovar."

Sean considered the new information while Tara sent the translation to a nearby printer. She stood up and walked over to it, grabbed the newly printed sheets, and brought them back to Sean and Tommy. "Just in case you need to take these with you."

She smiled and sat back in her seat and continued to analyze the tablet's translation.

"Tovar?" Sean wondered out loud.

"Already on it, Mr. Wyatt," Alex said. His fingers flew across the keyboard faster than anyone Sean had seen. The kid was easily typing a hundred words per minute.

"Please, don't call me that."

His comment didn't slow Alex at all. "Sorry, force of habit, Sean. It's how I was raised."

Sean smirked. Pushing forty years of age didn't bother him, but he still had a few years of thirties left and was in no hurry to give that up for the title of Mr. Wyatt and a seat at a bar where 1980s music played all the time. Not yet anyway. Alex was a good kid. Sean cursed himself in his mind. The fact that he and Tommy referred to Alex and Tara as kids validated the fact that he was worthy of the title.

The computers hummed as the internals worked at the speed of light. Less than ten seconds later, Alex motioned for the other two guys to come over to his side of the table.

"I think this might be our high priest."

He pointed at the screen covered in images of ancient scrolls. In the right-hand sidebar, the text translations were displayed in plain English. In several places, the name *Tovar* was highlighted in yellow.

"What are all these old scrolls and documents?" Sean asked.

"I'm not sure," Alex confessed.

"I am." Tommy leaned closer. "I've seen these scrolls before. They were found at the Hebrew monastery at Qumran."

Sean frowned. "Dead Sea Scrolls?"

"Sort of," Tommy shrugged. "These aren't part of the collection of the actual Dead Sea Scrolls. These are something else. But I recognize the signs of aging and the way they're written. The library that was discovered at Qumran was unique in many ways. It would surprise me if those scrolls weren't part of that collection."

"Bet me a Coke?" Sean grinned wryly.

"You're on."

Alex's fingers pounded away at the keyboard once more. Tara glanced around the side of her monitor to see how the faux drama would play out. Alex hit the return key and waited for a second before he pointed to the screen. "I'm impressed, Tommy. These were some of the historical records discovered at the monastery. It seems they weren't included in the Dead Sea Scrolls because they were considered mundane, due to the records having more to do with the day-to-day operations of the temple and the lineage of the priests.

Sean smiled over his shoulder at his friend. "I'll hit up the vending machine on the way out."

"Thanks, but I'm not thirsty right now," Tommy joked. With the next breath, he returned his attention to the matter of the tablet translation. "So, we think we know who the man was that Nehem was researching. Great. That still doesn't explain to us what the riddle means on the stone they found in his tomb.

He quoted the lines again, paraphrasing as he did so. "One to the east and one to the north. Belly of the beast? Seekers of light? Any of you have any thoughts as to who or what those might be?"

Sean found a chair nearby and rolled it close. He plopped down into it and crossed his arms, thinking deeply about the issue. "The problem with these pesky ancient puzzles is that people have been trying to solve them for thousands of years, without success."

"Yeah," Tara agreed, "but we can accelerate those thousands of years with the best software. It takes things we would have needed centuries to understand, and pieces them together."

She tapped a few keys on her computer and then clicked the mouse. "Most of the references for beasts in the *Bible* are related to prophecy. This says the term beast is used most frequently in the books of Daniel and Revelation."

Sean nodded. His knowledge of Jewish and Christian religions ran deep, way deeper than most people probably realized, with the exception being Tommy. "Yes. Both of those books talk a great deal about beasts that symbolize different countries." Despite his extraordinary Biblical knowledge, Sean moved on to the other part of the riddle. "Did you search for the seekers of light term?"

She pecked away again, and in a few minutes the screen changed once more. Her face twisted noticeably. Tara didn't try to hide her disappointment. "I'm finding a few different results, but not much. There isn't a group that goes by that name. It might have been an ancient society of some kind, but it will require more research before I can tell you definitively."

Sean looked over at his friend, and Tommy returned the questioning glance. "So," Sean said, "what do you think?"

Tommy studied the screen for several more seconds before speaking. When he did, his tone was low and secretive. "Whatever it is that Nehem is looking for was important enough to someone that they tried to kill us and burn our houses down."

"So we're for sure operating from the theory that it was his research that got us in trouble?"

Sean wasn't opposed to the idea, but it was a conclusion they were jumping to, and that wasn't always a good thing.

"It's the only theory that makes sense right now," Tommy defended. "It can't be a coincidence that I get an email from an archaeologist who disappears, and then a few days later someone is trying to kill us. No way that's a coincidence."

"I agree. So, what's our next play?"

Tommy considered the question and then sent it back to Sean. "I know what *I* think we should do. What do *you* think?"

Sean's mouth parted slightly in a narrow grin. "You know exactly what I'm thinking. We fly to Israel. Sooner or later, we have to find the people that tried to kill us before they hurt anyone else. And maybe along the way we can pay them back for destroying our houses."

5
Jerusalem, Israel

Arranging the flights to Israel took a little more doing than usual, even for someone like Tommy who had full-time access to a private company jet. The on-call pilot wasn't typically available twenty-four hours a day, though he did endeavor to be ready at a moment's notice. On this occasion, he was already asleep, and by the time he received the messages, it was early the next morning. The man was efficient, though, and had filed the flight plan and made arrangements with Israeli air traffic control so that they would have as little trouble as possible coming in.

The Gulfstream left Atlanta's Hartsfield International airport in midmorning. When it landed several hours later in Israel, darkness had already fallen across the ancient, sacred land.

Tommy had called his friend, Karem, who lived in the area, and asked if he could be their driver for a few days. Karem had been more than happy to oblige. The forty-two-year-old Israeli was the curator at one of the local antiquities museums. It was a small operation but one that saw tens of thousands of visitors visit every year. His museum contained several important items from Jewish history, including a few that were extremely rare.

Karem also had unlimited access to nearly every high-security site in the land. During Tommy's last visit, he'd taken the American to see the heavily guarded Isaiah Scroll, one of the most precious and sacred texts the nation of Israel possessed. The scroll had been written on an enormous sheet of thin copper. In the museum display, it was wrapped around a giant stone cylinder so that it could be read from beginning to end. The museum was basically bombproof, and in case of an attack, the scroll and its stone dropped several stories down into the ground, protected by hundreds of feet of concrete.

It had been an impressive sight, and one that very few outsiders were afforded the privilege of seeing.

Karem picked them up at the airport and drove them to the outskirts of Jerusalem where they'd arranged for a room at a hotel where Tommy had stayed once before. They were fortunate a room had been available, though it was one of the most expensive in the place. Luckily for the two Americans, money was no object. The finances Tommy had been left when his parents died years before were significant. Thanks to clever investments and shrewd dealings over the better part of the last decade, his substantial inheritance had grown to the hundreds of millions. With the money, his International Archaeological Agency had been lucky with countless opportunities to save hundreds of priceless treasures from around the world.

After a night of restless and precarious sleep, the two Americans woke up, showered, and got dressed. On the elevator, heading down for a quick breakfast, Tommy glanced over at his friend and shook his head disapprovingly. "Always with the khaki pants."

Sean glanced down at his pants and then back to Tommy. "What? They're comfortable. And the last thing I want to be wearing in this hot weather is jeans."

"You could wear cargo shorts like me."

"I prefer pants. So sue me."

Their banter ended as the elevator dinged. They walked through the lobby, a contemporary design with faded olive-green walls contrasted by dark-brown wood flooring. A beautiful young woman with chestnut hair stood behind the concierge desk, greeting people as they came in through the entrance or down from their rooms. Off to the left was a cafe where people were busily eating their breakfasts and talking about the things they looked forward to seeing.

Holy Land tours were big business in the area. Christians, Muslims, and Jews from far and wide came to see the places their respective religions so revered. Tourists were more than happy to pay out thousands of dollars to see the Via Dolorosa, the supposed site of Golgotha, the Mount of Olives, the great mosques, and many other sacred locations.

As the two Americans walked through the cafe and found a table, they couldn't help but laugh at some of the attire worn by the tourists. They sat down at a table near the window and looked over the menu, deciding to eat light and order some fruit, bread, and cheese for breakfast.

Tommy's eyes wandered around the room and then returned to his friend. "You know what? I'm sorry I gave you crap about the khakis. These people are dressed way worse than you."

Sean laughed and pulled a water bottle out of the canvas messenger bag he'd brought along. He twisted the lid off and took a sip before replacing it. "Yeah," he said, his eyes trailing around the cafe, "it's like fanny pack central in here."

Tommy snorted a laugh and nodded.

A minute later, a young man with a white button-up shirt and a black apron around his waist came by and took their order. He set a few glasses of water on the table and disappeared around the corner.

"Karem is meeting us here in twenty minutes?" Sean asked the question he'd already asked earlier regarding their rendezvous with the Israeli.

"Yes. And he'll be here. Karem is extremely prompt. When he says he will be somewhere, you can count on it."

Sean nodded and pulled out his phone. He checked a few messages in his email inbox, one of which was from Adriana. She was investigating a shipwreck off the coast of Ibiza, near Spain, and was trying to figure out where the ship had gone. She claimed that someone, a treasure hunter, had unrightfully taken the booty from the ship and had detonated underwater explosives to dispose of the evidence. From the sound of it, she was dealing with dangerous people, but he knew better than to tell her what to do or how to do it. Adriana was her own woman. If she needed his help, she'd ask. And he knew she probably wouldn't ask.

She was planning on coming to the United States to visit at the end of the month, so he hoped that whatever shenanigans she was up to would reach closure soon.

"Email from Adriana?" Tommy asked.

"Yeah," Sean said and put the phone back in his pocket. He didn't sound happy. Probably because he wasn't. He wished they could spend more time together, but he understood. She was a little younger than him, and was a wild, free spirit.

Tommy folded his hands on the table and tried to look sympathetic. "Everything okay with you two?"

"Yeah, we're good. She's just hunting down another lead right now. Sounds like she's dealing with some potentially dangerous people. But you know how she likes to roll."

"You worry about her, don't you?"

Sean's eyebrows lowered, but he couldn't deny it. "Of course I worry about her. I know she's good at what she does. Other than you and me, I've never met anyone more capable of handling the kinds of dangers we deal with. At the same time, you know as well as I do that eventually luck can run out."

Tommy leaned forward. "She'll be fine, man. Don't stress yourself out. Right now, we've got our own problems to worry about."

He was right. Sean knew it, too. They were about to embark on a path that would almost certainly be fraught with danger. The only advantage they had at the moment was the hope that whoever had tried to kill them still believed they were dead. If the would-be killers found out that they were still alive, the targets would be on their backs once more, and usually villains in Sean's line of work didn't make the same mistake twice.

A few minutes later, the waiter returned with their plates. The two quickly scarfed down the dates, grapes, raisins, and figs. The flattened bread reminded them of sourdough from back home, and the cheese was a mild, white variety that tasted remarkably similar to Havarti.

The little meal was surprisingly filling, and no sooner had they finished than Karem walked in through the entrance.

His face sported a full black beard that matched the thick hair on his head. He was diminutive, around five feet five inches tall, with dark creamy skin. His arms were hairy, and he wore a blue polo with khakis.

"Your friend doesn't seem to mind the khakis," Sean pointed out as Karem approached.

Tommy simply shook his head and smirked. "You still owe me a Coke, by the way."

He stood up, and Sean followed suit. The three shook hands and exchanged clichéd greetings before getting to it.

"The car is just outside," Karem said. "I figured you would want to see where Dr. Ben Asher was working first." He directed his next comment to Tommy. "If what you say is true, and Nehem was abducted, I fear anything of value in his temporary housing would have been stolen. It will still be worth a look, but I would not get my hopes up."

Karem was also a personal friend of Nehem. When Tommy told him what happened, his demeanor instantly became grave. Tommy explained who Sean was and why he was there, which made Karem feel a little better. Still, his hope was tempered by a strong sense of realistic expectation.

"We should be at the dig site in twenty minutes," he informed the Americans. "From there, perhaps you can find a clue as to who might have taken our friend, and why."

The ride to the valley just outside the city of Jerusalem was a short one, though it was hampered by the crawling traffic. Buses, vans, cars, and mopeds were everywhere. Summer months were a busy time for the area, and the tourist industry was booming, in spite of the conflicts going on with Islamist militant groups.

On the outskirts of town, the traffic thinned, and the three were able to reach the dig site without any trouble. There were ropes surrounding the area, protecting certain spots from a clumsy onlooker stumbling in and ruining the excavation. Around the perimeter, workers brushed away dirt and clay that had built up over the years as they meticulously continued their search for answers from the past. Some locals in large straw hats sifted dirt through screens and into a plastic bin.

It was still early in the day, but the sun already felt like a June afternoon in Tennessee, beating down on their skin like a warm fire in the sky.

They left the car in a gravel lot near the dig site and walked past the ropes to an area where the rolling earth steepened into a hill. Karem pointed to a particular section of the hillside where a dark cavity had been unearthed. It was the entrance to a tomb.

Two light-brown stone columns, one on either side, supported the entryway. Another stone sat atop the other two over the threshold. Piles of dirt and rock cluttered the ground on either side of the entrance, clearly where the crews had peeled away the layers of time to reveal the ancient doorway.

"This is what Nehem was working on," he said as they reached the tomb. "You can see the name engraved in the stone. *Tovar, high priest of Judah.*"

Moments like this were always reverent for Sean and Tommy. Standing in the presence of something that had recently been unearthed, not seen by human eyes for millennia, brought about feelings of humility and awe.

"So this is what he found," Tommy said quietly, almost to himself.

Karem nodded. "Please, take a look inside. I have made arrangements with the authorities for you to have as much access as you need."

The Americans didn't wait for a second invitation. Sean removed a pair of flashlights from his messenger bag, handing one to his friend and keeping the other. They switched on the lights and tiptoed through the doorway and into the cool darkness of the tomb.

The interior walls were roughly hewn, chiseled away without precision, a result of the workmen just trying to get the job done rather than worry with aesthetics.

Sean wondered about the interior tunnel. "I guess they didn't treat the high priest like other high ranking officials back then."

"Yeah. I was thinking the same thing," Tommy agreed. "Not the nicest tomb we've been in."

Karem was close behind the two Americans with his own flashlight. "Many of the priestly tombs were humble like this one. It was a precedent set early on in Jewish history that carried on until the temple fell for the last time."

The bright LED beams danced around the walls as the men proceeded deeper into the hillside tomb.

The cramped tunnel came to an end and opened up into a much larger chamber, though still not as vast as they would have anticipated for someone held in such high esteem by the Jewish nation. The room was circular, around fifteen feet in diameter. A stone coffin sat on the floor in the center of the room, coming up to around knee high on the Americans. A skeleton stared up at the wall from within the sarcophagus's confines, dressed in faded and tattered rags that once must have been priestly raiment.

Sean and Tommy shined their beams into the stone box, staring at the remains of the long-dead priest of Judah.

"So this is Tovar," Sean said, examining the bones from a few feet away.

"He's remarkably preserved," Karem said, pointing out the small amount of tissue still attached to the skull. "Nehem was greatly impressed by that. The stone tablet that he found on the chest of the body is gone. If we cannot find it at his quarters, then we must assume it was taken as well."

That would have been the same conclusion Tommy and Sean would come to as well.

Tommy wandered over to the end of the chamber closest to the head. He examined the walls and noted the symbol that was carved into the stone, two interlocking triangles that many people called the Davidic Star. He pointed his light to the wall on the right and noticed another symbol. This one, however, was not Jewish. It was something he'd seen before but didn't immediately realize from where.

"A symbol from early Buddhism," Sean said, answering his friend's unasked question.

"Yes," he said, embarrassed. "That's what I was trying to come up with. But why is it here?"

"There is one more," Karem interjected. He flashed his light past Sean's shoulders and onto the wall behind him. "A symbol from the Zoroastrian religion, the sign of Ahura Mazda."

Sean turned around and looked at the circular light on the emblem. Karem was correct. It was a symbol he'd seen before in Babylonian culture, mostly in temples and other religious settings.

He frowned as Tommy circled around the coffin and examined the carving. "It makes no sense," he said, definitively. "Why would there be symbols of other religions in the tomb of a Jewish high priest?"

Karem shrugged. "Perhaps he was a particularly tolerant priest."

Sean shook his head. "Maybe, but my gut is telling me it has more to do with that tablet. Did Nehem say anything about those symbols in the email — or to you in person, Karem?"

Both Tommy and their Israeli guide shook their heads. "Nope," Tommy answered.

"I wonder why that is." Sean took a step closer to the etched stone. "A Jewish priest who was buried, surrounded by a symbol from his own religion, an old one, and one that must have just been taking root."

Tommy agreed. "Yeah, Buddhism was in its infancy at that point. The first of their temples dates back to around the seventh century, perhaps a little earlier."

Sean looked around the room, still confused about the carvings. "Is there anything else in here, or is this it?"

Karem shrugged. "If there was anything, Nehem would have taken it. And if he did not, the men who kidnapped him could have. This area was not very secure while he was working here. Since his disappearance, security measures have been increased. Too late, I'm afraid." The last line carried the weight of regret.

Tommy kneeled down and examined the inner walls of the sarcophagus. Inch by inch, his light ran along the stone until he had nearly scoured the entire object. He was about to give up when he found something odd cut into the stone near the right foot of the skeleton. He squinted and leaned in a little closer to get a better look.

"You got something?" Sean asked, hovering over the spot where Tommy was looking.

"Maybe," he shook his head. "It's so small I can barely see it. And the angle is awkward. It looks like ancient Hebrew, though."

Sean took out his phone and handed it to his friend after letting his thumbprint unlock the screen. "Take a picture of it."

Tommy nodded and accepted the device. He gently dipped his hand into the box and pressed the button. The flash seared their vision for a second, blasting a blinding cloud of bright white through the chamber. Tommy looked at the image on the screen. "Got it," he said. "There's something else near the other foot. I'm going to take a picture of that too."

As he leaned in, he realized that the writing had been placed in a similar fashion, but the symbols were different. He took another picture and then handed the device back to Sean.

"What do you think?"

Sean studied each image for a moment. "Not sure. It's definitely some variation of ancient Hebrew or Aramaic. Karem?"

He passed the phone to their driver, who took a quick look. He slowly shook his head. "I have seen this before, but I would need a little time to analyze it and come up with a translation."

"Maybe we should send it to the kids," Sean suggested.

Tommy nodded. "Good idea."

6
Dubai

Mamoud ran his fingers along the edge of the ancient tablet. He sat at the end of a long dining table. Made from English oak, it had been imported years ago by his father. When Mamoud moved into the coastal mansion, he'd brought it with him. The stone tablet rested safely on a satin towel so as not to scratch the expensive table's surface. His finger moved from the outer edge of the stone to the inner lines and shapes. He had no idea what he was looking at, but he was quite sure of what it would lead him to.

The man at the other end of the table seemed bent on not giving him the interpretations Mamoud required.

"Are you familiar with some of the ancient torture methods of King Xerxes of Persia, Doctor?"

The older man opposite him trembled in his seat. His long gray beard looked like it hadn't been trimmed in over a year. The skin on his balding head was tanned both from weeks of being in the sun and a lifetime of work that kept him outdoors. His wireframe glasses rested atop a broad, almost droopy nose. Wrinkles above both cheeks also belied his age. The eyes, however, were keen and fierce. While his body trembled, the greenish-brown orbs told a different story. Two guards stood directly behind Nehem Ben Asher. One of them was Sharouf.

"I am familiar with much in regards to history, Mamoud. Though I prefer not to study such barbaric traditions as that." His voice was even and sharp.

Mamoud reached out and picked up a small silver cup. He put it to his lips and took a long sip of the hot tea. "That's a shame. They were truly quite adept at the art of inflicting pain on their prisoners. My ancestors come from a line that goes all the way back to Xerxes himself."

"All of our lines intersect at one point or another, Mamoud. What is your point?"

The young Arab ignored the insolence, instead appreciating the man's boldness. "I like how you are direct and to the point. That must be the scientist in you."

"I see no reason to be otherwise," Nehem said defiantly.

"Nor do I, Doctor, which is why I must ask you again why you won't do as my man asks."

Nehem took in a deep breath and tilted his head back. "The relics you seek belong to the kingdom of Israel. No one else. Even in the hands of the Israeli government, those objects could be of great danger to the world. They can only be given to the most careful and trustworthy individuals whose hearts are as pure as snow."

Mamoud raised an eyebrow and flashed a cynical glare. "Hearts as pure as snow? I'm not here for a lesson in morals, Doctor. I need you to decipher the tablet code."

"Why?" Nehem raised his hands off the table, a move that caused Sharouf to put his hand on the doctor's shoulder.

Mamoud raised a hand, signaling for his guard to release the hostage. "It's fine, Sharouf. He's of no threat to us."

Sharouf obeyed and took a reluctant step back.

"Why?" Mamoud repeated the question. "Because I am a lover of all things in history, and of all religions." He almost laughed at his own lie as it came from his lips.

Nehem snorted in derision. "What is the real reason you want the relics, Mamoud? You already have everything a man could want in this world. What would you need with those things?"

"If I told you, you wouldn't believe me, old man. But I will tell you this: You will give me the translation to the tablet, or I will make sure that before you die you experience more pain than you have ever imagined." He leaned forward, folding his hands and resting his elbows on the table. "Give us the translations to the tablet, and lead us to the relics, or I swear to you, you will wish you were dead."

The old archaeologist stared at him with an unwavering gaze. His nervous shaking had ceased, and he found new resolve in the threat. "You can do your worst to me, Mamoud. I will never give you the translations or the location of the Hoshen. They do not belong to you. I do not know what you want with them, but whatever the reason, I am most certain it is not for the cause of good."

Mamoud feigned disappointment. "Why, Doctor, you believe that I serve the forces of evil? You couldn't be more wrong about that. Just as you couldn't be wrong in your assumption that I can't make you tell me what the tablet says. And the fact that you mentioned not telling me the location means you've already figured that part out."

Nehem's demeanor shifted noticeably, to a much less comfortable affect.

"It's okay," Mamoud reassured him. "You are understandably stubborn. But your beliefs are misplaced. You think that I aim to torture you into submission?"

The doctor glanced over one shoulder and then the other at the guards behind him. "Why else would you ask me about ancient torture methods? I know your reputation. You are a cruel, evil man who will stop at nothing to get what he wants."

Mamoud rolled his shoulders. "Perhaps that's true, but I do it all for the right reasons."

"Greed is never a right reason."

"Greed? Oh, I'm not greedy. I have no want for anything, Nehem. Look around you. I live in a palace on the beach." He put his hands out as if displaying the surroundings to his unwilling guest. "I have everything I could ever desire."

"Then what drives you, Mamoud? Power?"

The young Arab stood up and walked deliberately to the other end of the table. His expensive Italian leather shoes clicked on the hard floor with every step. When he reached the chair where Nehem sat, he folded his hands in front of him, keeping them at waist level.

"All men want power, Nehem. I have that as well. I could snap my fingers, and a hundred people would do my bidding, no matter what the order. The reason for my search will be revealed to you soon enough, when you provide me with the translations and, apparently, the location."

Nehem's head went back and forth slowly. "I'll never tell you. You can torture me all you want. You'll not get your dirty fingers on those holy relics."

"I see." Mamoud started to spin around and walk back to his seat, but he stopped, instead putting one hand on the table and bending over, putting his face only a foot away from the older man's. The closeness made Nehem uncomfortable, but he forced himself to keep a straight face and not flinch.

"You are mistaken, Doctor, when you assume I was going to torture you." He stood erect once more and took a step back, turning to leave the room.

Nehem's mind raced. What was he insinuating? He thought fast, and one terrifying truth kept rearing its head in his eyes.

"I have no family," he said finally. "My wife died years ago. I am all alone now."

Mamoud stopped instantly and slammed his fist on the table. "Lies!" he yelled, his voice echoing through the high ceilings.

A tear formed in Nehem's left eye. His head kept moving back and forth in one last attempt to deny his captor. "Please. I beg of you."

"No more begging, Nehem." Mamoud still faced the other direction, keeping his back to the older man. "I will torture your daughter until every last ounce of her will succumbs to me. I will give her over to my men first, before the old techniques are employed. They will have their way with her, at my insistence. And I have many, many men in my service. When they are done, Sharouf here will begin his work. And he is very, very good at what he does. Xerxes himself would have paid dearly for his services."

There was no holding back the tears now for Nehem. They flowed freely like two broken dams. "Please. She's all I have in this world. Do whatever you want to me, but don't hurt her. Please." There was surrender in his voice. Mamoud had heard it before, many times. He always got what he wanted. That was the simple way of it. People could hold out sometimes, but in the end, everyone had a pressure point that could be used.

"Tell me what the tablet says, and I will spare your daughter. Lie to me, and I will personally take her as part of my harem, for a while. After I'm done with her, all the other things I said will come to pass. Now," he spun around and stared through his hostage, "are you going to tell me what the tablet says, or do I need to send Sharouf to the university where your daughter works?"

Nehem swallowed hard, tears still streaming down his already wet face. They hung momentarily in the tangles of his beard before falling to his thighs. He nodded. "Yes. I will tell you. But I have your word? No harm will come to her?"

"I swear it to Allah," Mamoud answered.

The old man paused. He didn't care what they did to him, but he couldn't risk any harm coming to the only family he had left on the planet, even at the cost of the rest of civilization. She would find a way to survive, somehow.

"The translation is a riddle."

Mamoud took another step closer. Sharouf's eyes widened behind Nehem's back.

"Go on," the wealthy Arab said.

Nehem's eyes began to dry out, and he wiped his face clean of the tears with his sleeve. "I don't know both locations with any certainty. But from what I understand about the translation, the objects you seek were taken to two places, far apart from each other."

"The first?"

"Again, I honestly do not know for certain. I only discovered the tablet shortly before your men showed up. I'd been working on the translation day and night. I only unraveled it this morning."

"You're sure you did the translation correctly?" The question left little room for doubt. If Nehem were trying to stall or fool Mamoud in any way, the consequences would be most dire.

The prisoner swallowed again. "Yes. I am sure. But the riddle is vague. I can only offer a guess as to where it might lead us. I need more time to figure out the first location."

"More time?" Mamoud looked at Sharouf. "Find the girl. Bring her to me."

Nehem shot out of his chair. The second he did, Sharouf's hand smacked down on his shoulder and forced him back into the seat with a thump. "I am not lying to you, Mamoud. I know what you would do to her. Please, the tablet translation is only part of the puzzle. The riddle lends a clue, but there is more."

"What do you mean, more?"

Nehem's breath came quickly in big heaves. "The tablet is a grid of twelve spaces. When you put the symbols into the different spaces, it produces a different result, a completely new combination of letters. The symbols alone can spell out the riddle once you unlock the cipher, but it could take weeks to get the correct sequence in the grid to spell out a name of any significance."

Mamoud considered what his hostage was telling him. He had no reason to lie at this point, unless he was stalling. He doubted Nehem would risk doing that, knowing what would happen if he suspected what the man was up to. The archaeologist was well aware of the actions Mamoud would take, and they would be severe. No, he was being honest. He could see it in the man's swollen, reddened eyes. There were no lies in them. Still, a few weeks wasn't good enough. He'd waited long enough for the war he was about to wage, and he couldn't begin until he had the two relics.

"You said there are twelve spaces on the grid, and that each one combined together will produce possible names of the places where the relics are hidden?"

"Yes. I believe so. I swear. I can't be sure. But I am confident."

A few weeks. He didn't have that kind of time.

"You have twenty-four hours."

A short, low vibration sound echoed like a rumble in the vacuous room. Sharouf stirred behind the prisoner, sliding his hand into his pocket. He pulled out his phone and stepped away from the table to an archway leading into the adjacent room.

He answered the phone in Arabic. "What?"

Mamoud's eyes narrowed as he tried to hear what the person on the other end of the phone call was saying, but all he heard was mumbled gibberish.

Sharouf nodded. "I see. Are you sure?"

He listened again to the report coming from the earpiece. When the person was done talking, Sharouf thanked them and ended the call. He put the phone back in his pocket and looked up at his employer. Mamoud stared at him expectantly, giving away nothing. Sharouf likewise kept his demeanor calm. Clearly, he was trying to hide something from their captive. He motioned with his head to join him in the other room.

Mamoud nodded and ordered the remaining guard to escort Nehem back to his room. "I would suggest you hurry, Doctor. The clock is ticking."

The guard stood the man up and ushered him out another entryway, into a foyer, and up a set of stairs. Once the sound of their footsteps had faded away, Mamoud followed Sharouf into the kitchen. They both cautiously looked around to make sure no one was within earshot.

"What is this?" the head man asked.

Sharouf kept cool, but a twitch in his eye belied that something was wrong. "That was my man in Atlanta. The targets managed to escape."

Mamoud's expression remained stoic while rage boiled up inside him. "Where are they?"

"My men have been working to find out where they went. They believe they may have stayed at a safe house or perhaps their IAA building over the evening."

"So you have no idea where they are right now?"

Sharouf looked down at his shoes for a second before locking eyes with his boss once more. "On a hunch, they were able to track the IAA jet late this morning."

"And where did it go?"

"Israel."

7
Dubai

Fury burned in Mamoud's eyes as he stared through his most trusted bodyguard. He had a million questions, but only one remained at the forefront of his mind. It hung on his lips like rain drops on the leaves of a tree, begging to drop from the weight of its burden.

"How did this happen?"

For the first time since Mamoud had met him, Sharouf's face expressed worry. It was slight, barely noticeable, but it was there nonetheless.

He didn't answer at first; instead, his eyes remained on the floor as he searched for answers. When he looked back up, his boss knew he had none. "I am not certain. But we know where they are headed."

"You only know they're in Israel!" Mamoud roared, his voice bouncing off the walls like thunder in a raging storm.

Sharouf took a deep breath. "There is only one reason they would have gone to Israel, sir. We know where they are headed. They will go to the tomb first, most likely. When they are done there, they will visit the archeologist's apartment to search for clues."

"And how do you know for certain?"

"It is the only thing that makes sense."

Mamoud's temper eased a little as he considered what Sharouf was saying.

The guard continued. "The only explanation is that, somehow, Nehem was able to contact them. We know that he sent an email to his American friend. Their escape and subsequent trip to Israel could only mean they are attempting to find Dr. Ben Asher."

Another thought occurred to Mamoud as his man was talking. "Is there any chance we could be implicated?"

"None. And we made sure there was nothing left in the doctor's apartment. I personally oversaw the search. All we could find was the tablet. Nothing else."

Mamoud nodded, but there was still a look of concern on his face. He stood still for a moment. A finger involuntarily scratched his beard on the right cheek. Then he ran both hands through his black hair, leaving them hanging on the back of his neck for a second as he sighed.

He let his hands down and walked over to a window that was nearly the size of the entire wall. It looked out onto the blue waters of the Persian Gulf, where turquoise turned to deep navy, speckled with intermittent whitecaps. A single puffy cloud hung in the otherwise perfectly clear blue sky.

Wyatt was like the cloud, lingering around, ruining what should have been a perfect plan.

If the cloud was permitted to stick around, others could join it, and before he knew it, Mamoud would have a storm on his hands.

He spun around and faced Sharouf, who had turned and watched his boss as he paced to the other side of the room.

"Do you still have any operatives in Jerusalem?"

Sharouf nodded. His lips barely parted in a knowing grin. "I have two stationed ten minutes away from Ben Asher's apartment. They're on standby."

"Call them. Have them pay the doctor's residence a visit. Make sure Wyatt and his friend don't get out alive this time."

Sharouf nodded and retrieved the phone from his pocket. He tapped the screen a few times and then put the device to his ear. After the second ring, he heard a voice on the other line. His orders were swift and direct. "Eliminate them both," he said, finishing the details of the command.

He ended the call and slid the phone back in his pocket. "They will take care of it. Both of them are highly trained. They used to work for Pakistani Special Forces. After today, you won't have to worry about the two Americans anymore."

"Good." Mamoud said and turned back to gaze out at the azure sea. While he had confidence in his right-hand man, that certainty was starting to wane. First, the mistake in Atlanta, and now he had two men Mamoud has never met carrying out orders in a faraway land.

He'd read the dossier on Wyatt and Schultz. Wyatt was a highly decorated former government agent. He'd worked for the United States Department of Justice, but some of his exploits had been hard to uncover. With Wyatt, it seemed there was more than met the eye. The report claimed that he was retired from government operations, and had worked with his friend, Tommy Schultz, at the International Archaeological Agency as a transport and logistics security agent. The title sounded made up, but there were rumors that the man was extremely dangerous, and usually armed.

Schultz, too, was no pushover. Information on him had been easier to come by but was somewhat disconcerting. While he was not as expertly trained in the deadly arts, several reports indicated he could handle his own if pushed into a fight. Schultz's IAA organization was well known all over the world, and he had personally been responsible for the recovery of some of the most priceless artifacts in history.

He stared out into the bright sunlight for a few more moments before spinning around and facing Sharouf. "Up the timeline for our preparations."

Sharouf seemed puzzled by the odd change of plans, and by the vagueness of the order. "How soon do you want them ready?"

"The cells should be ready to begin operations when you give the command."

The bodyguard's face contorted into a frown. "What if the archaeologist doesn't produce what you're looking for? Will we still move ahead according to plan?"

Mamoud considered the question for a moment before he answered. "We have spent too much money and time planning this. The moment has come for the West to pay for its insolence. We were told by the great prophet that the infidels must convert or be destroyed. They have chosen the latter. And we will be the tip of the sword that brings their destruction."

8
Jerusalem

Karem and the two Americans left the tomb and made their way back to the car. Five minutes later, they arrived at an apartment Nehem had rented for the duration of his research, however long that was going to take. The exterior looked like every other building in the area. Sean was always surprised at the almost Communist appearance of many buildings in the Middle East. It was especially surprising in Israel, considering the enormous amount of money that flowed into the country from tech startups, as well as research and development companies.

One app startup had recently been purchased by Internet giant Google for the hefty price tag of $1.3 billion dollars. Even after it was bought out, Google decided to leave the startup's headquarters in Israel, which kept hundreds of people employed and the money still rolling in.

The bland-gray sides of the building soaked in the warm rays of the morning sun as Sean and Tommy followed Karem through the parking lot and up a flight of stairs to the second floor. Once there, they continued forward until reaching a door on their left.

Karem had visited Nehem at his temporary residence on several occasions. He took a keen interest in what was going on with his research, and when the archaeologist had uncovered the strange tablet, his interest had only grown stronger. Karem seemed somewhat despondent as they approached the apartment door. He'd become friends with Nehem years ago, and the two had worked on many projects together. Now, it was a friendship that Tommy and Sean were grateful for, and one that seemed to cause Karem a great deal of concern.

When the three reached the door, they saw no evidence of a break-in. The doorknob was still intact, and there were no signs of forced entry. Sean put his hand on the doorknob and turned it. The metal twisted easily, and the door swung open.

Inside, it was a disaster area. Papers were scattered about on the floor, and the sofa and chairs were sliced open, their cotton innards strewn about chaotically.

"Someone has definitely been here," Tommy stated the obvious.

Karem and Sean both looked at him with a *no crap* expression.

"What was your first clue?" Sean teased.

"Hilarious," Tommy said. He walked through the opening and into the trashed apartment.

The refrigerator had been left open, and a puddle of water had collected at its base. The pantry door was open, too, as were several of the cabinets. A seat cushion was on its side next to a television that had been knocked onto the floor.

"They really left no stone unturned," Sean commented. "Whoever came through here was extremely thorough."

"Should we not call the police?" Karem asked with growing concern in his voice. "We should report this, yes?"

"You might want to hold off on that for a minute," Sean warned.

"Why? Now we know that someone vandalized his apartment, things were probably stolen."

"Agreed. But we need a few minutes in here first to see if they missed anything."

"Missed anything?" Karem was adamant at this point. "Look around. They destroyed the whole place. How could they have missed anything?"

Tommy had drifted over to a desk in the corner. It was void of anything. The paperwork, pens, stationery, and everything else that belonged to it had been cast onto the floor in the hurried search. The drawers had been pulled out and thrown into the pile too. The only drawer that remained was the center one over the chair space.

He'd worked with Sean enough to know where to look when other people thought they'd searched everywhere. While the men who took Nehem might have scoured his research, torn through his furniture, and believed they found what they were looking for or not, Tommy and Sean knew that the cleverest people in the world always found a way to hide their most important information. Usually, it was right under the searcher's nose.

"Nehem knew I would come here," Tommy said, interrupting the other two and their argument about calling the police. "He knew I would come to Israel, looking for him. He was afraid. I thought when I read his email that was maybe the case. His typing seemed hurried, his tone concerned. If he knew someone was coming for him, he wouldn't have just sent the photos of the tablet to me. There was something else."

He scratched his head and sat down in the humble wooden chair near the desk. He pulled out the center drawer and felt underneath it, on the bottom of the workstation's surface. His fingers ran along the smooth wood but found nothing. Tommy had hoped there would be something taped to the underside of the desktop. Unfortunately, his guess was wrong.

He didn't give up. He stood and stepped over to the back of the desk that was flush against the wall. Pressing his back against the wall, he leveraged his weight and moved the workstation back six inches so he could see the front panel. As the surface was exposed to more light, he saw that there was nothing there.

Tommy sighed but tried to keep the disappointment from creeping into his thoughts. "Guys, flip over that sofa, and see if you can find anything underneath it."

Sean nodded and motioned for Karem to help. The Israeli was indignant at first but surrendered and bent down as Sean stepped around to the other side and lifted the heavy piece. The two men tipped it over, revealing the woven polyester underside. Otherwise, there was nothing helpful to be found.

Tommy sat down in the desk chair and let out a long sigh. Whoever had come here before them had cleaned the place out. If there was a clue as to what it was Nehem was working on or who might have taken him, it was long gone by now.

Sean scratched the back of his head as he surveyed their surroundings. "I'm going to check the bathroom and the bedroom. Come with me," he said to Karem.

Despite what he thought was best, Karem obeyed and followed Sean to the back of the apartment and into a bedroom that couldn't have been more than twelve feet square. There was a small master bathroom attached to it with what looked like the cheapest faucet and sink the largest wholesaler had to offer.

Sean scanned the wrecked bedroom for clues. The cotton had been ripped out of the pillows and tossed aside. The mattress was removed from the box spring and lay at an angle over the edge of the latter.

The nightstand's drawers were pulled out and emptied onto the floor. A few notepads, pens, and some prescription pill bottles were all that the act had produced. Sean looked over at a nearly empty closet. The clothes had been searched and dropped on the floor. He could almost see the invaders going through the process in his imagination.

"Well?" Karem asked. "See anything?"

Sean shook his head, perplexed. "No. They've been through all of this."

Back in the other room, Tommy sat in the chair, with his head in his hands. To the untrained eye, he would have appeared distraught. The fact of the matter was that he was thinking hard about the situation. Nehem would have left a clue in a place that no one else would have considered.

Tommy closed his eyes and imagined the day of the abduction. *Nehem would have been sitting here at his desk, working on a translation for the tablet. The abduction would have happened here because the kidnappers wouldn't be so foolish as to try to take him with so many people in view at the dig site. It had to be here.*

He watched through his mind's eye as the men came in and started trashing the place while Nehem just sat in his chair, patiently waiting until they snatched him up and took him away.

At that moment, the solution struck Tommy as he felt the hard surface of the chair underneath him. He stood up and flipped it over. Stuck to the bottom of the seat was a sheet of paper held by a few strips of Scotch tape.

He pulled on the paper's edge, careful not to let the tape tear any of it. He stood up and looked at the image drawn on the paper. It was a drawing of the tablet, but it had some significant additions. Arrows had been drawn from the symbols at the bottom of the page, connecting them to certain spaces within the grid.

Tommy's mind raced. Nehem hadn't left him with the translation of the riddle. Why? That would have made more sense. Instead, the man had left directions for something else, another way of figuring out the translation perhaps.

His eyes probed the page for answers. The gears in his brain turned faster and faster. Then the realization hit him. Nehem wasn't trying to give him the translation to the tablet's code. He knew that Tommy would have already been able to figure that out with technology. Not only that, but if he'd left the translation under the chair and the kidnappers had found it, they would be that much closer to whatever it was Nehem was trying to keep hidden.

Tommy's eyes grew wide as the solution came to him in an instant. The tablet wasn't just one code. It was two. The riddle was only half of the solution. Without deciphering the grid, finding whatever the tablet was linked to would be impossible. The symbols, the lines, the code, the grid, all of it became suddenly clear.

"Sean," he shouted, trying to contain his excitement, "I think I have something!"

9
Dubai

Cameras in two corners watched Nehem's every move. He stared up at the one nearest him from the meager desk chair he'd been given. The workstation was little more than a rickety folding card table. The chair looked and felt like it was thirty years old, a relic from a rundown office that had long since closed down. The rest of the room was sparsely decorated, which was a major contrast to the opulence the rest of the mansion displayed. Nehem figured it must have been used for storage most of the time. It was one of the few rooms in the palatial residence that didn't have a window. A narrow cot with a thin brown blanket and white pillow sat in one of the other corners.

The only expensive item in the room was the laptop he'd been afforded for his research.

Now, Nehem lowered his eyes and gazed at the vibrant, bright computer monitor. The glow of the screen illuminated his face and part of the wall, almost more than the solitary light fixture in the center of the ceiling. He'd bought himself another day. More importantly, he'd been able to make sure his daughter was safe. They could do whatever they wanted to him, but Nehem had to make sure she would be okay. Nothing else mattered now.

His hope, his only hope, was that his friend in America got the email and was able to solve the code on the tablet. He knew that Tommy had the most sophisticated software on the planet, capable of deciphering nearly any complex sequence. If he was able to solve the riddle, there was a chance he would head to Israel. That all hinged on the assumption that he caught the last part of the email.

There hadn't been time to elaborate on what Nehem meant by his warning. The men were outside his apartment and on their way up. With only seconds to spare, he was able to get the email away to his friend in the United States. At least Mamoud's men had possessed the decency to knock. They gave him the chance to give himself up or they would break down the door. He chose to go easily, thinking that it would be better for him in the long run if he didn't resist.

When Mamoud's men entered the apartment, led by the one he called Sharouf, the group of mercenaries ripped through everything in the apartment while Nehem sat idly by in his desk chair, watching helplessly. They'd taken the tablet, which he knew there was no possible chance he could hide. The three-thousand-year-old piece of stone was taken from his tiny breakfast table where he'd placed it on a towel. Part of his plan was to keep it in plain sight, knowing that the only people who could translate it were his friend in America and himself. Had he claimed to not know the whereabouts of the tablet, the men might have simply killed him right then and there.

"Is there anything else?" the one called Sharouf had asked.

Nehem had slowly shaken his head and watched as the other men finished tearing apart his belongings.

When they were satisfied they had what they needed, they'd put a pillowcase over Nehem's head and taken him down to their van. The next day, he'd woken up in this cramped little storage room.

Over the days that he'd been held hostage, Nehem knew what Mamoud Al Najaar wanted. He knew that the wealthy young Arab wanted the symbols to be interpreted, and he knew why. Nehem may have just been an archaeologist, but he was no fool. The reasons why someone would want the relics he searched for could be many in number. If anyone who'd studied the *Bible* or the *Torah* took note of the relics, they could easily wonder what possibilities awaited if the two were found and reunited.

Of course, neither Scripture discussed what happened to the Hoshen and the Urim and

Thummim when the Babylonians came. Both sacred texts seem to just cease mentioning the items, much like the Ark of the Covenant.

Nehem knew exactly what Mamoud wanted to hear. Unfortunately, he didn't know enough about the man to come to a logical conclusion. All he could do was hope that Tommy could figure everything out before it was too late.

Nehem tapped on the keyboard and moved the mouse around, pretending to examine the grid on the screen. Next to the monitor, the stone tablet sat like a heavy, priceless paperweight on the desk's surface.

He was pretending because everything he'd done up until now was part of a plan to stall. Nehem didn't tell Mamoud that he had already figured out the riddle in the symbols. He'd discovered the translation shortly before sending Tommy the email. He didn't actually need his friend's help. He had all the same technology. But Nehem didn't entirely trust the Internet, either. If he sent an email out with specific locations and with the translation of the riddle on the stone, it could be hacked and spread around the world within an hour.

There were going to be enough hurdles. Worrying about a thousand treasure hunters didn't need to be one of them.

So instead of including the key to the symbols on the tablet, and the way in which they could be used with the grid, Nehem played it safe and sent copies to Tommy, knowing that the American would be one of the few people in the world with the software powerful enough to break down the extensively complicated cipher. Along with that, he'd left another clue that Sharouf and his men had missed.

Nehem suppressed the laughter that tried to escape from his lips, aware that the cameras were always watching for any unusual behavior. Even in a dire situation like the one in which he presently found himself, he could see humor in some things.

He moved the mouse around again and picked up a pencil, pretending to write down something important. They were meaningless symbols, but the men behind the cameras didn't know that. Nehem already had the solution to the code, and to the grid. He knew exactly where to look for the first of the two relics, though where it was hidden once they got there could prove to be tricky. At the moment, that didn't matter. All that mattered was that Mamoud believed he was working on a solution, and that he would be able to provide it within the next twenty-four hours.

Nehem wrote down another phrase in Old Hebrew and set the pen down again. The newest lettering spelled out an insulting line, directed at his captors. They would never know what it meant anyway.

When his twenty-four hours were up, he would present the solution to the first part of the riddle to Mamoud, and not a minute sooner. All Nehem could do was hope that he'd bought his friend enough time to catch up, if Tommy was even on the trail at all.

He wondered where the American might be and whom he had with him. Nehem put his hands over his head and stretched. A yawn escaped from his gaping mouth. His eyes wandered over to the clock on the computer monitor.

His deadline was hours away. He said a silent prayer that his friend would hurry.

10
Jerusalem

Tommy's finger traced the arrows on the sheet of paper. He'd put it down on the desk and waited for Karem and Sean to return from the bedroom so he could show them what he had found.

"These symbols fit into the grid to spell out different possibilities. The riddle was only half of the solution." He relayed his theory to his friend and waited to hear what Sean had to say.

Sean examined the paper and nodded slowly. "Finally," he said, relieved. "That makes perfect sense. The riddle, though revealing, was vague about actual locations. You think this spells out where to go next?"

"It has to," Tommy said. "It's the only thing that makes sense. The riddle gives a clue, but the grid will tell us exactly where to look. That's why it was so hard to figure out. We only had half the information."

Karem had been standing by, listening to the two. "Does this mean you know where Nehem is?"

"No," Sean said. "But it gives us some insight as to where we should look next. If someone who wants what he was looking for took him, they will force him to lead them to it. Nehem left us this clue so we can track them down." He hoped he was right. The truth was, Nehem and the people who took him could be anywhere at that moment. He wasn't about to tell Karem that, though.

Sean turned his attention back to his friend before the Israeli could say anything else. "You think you can figure that thing out?"

Tommy stared at the paper. "I think so. It's almost like a three-thousand-year-old word jumble." He found a blank piece of paper and set it next to the drawing.

"Based on the key that Tara and Alex discovered, if we apply the letter sequence to the symbols on this sheet, we should be able to get several different combinations of words in Old Hebrew. Once we have those, we can take a picture and send it to the lab for the kids to analyze."

Karem stepped forward. "You mean you two don't read Old Hebrew?"

Sean and Tommy stopped what they were doing and turned back to their guide. They simultaneously shook their heads.

"No," Sean said. "Do you?"

"Sean, I am the director of antiquities and head curator of one of the most prized museums here in Israel. I have access to rooms and galleries that even high members of state don't have." He grinned at the other two. "In short, of course I can read it."

Tommy smiled and motioned him to come closer. "Perfect. Get over here."

He spent the next fifteen minutes drawing out a grid of his own to mirror the one Nehem had left, inserting the corresponding Hebrew letters into different areas and substituting them for the odd symbols.

As he followed the directions left by the Israeli archaeologist, Sean watched intently. An eerie silence hung in the room, and every time a sound came from outside, whether it was a door slamming shut or a neighbor yelling, all three men started and looked toward the entrance. At one point, Sean walked over and secured the door, locking the deadbolt and the lock on the doorknob. He knew that these measures wouldn't hold up to someone who wanted to get in badly enough. Still, it was enough to slow them down by a few seconds. In a fight, a few seconds could mean the difference between life and death.

He patted the ankle holster carrying his weapon of choice, a compact Springfield XD .40-caliber. It was a habit he'd adopted years ago. Even though he could feel the gun there, it always reassured him to feel it with his hand. Normally, he'd rather have a full-sized weapon, as they were more accurate and just felt better in his hand, especially when fired. This particular situation called for concealment, though. Since he was officially a government agent again, he would likely have no trouble with the Israelis for carrying a firearm, but if he had his choice, Sean would prefer not to have to use it.

Satisfied he'd done what he could with the door, he returned to the workstation where Tommy worked diligently with the code. Karem stood directly over him now, looking over his shoulder like a little kid watching a magic trick.

"If you want, you can start speeding this up by translating these to English," Tommy said to their guide. He never looked up from his work but slid a nearby pen over to the left side of the desk.

Karem nodded. "Good idea."

He grabbed the pen and a piece of paper off the floor and shifted to Tommy's left. Karem started working on the translation, putting the word clusters in the order they found them on the grid. Rather than a direct substitute of letter for letter, the symbols produced different word groupings, which were more representative of the original language. Some of the letters were dummy letters, sounds that would have been included in the primary language but now would be left out, especially when changing to English.

As he jotted down the meanings, he crossed out letters he deemed irrelevant and connected letters he thought might go together. After five minutes of working, though, things still didn't seem to coalesce.

"I don't understand," Karem said, frustrated. "This just looks like nonsense."

Tommy was almost finished with his part of the task and glanced over at the work Karem had done so far.

Sean looked over it as well, standing behind the other two. His eyes narrowed to slits. "You've got it," he said evenly, trying not to sound too excited.

Tommy and Karem looked back at him over their shoulders. "What are you talking about?" the Israeli asked. "It's just a bunch of gibberish."

"No," Sean shook his head and pointed at a particular section. "Take the top line, go across, and then down. Tommy, if I'm not mistaken, it looks like that's forming the name of the oldest Buddhist temple in the world."

Tommy cocked his head and stared at the sheet. Sure enough, it was plain as day. "I don't know why I didn't see that."

"Well, it's a strange name," Sean said in an attempt to make his friend feel better about not seeing what appeared obvious to him.

"Yeah, but it's one I know. Heck, I've been there before."

Karem still seemed lost. "Are you certain that is the name you're looking for?"

"It makes perfect sense," Sean said. "Think about it. The riddle suggests a place to the east with the seekers of light."

Tommy's eyes widened at the epiphany. "Of course. Buddhists are seekers of enlightenment."

"Bingo."

"And this place," he tapped the paper, "has a high tower."

"Lots of towers, actually."

"Right."

Karem interrupted again. "So you're saying that what Nehem was looking for is at the Buddhist Temple of Borobudur?"

"It would appear so, professor," Sean answered.

"But why there?"

Silence soaked the apartment again as the three men pondered the question. Karem had a good point. Why would a relic of Jewish history be hidden there?

"Maybe the answer lies in figuring out what it is he was looking for," Tommy said, breaking the dead silence once more.

"Fine," Karem agreed. "How are you going to do that?"

"Easy," Sean said, staring at the floor to the right of the desk. "It's been right in front of us the entire time we've been here."

The other two followed his eyes down to where a print of a painting lay among the debris. It was a picture similar to some Sean had seen when he was a boy in church. The artist had painted the image of the Israelite high priest in full regalia as he offered a sacrifice. His arms were extended high to the heavens, his head tilted back, and his eyes gazing into the sky. On his head was a fluffy white hat with a golden crown around the base. Sean immediately recognized the white linen ephod, or robes, that the priests of the time wore. In the background, thousands of people kneeled reverently. But none of that was what drew the attention of the three men in the apartment. They all stared at what the priest wore over the ephod.

The shining golden breastplate hung over the priest's chest, supported by golden chains that went over his shoulders. Additional chains secured it around his waist to keep it stable as he performed the rituals required of his position. Sean knew he'd recognized the pattern of the stone tablet before. It looked almost identical to the breastplate, except that the one the priest wore featured twelve stones, each of unique color and clarity. Two additional stones in the priest's hands caught Sean and Tommy's attention.

In the right, a stone as black as onyx; in the left, a stone that looked like white quartz, smoothed down into an oval shape. The artist's rendering displayed an odd glow hovering around the hand holding the darker of the two stones.

"The Hoshen," Sean said in a hushed tone, breaking the silence that once more pervaded the room.

"And the Urim and Thummim," Tommy added, referring to the stones in the priest's hands.

The two looked back at the sheet Nehem had drawn and then down again at the print.

Karem looked perplexed. "Why would Nehem be looking for those things? They are sacred, hidden thousands of years ago by the priesthood."

Sean and Tommy turned to him with questioning eyes. "How do you know that?"

He shrugged. "It's the only explanation. When the Babylonians invaded the Holy City, they took everything of value. The temple was ravaged and looted of most of its treasures. The priesthood had set security measures in place in case of an invasion. The Ark of the Covenant was the first priority. They built a contraption into the temple that would allow the Ark to drop down below ground. It worked with counterweights made from heavy bags of sand."

"Stay on track, Karem. What else do you know about these things?" Sean pointed at the print again.

"Honestly, not that much. There are only legends, myths really, that surround the whereabouts of the Hoshen and the two sacred stones."

Sean crossed his arms and waited. Tommy mimicked him, coercing Karem to keep talking.

When he did, he stuttered at first but gained clarity as he went on. "From...from what I have learned about those objects, they were a form of divination the high priest used to gain insights into important matters of state."

"Divination?" Sean asked. "You mean, like, they would use it to get answers from a supernatural source?"

Karem nodded. "Again, this is what the Scriptures say, though we never spent a great deal of time and energy on the subject. Most of our teachers and rabbis brush over those parts of the texts, claiming they are unimportant."

Tommy listened carefully before interjecting. "Wait a minute. I thought that using divination was forbidden in Jewish and Christian religions. Aren't there several texts that talk about that?"

"Yes," Karem gave another nod. "We do not condone divination, necromancy, cleromancy, or astrology. Those things are forbidden. But to the ancient Hebrews, divination was the way they sought answers from Yahweh. They occasionally used cleromancy, or lot casting, as well. Only the high priest was permitted to engage those kinds of techniques, and they typically were done prior to a sacrifice, like in the image you see here." He pointed a finger at the print.

Sean spoke up again. "You said that they used these objects to seek answers from Yahweh. What kind of answers? I mean, how did it work?"

Karem took a deep breath and sighed then shrugged. "No one knows for certain. There are many accounts of using the Hoshen with the sacred stones to seek answers to questions. Some histories indicate that the stones were placed on top of the breastplate. When they were positioned correctly, the priest could ask questions, and the Urim or the Thummim would move to a specific jewel."

"Wait," Tommy stopped him. "You mean, like on a Ouija board?"

"Most certainly not," Karem sounded defensive for a second. "Those things are strictly forbidden, and related to contacting the forces of darkness. It would be considered necromancy."

"I meant no offense," Tommy sounded apologetic, "but what I meant was, on a Ouija board, people say the thing moves on its own.

You're saying these stones move by themselves?"

"That was one account, yes. However, the priest did not have to be touching them for the stones to move."

Sean had another question. "You said the stones moved to a specific jewel. From what I understand, each jewel represented a tribe of Israel. That would make me think that the questions typically revolved around answers they sought for the tribes? And I thought the priest had to be wearing the thing. If that is the case, how did they move without him holding them?"

"Typically yes, that would have been the case. In most instances, the high priest needed to know who a scapegoat was, who had done something wrong, or who should receive what reward after a battle. Of course, the moving stones is only one method that was recorded. The priest would have to put the breastplate down on a table to perform the ritual in that manner. The details, however, are extremely sketchy."

The two Americans gave a look that urged him to continue.

"Fine. The other method they used caused the stones to light up. That's why this artist's rendering shows a halo of light around the hand holding the darker stone. According to the records, the light effect was more frequently referred to when the priest was asking *yes* or *no* questions. If the answer was no, one stone would light up. If it was yes, the other would illuminate. There were also instances where it was said that the other stones on the Hoshen would light up during certain inquisitions. Other than that, there is nothing else I know about the relics."

A quiet calm fell over the room once more. Sean and Tommy mulled over the information Karem had given them. It seemed like he was talking about some kind of magic, though the two Americans knew better than to insinuate that. Growing up in a Christian church, both of them had heard all kinds of stories from the *Bible*. Miracles and unexplainable events were commonplace. Now, the possibility of finding two of the objects that seemed to revolve around something miraculous sent goose bumps across their skin.

Two more questions still needed answering, though.

"So," Sean spoke first, "the question is, who wants these things badly enough that they would kidnap an archaeologist to find them? And second, what do they want with the relics?"

Karem answered him. "Nehem must have been looking for these artifacts to preserve their historical value. I do not see why he would do otherwise. However, in the wrong hands, the Hoshen and the sacred stones could be a powerful force."

Sean and Tommy paid close attention to what he was saying, both minds racing with horrific scenarios even as Karem explained. "If someone, say a terrorist organization or insurgent group, were able to get their hands on those objects, assuming they do what the Scriptures say, it could spell doom for millions of people. They could find the answers to questions about military positions, stock market information, technology, and who knows what else. Use your imaginations. They would be able to effectively shut down global commerce. Armies would be rendered ineffective. Computer viruses would run rampant through the web. It would be worldwide chaos."

Those were some of the scenarios Sean was considering, even as Karem was speaking. "That's assuming these things actually do what the texts say they do. Right?"

"Correct." Karem answered quickly, but something in his voice told the other two that he wasn't confident in his response.

"We've dealt with future-telling devices before," Tommy attempted to lighten the mood. "It didn't work out so well for the bad guys." In his head, he recalled the events in Greece.

"Look, we're missing the point," Sean tried to guide them back on track. "Whether the Hoshen and those two rocks actually do what the *Bible* says they do doesn't matter at this point. We need to find whoever took Nehem and get him safely home. If we happen to recover a couple of priceless Israeli treasures along the way, great. But we need to focus on finding Nehem."

Karem and Tommy nodded their agreement. "Where do we start?" Tommy asked. "We don't exactly have a lot of leads."

"Sure we do," Sean corrected. "We know where to look for the breastplate." He leaned down and picked up the print. "Call the pilot, and tell him to make a flight plan for Indonesia."

Tommy didn't wait to be told twice. He reached into his pocket and pulled out his phone. A few seconds later, he was conversing with their pilot who was waiting around in Tel Aviv, probably at an Internet cafe. It only took a minute to relay the information. When he was done, Tommy looked at the other two. "We're good to go. Need to get back to the airport. He said the plane will be ready within the next two hours."

Sean folded the print and put it in his back pocket. Tommy took the two sheets of paper with the symbols and the translations and folded them carefully, putting them inside one of his cargo pockets.

The men turned to leave, but a noise stopped them in their tracks. Across the room, the doorknob was jiggling. It was slight, barely noticeable, but it was definitely moving back and forth.

Someone was trying to get in. And they were trapped.

11
Jerusalem

For one second, all three men inside the apartment froze. They turned their heads, looking to one another for an answer. Tommy shrugged as Sean glanced at him. Sean, however, wasn't a man of indecision. He acted quickly, his thoughts in perfect sync with his actions.

He motioned for Tommy to come to the door with him. His friend shook his head and mouthed the word *No*. Sean pointed at the side of the door closest to the hinges, instructing him to stay behind the opening once the intruders came through. That way, he could attack from behind.

With a clearer understanding of his role, Tommy nodded and tiptoed over to the other side of the entrance. Sean pulled the gun out of his ankle holster and pressed his back against the wall. Karem still stood by the desk, uncertain of what he was supposed to do.

Sean urgently motioned with his hand for the man to go hide in the bedroom in the back. Reluctantly, Karem obeyed. He knew his strengths, and he realized that he would be of little assistance in a fight.

The door jiggled more violently. Karem hurried to the back of the apartment and disappeared into the bedroom, closing the door behind him.

A sudden jarring thud came from the door, and a man's shoe and leg followed through as the portal gave way to the heavy kick. Sean pointed his weapon but didn't fire. If he were to miss, Tommy was now behind the door, and even though it could potentially stop the bullet, he didn't want to chance shooting his friend. Sean's thought was to use the gun as a way to get whoever came through the doorway to stop and surrender.

Unfortunately, it didn't go down that way.

A man with a scarf over his face came through the door and only lost his balance for a split second, recovered quickly, and jabbed his own handgun at Sean's chest. The long barrel of the silencer made the weapon awkward and unbalanced, a fact that played to Sean's advantage in the moment it took the man to aim. Sean dropped his right hand and reached out with the other, grabbing the elongated barrel and yanking it to the right just as the intruder fired. The muffled pop sent a round harmlessly into the drywall. Before he could squeeze off another shot, Sean jerked the man toward him. Using his momentum, he planted his forearm squarely in the attacker's nose.

Behind the mask, the man grunted. He stumbled backward, dizzied by the shattered nose and the pain shooting through his skull. His eyes instantly watered, and he instinctively put his hands to his face. Sean took a step forward and was about to send his boot into the intruder's gut when another man came through the door. Tommy had been waiting in his hiding spot, anticipating the right moment. Seeing the second attacker coming through, he took that as his cue and shoved the door hard as the next man tried to aim his weapon at Sean.

The door crashed into the man's side, jarring the arm that held the gun. The barrel puffed a thin cloud of smoke, and the bullet zipped through the wall on the other side of the room by the desk. Tommy yanked the door back and moved quickly around it. Using the element of surprise, and the attacker's imbalance, Tommy punched him in the jaw with a right hook. The blow sent the man stumbling back through the door, but he kept his weapon in hand and regained his composure a moment later. Tommy's stocky frame wasn't the most agile, but he managed to duck to the side as the gun fired again. He sidestepped and then quickly slammed his elbow into the man's forearm. Reaching over his elbow, Tommy grabbed the gun's lengthy barrel and twisted it hard, using his momentum to wrench it from the intruder. As he did, the masked man spun his body and brought his leg up, snapping the top of his foot into the target. His boot struck Tommy in the face and sent him reeling backward until his back struck the wall in the corridor, outside the apartment.

Inside the apartment, Sean lashed out at the crippled attacker while the man's hands were still grasping at a bleeding and broken nose. He jumped forward and kicked out, aiming for the man's ribs, but somehow the intruder was aware enough to step back and grab Sean's shoe before it reached the target. In the same quick motion, the man twisted the foot to the left and pulled hard. The move caught Sean in midair and sent him in a spin, crashing to the floor. A sharp pain shot through his shoulder as it struck the hard surface. Sean didn't have time to hurt, though. The intruder had regained his vision and stomped hard with his boot, intent on crushing Sean's face.

He rolled out of the way, put his hands on the floor, and swept his right leg out as the attacker tried the move again. Sean's leg clipped the man's ankle, and combined with his weight, sent him toppling backward onto the floor, landing hard on his shoulder blades.

Sean spun to a crouching position as his opponent lifted his legs and, pressing his hands against the floor, leaped acrobatically back onto his feet. Sean's shoulder ached. He had to keep focused, though. The other man was hurting too, blood oozing from his crushed nose down into the black scarf.

The man put his hands up in a position Sean recognized. The intruder was evidently trained in the martial arts of hand-to-hand combat. Sean waited for the attack he knew would come. There was a momentary pause, a second of nervous anticipation. Sean's heart pounded in his chest, and his lungs heaved rhythmically. Then the man launched his attack.

He lunged forward with a kick. Sean raised his right knee and blocked the strike with his shin, sending a fresh pain through his entire leg. He stayed focused though as his opponent lashed out with a fury of blinding fast punches. One after the other came at Sean like lightning. His hands were just as fast, though, and he parried and blocked each one. A quick knee aimed at Sean's midsection followed the blizzard of jabs, but the man overcommitted and stepped right into a counterpunch. Sean's fist came to a snapping stop three inches behind the target as the man's head cracked back. The blow caused him to waiver for a moment. Sean didn't hesitate. Like a shark with blood in the water, he attacked mercilessly, first with a foot to the abdomen, then a knee kick to the face. The bloodied man staggered backward, miraculously still on his feet. Sean pounced, pressing the attack further, and grabbed the back of the man's head while in the same motion jumping hard and bringing his knee up. The hard kneecap struck the man's chin with such force that Sean could hear teeth chipping and bone breaking. The attacker fell onto his back. His eyes rolled into the back of his head, and his body went still.

Outside on the second floor landing, Tommy grappled with the second attacker. The man had jumped at him, attempting to kick him in the throat, but Tommy had grabbed him out of the air and now was desperately trying to get the guy into a submission hold.

The intruder was slippery, though, and every time Tommy thought he was about to close the deal, the man escaped his grip. Tommy spun the attacker around and wrapped his forearm around the guy's throat in a chokehold. The victory was only temporary, though, and the man jerked his elbow into Tommy's ribs three, four, five times before the knife-like pain weakened him enough to let go.

Tommy instinctively grabbed at his midsection. The other man took a step away, grasping at his throat and heaving for fresh air. He started to spin around and renew his attack; however, Tommy recovered first and charged. He lowered his shoulder and plowed into the target like an all-pro NFL linebacker at full speed. The man's eyes widened as Tommy's shoulder dug hard into his abdomen. The momentum drove the two precipitously toward a railing near the stairwell. Tommy kept driving his legs hard, in spite of the burning in his thighs. The other man's feet shuffled backward, helpless against the larger American's power. He tried to beat Tommy's upper back with his elbow, but it was too late. The man's tailbone struck the top of the railing, and in one continuous motion, Tommy forklifted him up and over.

The intruder shrieked for a second until his body clumped onto the concrete below. Tommy put his hands on the railing and looked down. His lungs screamed for air, and he drew in huge breaths. Below, the man's right leg was bent at an awkward angle, clearly broken. The man didn't move, but Tommy doubted he was dead. The fall was less than fifteen feet. If he didn't land on his head, he would likely still be alive.

Back in the apartment, Sean reached down and felt his opponent's neck. There was a faint pulse, barely detectable and extremely slow.

Sean hurried to the door to check on his friend and saw Tommy leaning over the railing, still gasping for air. Sean noticed the other attacker was gone and realized where he must be. Tommy heard the movement at the door and twisted around quickly, ready for another fight. When he saw it was Sean, he visibly relaxed. His friend joined him at the rail and looked down at the body.

"He dead?" Sean asked.

"Not sure," Tommy said between breaths. "Doubtful, unless he landed on his head."

"That leg is definitely broken." He motioned with a nod at the black pants bent to the side.

"If he's not dead, he's going to wish he was when he wakes up. That's probably a compound fracture."

Sean nodded, taking a moment to catch his breath as well.

They heard a commotion back in the doorway and spun around with fists in the air, ready for another round. Karem stood on the threshold with eyes wide and mouth agape. He looked back into the apartment at the body on the floor and then again at the two Americans.

"Is he dead?" Karem asked in a trembling voice as he jerked his thumb at the man on the inside.

In the ruckus, the two friends had forgotten he was still inside the apartment.

"No, not yet," Sean answered. "But he'll be out for a while."

Karem walked onto the landing like a zombie. When he reached the railing, he looked down and saw the second man. He put his hand over his mouth as if to prevent himself from vomiting. "Is he...?"

"We don't think so," Sean answered. "But we'll go check in a minute."

"His leg..."

"Oh it's broken, guaranteed," Tommy said. His breathing had finally slowed from the struggle.

Karem stared blankly at the two friends, then down at the man below, and back at the Americans again. His lips trembled as he spoke. "Who *are* you two?"

Sean glanced at Tommy and then back at Karem. "It's a long story."

12
Tel Aviv, Israel

A shell-shocked Karem dropped Sean and Tommy at their hotel on the edge of the city. The drive back had been relatively quick. Karem, it seemed, had no desire to spend any more time with the two Americans.

They didn't blame him. After all, they tended to be bullet magnets on occasion. The sooner Karem could be done with them, the safer he would be.

The drive from Jerusalem back to the thriving coastal metropolis of Tel Aviv took just over an hour. Sean had been to the city several times during his first go-around with Axis. Even in the last decade, he'd been shocked at how quickly it had grown. The surrounding metropolitan area boasted around half a million people. New buildings were being constructed in perpetuity. The city, it seemed, was in a massive state of expansion, in spite of living under constant threat.

Tel Aviv had become one of the world's trendy places to visit. High fashion could be found everywhere, with women walking in brightly colored dresses to and from expensive clothing shops and boutiques. Restaurants and bars were thriving, especially over near the sea. Tel Aviv's beaches had become one of the country's top destinations and seemed to attract the most beautiful people, anxious to bathe in the constant warmth of the Israeli sun.

As Sean and Tommy got out of the car, thanking Karem for his help, the smells of the city simmered together with the salt air of the sea. A cornucopia of food scents wafted over the two Americans, flooding their nostrils with the aroma of fresh pita bread, falafels, schnitzel, sabih, shawarma, and a flaky, round pastry known as malawach. His nose reminded Sean of how hungry he'd got since leaving the hotel earlier. A shawarma stand across the street called his name. He could see the spit of lamb meat turning slowly over the cooking heater. There was no time to eat right now, though. He would have to settle for something on the flight.

The two hurried up to the hotel room and gathered their few belongings. Traveling light had been their choice. It made getting around easier, and quick getaways even more so.

Sean grabbed his laptop case, rucksack, and messenger bag. Tommy grabbed his backpack and laptop bag. They were checking through their things when Tommy's phone started vibrating. He looked down at the screen and hit the green button.

"Hey, kids. What's up?"

Tara's voice came through the earpiece first. "We looked up those engravings you sent. Where did you find those anyway?"

"The high priest's tomb of early seventh-century Israel. Why do you ask?"

Tommy's blunt and surprisingly exact answer caused her to pause for a second. "Okay...anyway, this language is really old. It took our computers a bit, but we were able to get you the names."

"Names?" Tommy raised an eyebrow and looked over at Sean. "I'm going to put you on speaker so Sean can hear." He tapped another button on the screen and set the phone on the bed.

"Can you both hear me?"

"Yep," the two said simultaneously.

"Like I was saying, the two words you sent us to translate are names."

"What names?" Sean asked. "Who are we talking about here?"

Alex jumped in on the other end. "The first name was one we didn't recognize. It's a historical Jewish name, not used very frequently anymore, but back around three thousand years ago it was fairly common. The name was Lamesh."

Sean and Tommy glanced at each other, but neither had any clue who that might have been.

"The other one," Alex continued, "is definitely one that you'll recognize. We aren't 100 percent sure if it's the same guy, but based on what Tommy said about the timeframe of the high priest's burial, it would be a logical conclusion to jump to."

"What's the name, Alex?" Tommy pressed, trying to be polite. His assistant tended to ramble from time to time.

"Oh, sorry. It's Daniel."

Tommy and Sean gave each other an intrigued glance.

Sean spoke before Tommy could. "Daniel? As in, the Old Testament prophet, Daniel? Like Daniel in the lions' den?"

"That's what we believe," Tara jumped back in. "We can't confirm that was the guy the name is indicating. There may have been thousands of Daniels around that time. However, based on the fact that this Tovar was a high priest and that he would have likely had connections with a known prophet, I would say it's highly probable that it's the same Daniel from the *Bible*."

Sean and Tommy pondered the implications.

"Is it possible that Daniel was one of the guys the priest sent away to protect the relics?" Sean was talking to Tommy, but the two on the phone also heard him.

"What?" Alex asked awkwardly.

"Sorry," Tommy offered. "Earlier, we figured out what the riddle meant. At least we think we did. Tovar sent two men, each with a precious temple object, to two places far apart from each other."

"Why?" Tara asked.

"To protect the relics from the invading Babylonian army," Sean explained. "The items were considered to be extremely powerful, and if they were to fall into the wrong hands, it would have meant catastrophe for the entire world. At least that's what we've gathered from the records." He embellished a little, but it was based on what Karem had told them. "One of the relics is called the Hoshen; it's the breastplate that the high priest wore in the temple. The other is two stones known as the Urim and the Thummim. They were probably kept together, from what we can tell."

Tommy cut back in. "If Daniel was one of the emissaries used to protect one of the relics, he would have had to have been the one sent back into Babylon."

"Thus the part of the riddle that talks about the belly of the beast. Several places in the *Bible* refer to Babylon as the beast — in Daniel and Revelation, in particular," Sean added.

"Right," Tommy agreed. "Daniel spent a great deal of time in Nebuchadnezzar's court before and after the second invasion of Jerusalem. It's entirely possible that the king sent him to parlay with the king of Judah to negotiate terms. If Daniel had a chance to get to the temple and meet with the high priest, he would have. In fact, I'd say that was his first priority, unbeknownst to Nebuchadnezzar."

A silent pause came over the room. After a few seconds, Alex came back on the line. "Do you guys always think this way?"

Sean stole a quick glance at his friend and smirked. "Doesn't everyone?"

"Um, no. Not really. I guess that's why you guys are the best at what you do." Tara's said. The compliment made both of them blush a little.

Tommy ignored it. "There was something else when we were in the priest's tomb. Three emblems were carved into the stone at three specific points surrounding the sarcophagus: the Star of David, an image of Ahura Mazda, and one other emblem. The first two were pretty obvious, but the last one was tricky. It's a Buddhist emblem, from what I recall, a picture of two fish."

He waited for a moment before Alex's voice came through again. "In the Buddhist religion, the two-fish symbol is meant for one who is willing to face a difficult trial, essentially what could be a lifetime of sacrifice and suffering. Many monks considered it to be their divine obligation to take on such an existence. I wonder why that and the Babylonian symbol were there."

"Ahura Mazda," Sean spoke up, "was also said to have gone through great trials along his journey. Tovar must have known he was sending these two young men on an extremely dangerous mission. They would be on the run, always looking over their shoulders for the rest of their lives. It was a great sacrifice they had to make to protect their people."

It was a sobering thought, and one that brought about silent reflection to the four on the phone.

"Is there anything else you two have for us?" Tommy asked.

"That's it for now. Sorry we couldn't get you more information." Tara sounded apologetic.

"You did great. This, combined with what we figured out, means we definitely have something to go on."

"So you found the answer to the code. Where to next?" Alex sounded genuinely curious.

Sean answered. "Java in Indonesia. The world's oldest Buddhist temple is there, a place called Borobudur. From what we can deduce, it was the hiding place of one of the relics. We're not sure which one, though."

A pause hung in the room for a few seconds, and then Alex spoke up again. "It looks like this Buddhist temple is a UNESCO world heritage site. It was abandoned a long time ago, when most of the people in the area converted to Islam. Have either of you ever seen this place?"

Tommy and Sean passed each other a questioning look, and both shook their heads. "Actually, I have once but I didn't get to roam around much. There were...extenuating circumstances," Tommy said.

Sean raised an eyebrow at the curious comment.

"Oh, wow. Okay," Alex interrupted. "I'll just assume you don't know much about the site. You should know that it's a huge facility. I can't imagine how many hours it took to lay all those stones. Not to mention how many people were used for the labor."

"Anyway," Tara cut him off, "good luck, and let us know if you need anything."

Tommy grinned. "Will do, Tara. Thanks to both of you."

He ended the call and slipped the phone back into his pocket.

Sean eyed him suspiciously as he finished collecting his things. "You really haven't been to Borobudur?"

"Shocking, I know."

"I mean, I guess you can't see everything. Or can you?" He stuffed a Ziploc bag containing his toothbrush and toothpaste into one of the bags. "I heard about a blogger who visited every country in the world."

"That's impressive," Tommy said, pressing his lips together.

"Yeah. I would have thought together we could have at least done that."

"We're not dead yet."

The words hung in the hotel room's industrial, filtered air.

"Here's hoping that doesn't happen anytime soon."

13
Dubai

Sharouf held the phone to his ear. All he heard was the intermittent ringing of the device on the other end. No answer.

He'd tried calling four times over the course of the last forty minutes. For some reason, his men weren't answering. With each subsequent failed call, Sharouf's anger grew, and his frustration built.

He ended the call and stared at the phone for a few seconds, trying to understand why no one was answering. At the moment, Sharouf was alone. Mamoud was busy handling a few business matters and had retired to his office to take care of things, leaving Sharouf to make sure things in Israel were going according to plan.

When Mamoud had recruited him, Sharouf had come at a hefty price. His reputation with various paramilitary groups and private security organizations had preceded him. Mamoud gave him a room in the mansion, not as luxurious as his own, but better than Sharouf had ever called his own. The downside was that he had traded his freedom for a life of ease and wealth. Most of the time, he didn't need to do much, occasionally encourage someone to leave the premises. Rarely, he had to eliminate a problem.

Now, he stared out his window. He'd kept his room minimally decorated compared to the rest of the home. His black wooden bed was covered in plain white sheets. The only other furniture in the room was a small chair made of maple, which he used simply for putting his shoes and socks on in the morning. The last piece of decor was his prayer mat that sat under the window. Despite the ruthless and often cruel nature of his job, Sharouf believed himself to be a deeply religious man, which was another reason he chose to work for Mamoud. The two were like brothers when it came to their ways of thinking. They believed in the old ways, the ways of the Saracens and the sultans of old. Only through the sword could peace be achieved. The peace they sought, however, was through the destruction of the West.

Sharouf had a special hatred of the Americans.

He'd served a tour with one of the private security companies in Iraq during the American occupation there. He'd watched as the American soldiers treated Muslims like subhumans, killing first and asking questions later. They cracked jokes and made bets on how many Muslims they could kill in a day, all the while thinking that Sharouf didn't speak English. Every word and every action that came from the Americans seeped deep into his soul. He stored the experiences and the things he learned in the vault of his mind to be called upon later, when the time was right. In a black Denali with several other security team members wasn't the right place or the right time.

Now, however, things were changing. Mamoud was giving him his chance for payback, and he must not fail. His employer shared Sharouf's vision, and more importantly, possessed the resources to make it happen.

But things, evidently, were not going according to plan.

One thing Sharouf had learned a long time ago was never to put all his eggs into one basket. He had confidence in the men he'd sent to eliminate Wyatt. If that hadn't been the case, he would have sent others, or simply more men. But even the best-laid plans fell apart from time to time. Sharouf was well aware of this, which was why he'd not entirely played his hand yet. Sometimes, it was best to hold a card for later.

He scrolled through his contact list and found the name he was looking for, tapped it, and waited for the phone to ring. The man on the other end answered instantly.

"Your men are dead."

Sharouf recognized the voice as one of his trusted mercenaries, but the news with he provided when answering the call was direct and troubling.

"Both of them?"

"Yes."

"What happened?"

The voice relayed how the other two went into Nehem's apartment to ambush Wyatt and his companions. He hadn't seen what happened inside, but he did see when one of the men was pushed over the railing to the ground below.

"The fall killed him?" Sharouf asked.

"No. His leg was broken. The police were on their way. I had to kill him myself." The voice was cold. Clearly, taking another human life meant absolutely nothing to him. He may as well have squashed an ant.

"What about the other?" Sharouf tried to sound businesslike, masking the concern in his tone.

"He was basically dead when I found him lying on his back in the apartment. He was unconscious, barely breathing. His jaw and nose were broken, probably making it hard to breathe. I helped him stop breathing."

Sharouf listened carefully to the vague account. His observer had handled things exactly as he would have. Loose ends were not tolerated. It would have made for a sticky situation if his assassins had been taken to a hospital and kept in custody. If one were to talk to the police and tell them who he worked for, Mamoud's carefully woven anonymity would be exposed, and his entire operation would crumble like a paper-thin cracker under a boot. Sharouf himself knew that were he to fail, death was the only way out. No hospitals. No police. Even he could not be permitted to become a potential loose end. So delicate were the plans Mamoud had laid.

"It would seem the Americans are going to be more trouble than we first suspected," the man said.

Sharouf would not admit that he'd underestimated Wyatt and his companion. To do so would appear weak and ill prepared. He could afford neither. "Our men may have underestimated them, but I did not. Wyatt is a highly trained killer, and his friend has been in more than a few fights. If they were careless, our men deserved what they got. While it is unfortunate, we must move on. Tell me, where did they go?"

"I put a GPS tracker on their car. After I took care of the two problems, I was able to track them to Tel Aviv. They were staying at a hotel on the edge of the city. According to the tracking device, the car they were in stopped at the hotel and then went to another address on the north side of town."

"A decoy?"

"No," the voice said. "They had a driver. He dropped them off and probably went home. I stuck around, assuming they would probably be in a hurry to leave."

"And were they?" Sharouf scratched his chin as he listened to the account.

"Yes. They came out the front doors around ten minutes after I arrived. They got in a car that took them to the airport. That is where I am sitting right now."

Sharouf weighed the information. The Americans left in a hurry. At least that was what his observer was telling him. That could mean a few things. One, they were afraid after the failed attack and decided to get out of the country while they still could.

He wanted to believe that was the case, but Sharouf was no fool. People like Wyatt and

Schultz weren't easily spooked. It would take more than a couple of hired guns to scare them off.

The other possibility, and the likelier one, in Sharouf's mind, was that they had figured out a piece of the puzzle. If he could find out where they were going, Sharouf could circumvent the slow work Nehem was doing. It was a hopeful plan, but it could work. All he needed was to know where Wyatt was headed.

"Do you know where their plane went?"

The man on the other end took a deep breath and sighed. "No."

Well, it was worth a try.

"But," he continued, "I did see the plane they flew in."

Sharouf perked up, his right eyebrow rising slightly. "Go on."

"It was a private jet, kept in one of the hangars on the outskirts of the tarmac. Easy enough to spot since it was parked alone. As it took off, I was able to write down the numbers on the side of the tail."

"Give them to me."

14
Dubai

The door to Nehem's room burst open, and Sharouf entered like an angry bull. He stormed across the small space to where Nehem sat at his desk, surprised but not scared. Not yet anyway.

Sharouf drew his pistol from his side and aimed the weapon at Nehem's head. "Time's up, Doctor."

Nehem's face waxed pale, confused and worried. "What are you talking about? I still have several hours left."

The Arab looked over at the cot against the wall and noticed the sheets and blanket were not folded, instead lying in a crumpled heap as if someone had just got out of bed.

"You sure sleep a lot for someone whose life is on a timer. We watched you waste your time and ours," he motioned to the cameras. His eyes narrowed, and he brandished the gun at the archaeologist who was now starting to cower a little. "You know what I think? I think you have been lying to us. I believe that you already know where the relics are. Either you tell me right now, or I will kill you. After I kill you, I will kill your daughter. And I promise you, she will take a long time to die."

Nehem trembled, but he would not surrender easily. "You cannot kill me. If I die, your boss will never find the relics. They will be lost to the annals of time forever. And whatever it is you have planned will fail."

"Interesting," Sharouf said. "I find it odd that the Americans you contacted are on their way to Indonesia right now. You wouldn't happen to know why that is, would you?"

Nehem tried to keep his face expressionless, but he failed miserably. Like a bad poker player at a table full of seasoned gamblers, his eyes gave away what he was so desperately trying to hide. There was a glimmer of hope, though. If Tommy was on his way to Indonesia, that meant he'd figured out the code. He was on the right path. At the very least, if Nehem was going to die, he could do so with the knowledge that Mamoud Al Najaar would never possess the holy relics.

Sharouf pressed the gun to Nehem's forehead. "Tell me where they went, exactly, and save the life of your daughter."

Cautiously, Nehem moved his hand backward to the surface of the desk and tapped on a sheet of paper next to the keyboard. "That is where they are going," he said in a weak voice. "It is an ancient Buddhist temple in Indonesia, in the Java region. You will find one of the relics there."

"Which one?"

Nehem forced a laugh. "I don't know. The clues the high priest left were vague for a reason. Whoever finds the relics will only know what they have found when they find it."

"So you do not know if it is the Hoshen or the sacred stones at this place?" Sharouf pulled the gun back a few inches. He looked over at the writing on the paper.

"No. No one could know that. I'm telling you the truth. But you should also know this. If the Americans are on their way, you will never catch up to them. They are far smarter than you. Once they arrive, it will not take them long to discover the relic. And when they do, your boss will have failed."

Sharouf considered the man's words for a moment. He stared into the fearful eyes of his prisoner without sympathy. The hand with the gun flashed to the left, smacking the side of the weapon against Nehem's temple. The man crumpled to the floor. A few seconds later, a thin cut oozed crimson down the side of his face and underneath his eye.

Sharouf turned to the two guards he'd brought and ordered them to take Nehem downstairs to the car. "Make sure he doesn't cause you any trouble when you get him there. We have a long flight ahead of us, and the last thing we need is more delays."

The men nodded and hustled into the room. They scooped up the unconscious hostage by the armpits and dragged him through the open door. When they were gone, Sharouf stepped over to the desk and picked up the sheet of paper. He stared at the name written on it.

Borobudur.

His lips creased ever so slightly into a knowing grin. He'd been correct about the prisoner keeping the answer from them. He was stalling to give the Americans a head start. Unfortunately, that would not be enough to save them.

He pulled out his phone and sent a text message to Mamoud, letting him know that whatever business he was taking care of would need to be put on hold for a moment, that he had something his boss wanted.

Mamoud replied after a minute, telling Sharouf to come to the office at the other end of the compound.

They were heading for a showdown with Wyatt and Schultz.

Sharouf cracked his neck to one side and then the other. He would be ready.

He left the room and walked fast from one end of the mansion to the other, where he knew Mamoud would be waiting. Sharouf had taken the liberty of ordering the archaeologist to be transported down to a car, figuring that is what his boss would have wanted.

When he reached the massive double doors to Mamoud's office, he pulled on the cylindrical bronze handle and stepped inside.

The wealthy young Arab sat behind an enormous mahogany desk. A woman in a miniskirt and a black skintight top stood waiting nearby. She looked like a common prostitute in that tacky dress. Perhaps that was what Mamoud's tastes desired for the day.

The boss motioned for her to leave. She hesitated for a second, to which he ordered, "Leave us."

The girl hurried out the door, her high heels clacking on the hard tile floor as she clumsily tried to run.

Mamoud waited until the door closed behind her before he spoke. "I assume you have news, especially since you know I have financial assets I have to look after, not to mention the war I am preparing to wage."

"I would not have bothered you if it weren't vitally important." He paused for a second and then said, "The first relic is in Indonesia. I forced Nehem to give it to us."

"Forced? He had a deadline."

"My apologies, sir. But he was playing you for a fool."

Mamoud's eyes narrowed, but he remained calm.

"He was stalling. I had eyes on him all day. He hardly worked at all, even took a nap at one point. I reasoned that the only purpose he could have in doing so was that he already knew the answer we were looking for and was holding out until the last possible moment before giving it to us. When I came to this conclusion, all I had to do was apply the right amount of pressure."

Mamoud considered his guard's words. Sharouf had done the right thing. Now he wanted to know what his next plan was for the Israeli. "Did you kill him?"

"No. I ordered him to be taken to a car downstairs. With your permission, I will fly to Indonesia with my team and recover the relic."

The last part didn't seem to please Mamoud. "I need you here. Send your chief of security. Have them recover it and bring it here."

Sharouf had worried the man would say that. There could be no hiding his true intentions. "Wyatt and his friend escaped Jerusalem. They made it back to Tel Aviv and flew out late in the afternoon."

Mamoud leaned forward, putting his elbows on the table. "And where did they go?" His voice stayed low, barely audible as it passed through clenched teeth.

"I had another man stationed at the Jew's apartment to make sure everything went according to plan. When I did not get a status report from them, I contacted the observer. He followed them back to the airport. He couldn't get access for obvious reasons, but he kept an eye on the plane and knows where they're headed. With that information, I coaxed Nehem to tell me exactly what he'd been hiding."

Sharouf placed the piece of paper on the desk in front of his employer. Mamoud examined the writing for a few seconds and then lifted his eyes again. "Take him there. Now. See to it, personally, that the Americans do not escape this time."

The guard nodded, spun on his heels, and strode out of the room. Mamoud picked up the paper. He leaned back in his high leather chair and gazed at the strange name Nehem had provided. After a few seconds, he set it back down next to a series of papers he'd been looking over.

Most of them were invoices from legitimate businesses. At least that was what he wanted them to look like. The largest bill of all was from a pharmaceutical company with a price tag of just over three million dollars.

The phone on his desk rang loudly and danced across the surface as it vibrated. He reached over and picked it up.

"Have the shipments arrived?"

"We're loading them into the warehouses now. Will this be the last of them, or should we continue buying more storage properties?" The voice on the phone wasn't of Arab descent. It sounded distinctly Spanish.

"If any good opportunities arise, you have the green light to buy. At the right price, of course."

"Of course."

"And what of the training of my men?"

"All two hundred pilots are getting better each day. Each has logged over a thousand hours. They've mastered the simulators and are ready for some test flights when you say the word."

Mamoud thought about it. It would be risky. If there were any spy planes flying in the area, or even less detectable, satellites, his operation could be in jeopardy. His eyes wandered out to the gulf and gave him an idea.

"Have them fly low-level test missions over the water. If anyone is watching, it will be unlikely they'll have their eyes on the water. Be sure to keep them low."

"Understood. Less chance of being noticed on radar. A good plan."

"Keep me updated on their progress. Have them ready to fly within the next week."

He ended the call and set the phone back on the desk. Once more, Mamoud leaned back in his high leatherback chair.

Soon, he would have the war his father had wanted. Soon, the devils in the West would feel the wrath of Allah.

15
Atlanta

"All right, Emily. I only have a few minutes before I have to give a speech, and the pressroom is at least a three-minute walk from here. Something must have got you spooked for you to call me on this line."

The president of the United States stared at Emily from her widescreen computer monitor. Only she and a few others in charge of top-level agencies had access to the number she'd called. After a quick linkup, the president appeared on the screen through a secure network line. Some of the techies called it the Internet subway. No civilians had access to it, and for good reason.

"We've noticed something strange going on in Dubai lately, sir," she cut right to the chase, which was something she knew Dawkins would appreciate. A farmer at heart, the president knew bull when he saw or heard it. When time was short, he preferred to dispense with pleasantries and get straight to dancing.

"Define strange, Director Starks."

Emily Starks had been the director of Axis for the past several years. The ultra secret agency was an Atlanta-based arm of the Justice Department that handled counterterrorism, counterintelligence, and internal investigations. They were occasionally called upon to handle dirtier jobs that the CIA, FBI, and NSA didn't want to touch. Axis operated with only eleven agents to keep things simple and clean, and deniability much more plausible. Recently, another agent was added to the list, although he was to be used sparingly, at his request. She'd often wondered why eleven and not ten or twelve agents but finding that answer had proven impossible.

"Based on CIA reports, there have been several shipments being dispersed to recently purchased warehouses on the outskirts of the city. One of our people on the inside of an arms ring said that something big is going down soon. They aren't sure what, exactly, but someone has been buying a lot of weapons."

"A lot, Director Starks, is a fairly vague number."

"Yes, sir. I apologize. Over two hundred million dollars worth of weapons is the report I'm seeing."

The president's face scrunched up. He wrinkled his nose before speaking again. "So who are we talking about? I'm assuming it's not insurgents. They don't usually have that kind of funding."

"That is correct, sir. However, we are not certain what affiliation this buyer has. Word from our guy is that it's a man named Mamoud Al Najaar. He's a wealthy business owner in Dubai, though he is only involved with a few actual enterprises."

"Where did he get all that scratch from then?"

Emily didn't need to glance at her notes. She'd already memorized everything after one read through the report. She kept them with her just in case, but rarely needed them when relaying information up the chain. "Al Najaar inherited a substantial fortune when his father passed away several years ago. It seems his father sold the family oil fields to one of the larger conglomerates. They made billions from the sale. Since then, his net worth has nearly doubled from investments and the few businesses he's taken on."

Dawkins didn't appear convinced. His wise, narrow eyes displayed his dubious thoughts on the matter. "What would his motive be? He's obviously a capitalist."

"More than you know, sir. His lifestyle is heavily influenced by the West. He keeps a stable of women in his beachfront mansion, has wild parties, and was even educated in the UK."

"Yet it seems like he's preparing for a war."

"Certainly contradicts his risqué exterior," she agreed. "He's something of an enigma."

"Director, do you want my permission for something regarding this Al Najaar, or did you want to keep me in the loop?"

Emily smirked. "A little of both, sir. As I said, we have an agent keeping a close watch with some high-end arms dealers. I don't have anything to request at the moment, but if things get shady, we may need backup."

Dawkins' expression remained firm. "Understood. Will that be all, Director Starks?"

She nodded. "Yes, Mr. President."

"Keep an eye on it, and let me know if anything changes. Play this one close to the chest. We don't need to piss off the UAE by storming in there and kicking up a bunch of sand under their noses without a good reason."

"I agree. Good luck with your speech, sir."

He smiled and nodded. "Thanks."

The screen went black. She turned off her own monitor and folded her hands in front of her face. Her eyes stared across the room at the grained finish of her wood-paneled walls.

Emily sighed, frustrated. She needed answers, and the president hadn't offered any. He seemed almost ignorant of the man she'd said they were watching closely. President Dawkins had a lot on his plate, and as he said, he was about to give a speech.

She suppressed her insecurities. He trusted her. That was the biggest thing to remember. With that in mind, she sent a text message to her guy in the field, instructing him to lie low and pay attention.

He'd reported in regularly with details of what was happening. If anything changed, she wanted to know about it, and fast. What concerned her most was what her man *didn't* report. He said there were dozens of forty-foot steel shipping containers arriving each day, but he had no idea what was inside. It could have been anything. Rockets. Long-range artillery. There was no way to know without seeing inside the containers.

Concern began to swell in Emily's mind as she considered the implications and the words of the president hung in her ears.

It seems like he's preparing for a war.

16
Yogyakarta, Indonesia

Before the sun had even reached the treetops, a heavy humidity swamped the region around Yogyakarta. To Tommy and Sean, it almost felt like being back home in the Southeast. It reminded them of Charleston, South Carolina.

"This is just like the weather down on Kiawah Island," Sean commented as they got in the small rental car they'd picked up at the airport.

Renting a car in Yogyakarta wasn't recommended by many people. With so many rickshaws, cabs, bicycles, motorcycles, and mopeds on the streets, getting around in a car could prove nearly impossible at times. Still, once they were out of the city, having their own mode of transportation would be vital.

The Americans had landed late the previous evening. The meal aboard the plane had satiated their need for food in the interim, but upon arriving, a quick snack of rice and vegetables from a street vendor filled their empty stomachs before bed.

Sean usually preferred not to eat late at night, but he knew they might have to rush breakfast the next day. His foresight proved correct, as they were only able to procure a handful of nuts and dried fruit during their rushed attempt to beat the early morning traffic.

Their hotel was one of the less fancy places either of the Americans had stayed in for quite a long time. It stood three stories tall and was clearly in the decline. Pinkish paint on the exterior walls noticeably flaked away in numerous places. The lobby was little more than a foyer with a counter, two potted plants on either side of the main desk, and a set of stairs that went up to the higher levels. No elevators were in sight.

For all it lacked in amenities, the hotel's rooms were, at the very least, clean. The pillows, though flimsy and beaten, were placed neatly at the head of the beds atop fresh linens. The interior walls resembled those outside the tiny slit of a window, the paint peeling away in various spots.

Sleep had come easily for the men in spite of the noises from the street below. They'd been so tired, both from their travels and the stress of fight or flight, that once their heads hit the pillows, they were out cold until their phone alarms woke them up the next morning.

In the car, it took forty minutes just to get to the outskirts of the city's artificial walled canyons. Once they did, however, the traffic thinned to a trickle. Eventually, they found themselves driving along a roughly paved road and away from the sprawling Indonesian town.

Palm trees sprouted into the sky in random spots along the road. Others lined the rice fields and farms, waving intermittently when the breeze picked up. Farms popped up between the rolling hills of the countryside, the scenery a variety of green grasses and heavy forests of leafy trees.

Their speed on the main road was faster than in the city, though occasionally Sean was forced to slow down. The side of the road carried almost as much traffic as the asphalt. Farmers with ox-drawn carts, beasts of burden laden with full baskets, and pedestrians made driving too fast a potentially dangerous proposition. In spite of the stop-and-start driving, the journey to the temple only took another twenty minutes after leaving the city.

The massive fortress-like facility rose up from the flats like a massive ziggurat, its dark façade set against a backdrop of shadowy, mist-covered mountains in the distance. Hardwood trees, thick with dark leaves, surrounded the immediate area of the temple's periphery. As the two men drew closer, more of the building's details revealed themselves.

A conical stupa towered over the site, its shape like an enormous bell sitting atop the temple's highest point. Dozens more smaller stupas came into view. The dome-shaped stone formations were originally built into the temple's surface to pay tribute to the stars in the heavens, a sort of celestial representation on Earth. The charcoal-gray and deep-maroon colors of the temple stones were arranged in a specific pattern, keeping the balance between dark and light, yin and yang.

Sean turned the car into a parking lot three hundred yards away from the base of the temple complex. He found a spot under a shady tree with huge, leafy branches. Tommy started to get out of the car, but Sean stopped him, grabbing Tommy's shoulder as he switched off the ignition.

"Hold up," he said. He double checked the Springfield compact strapped to his ankle and then pulled the cuff of the pants back down to his shoe tops.

Tommy shook his head. "I really hope we don't need those," he said wistfully.

"Me too, but better to have them and not need them than the other way around."

"I know." Tommy jerked up a pant leg, showing off his own weapon. He tugged the pistol from its holster and gave it a quick check, sliding the magazine out, making sure it was fully stocked with rounds, jamming it back into the base of the gun, and then pulling the slide back to chamber one of the hollow points.

"Judge not," Sean said smugly after he'd buckled the weapon back in its place.

The two got out of the car and shut the doors. They both instinctively surveyed their surroundings, their eyes keen to the possibility of trouble. Neither had noticed a tail on the way out of the city, though spotting one would have proved difficult. Even with traffic thinning considerably outside the city limits, there were still quite a few travelers on the road, and someone following them could have easily blended in with the seemingly endless array of old vehicles.

For the time being, all they could see were curious tourists milling about the grounds. A young Indonesian couple sat underneath a nearby tree, using its gigantic trunk as a backrest. Dozens more people with cameras, backpacks, fanny packs, and day bags moved aimlessly around the area. Some stared at a few of the hundreds of reliefs carved into the building's stonework. Others climbed staircases, searching little alcoves and nooks for secrets previous visitors may have missed.

There was one secret Sean and Tommy hoped everyone had missed.

Sean opened the rear door and reached into the backseat. He grabbed his rucksack and slung it over his shoulder. He unzipped the bag halfway and did a quick inventory of the tools inside: a yellow nail claw, a wooden hammer, an old paintbrush, and a few other miscellaneous items were all there. Some of the objects had been at Tommy's request. The nail claw had been a particular point of interest for Sean.

"You never know if you're going to need to pry something loose," Tommy had explained.

Sean had simply shaken his head in derision and loaded the bag with the odds and ends his friend requested. He'd been on enough digs with Tommy to know that his friend knew what he was talking about. If Tommy thought they needed a nail claw, then there must be a reason.

"Looks like a lot of steps to get to that tower on the top," Tommy pointed at the central stupa. He squinted into the sun despite the aviator sunglasses covering his eyes.

Sean followed his stare up to the temple's pinnacle. "Yep. Might as well get it over with."

The two made their way through the first outcropping of trees and onto the giant pad where the temple's foundation was built. They walked past a group of people who were speaking German, led by a local. Their guided tour had just ended, and they were descending the last of the steps as Sean and Tommy began their ascent. On the first mezzanine, a relief stretched across nearly the entire face of the lower wall. The engravings depicted one of the lives of Siddhartha. As they climbed the stairs, they saw more reliefs similar to the ones below, and along some of them, concavities featuring important points in the Buddha's life before he reached Buddha status. There were seventy-two stupas in total, each one laid out in a mandala pattern, rising upward amid the carvings, statues, and walls.

"Where'd you find that hotel?" Sean asked Tommy as his breath came in short, quick bursts from the climb.

"You didn't like it?"

Sean rolled his shoulders. "Wasn't the nicest I've been in. Of course, I've been spoiled for the last decade or so. I'm assuming you had a reason behind booking that joint."

"We needed to lie low, right?" Tommy said between gasps. They were only halfway to the top, and already he was breathing hard. The early morning heat and humidity were doing nothing to ease those symptoms. "There are several much nicer hotels in the city. In fact, there are some really nice ones only a few miles from here." He jammed his finger off in a random direction. "After our recent exploits, I figured a little low key would be better."

Sean had to admit his friend was probably right. But if someone were following them, it wouldn't make a difference where they spent the night. Whoever was after them was desperate enough to set their homes on fire and send a pair of mediocre hit men to take them out. He couldn't help but wonder what the next play might be.

The two Americans crested the high point and took a second to catch their breath. On the drive up, the temple had seemed like it was a huge piece of construction. Standing at its base, it seemed much smaller. After the climb, however, Sean and Tommy had reverted to their original opinions on the matter.

The view from atop the temple's high platform was much more spectacular than either had anticipated. The vast multicolored countryside stretched out in all directions. Yogyakarta stood in the distance, a tribute to the metropolitan growth of the Indonesian people. In the other direction, the mountains loomed beyond the haze of the humid plains and rolling hills carpeted with lush green trees.

"Not a bad sight from up here," Sean commented. "Whoever built this place sure picked a good spot."

Tommy put his hands on his hips, still catching his breath. "Yep. They really did."

Sean frowned at him, mocking disdain filling his eyes. "You okay? That was like a four-minute climb. It wasn't that bad."

"It's...the...humidity," Tommy answered. "You know what? Just...shut up, and look at the clue again. It said something about the high tower."

"It rests in the high tower with the seekers of light," Sean quoted the riddle. "And I'm assuming that stupa over there is the one they meant."

"Right."

The progression of the temple's reliefs, sculptures, alcoves, and stupas were all representative of the Buddha's life leading up to his enlightenment. The largest and tallest of the stupas represented him achieving Nirvana. An interesting piece of history, to be sure, and an interesting choice as a hiding place for a Jewish holy relic.

The two Americans walked over to the structure. Sean ran his hand along the smooth stones. "This dates back to the time of the Babylonian Empire," Sean said, a hint of reverence filling his voice. "While they were constructing this, far off to the west, Nebuchadnezzar was tearing Jerusalem apart."

"It's always strange to me to think about the things that went on during the same points in history, but in different places. These people probably had no idea what was happening over there."

"Other than the high priest's apprentice showing up here with a priceless relic."

"Well, obviously. At least, we hope."

"Right." Sean continued to circle the enormous stupa until he found the entrance. It was barricaded by a metal door and locked with a padlock.

They'd done their research before arriving in Indonesia. Only a Buddhist priest of high standing was permitted into the main stupa. Because of the strict rules about entry, there was little to no information to be found about what the inside looked like or what was there.

Sean reached into his rucksack and looked around before producing a small black tool with multiple attachments. It looked like a Swiss Army knife on steroids. He'd been picking locks since his early days with Axis, but he was nowhere as good as Adriana. Moments like this he wished she were with him. Although, if he was honest, he wished she was around for most moments.

"Keep a lookout," he said to Tommy as he ducked into the archway, shaded from the bright morning sun.

"Yeah. Probably don't want to get busted breaking into a Buddhist holy site." Tommy muttered the words as he turned his back to the entrance and watched the area.

Sean grabbed the padlock that hung from the latch. The iron door looked to be over a hundred years old, but that was just a guess based on the corrosion of the metal. The lock was a blackened hunk of metal that had seen better days. Little speckles of rust dotted the loop and lock housing. He spied the opening in the lock's base, analyzing which component of his lock-picking tool he should use. The decision made, he flipped out a thin blade no larger than the prong of a fork and pulled out a removable metal pick from the other end.

Holding the lock carefully with two fingers, Sean inserted the pick and the blade. It took three tries before he finally heard the mechanism click. He twisted the tools to the left, and the lock slackened. He unhooked the padlock, set it on the floor next to the wall, and grasped the iron latch. When he turned it, it squeaked alarmingly. Sean winced and glanced back at Tommy, who had heard the noise but kept surveying the immediate area for any witnesses.

A click came from inside the heavy door, telling Sean it was free. He leaned into it with his shoulder and cautiously pushed. Surprisingly, the door swung open easily and didn't creak nearly as loudly as the latch had. A wall of cool, musty air greeted him when he stepped inside. He took a quick inventory of his surroundings.

The walls curved inward until they formed a dome at the top. Each stone was placed perfectly in line with the ones above and below it, creating a flush, smooth surface. A shrine to the Buddha sat in the center. A stone sculpture of the smiling man with arms hovering over crossed legs sat amid an array of burning candles, flowers, and bronze vases. The sculpture sat atop a stone box that had been carved from a separate piece of rock.

Sean allowed himself a feeling of smug relief. The flickering candles that cast an eerie yellowish light on the walls meant that the priest had been in recently, which meant he wouldn't return for at least a few more hours.

He moved around the circular room, passing a rug that had been rolled up and placed against the wall. No other furniture or items of interest were lying around. When he reached the backside of the statue, Sean stopped and scratched his head. There was nothing here.

He scanned the walls first then the floor, desperately searching for anything that might give them a clue: a symbol, a word, a hieroglyph. But there was nothing.

A second before he was about to walk around to the entrance and tell Tommy to have a look around, he noticed something in a peculiar place. He stepped closer to the statue's back and kneeled down to get a closer look. It was almost unnoticeable at first. How he'd seen it in the first place was a minor miracle. A tiny circle had been carved into the back of the stone box. Inside the circle was a familiar emblem.

The Star of David.

17
Yogyakarta

"Tommy," Sean hissed through the stupa's entryway. His friend spun around with a look of concern carved onto his face. "Get in here." Sean waved his hand frantically, motioning for Tommy to look at what he'd found.

Tommy took a hesitant glance around and then hurried inside.

"Close the door behind you," Sean ordered. Tommy spun around and did as told before scurrying around the statue to where Sean stood anxiously waiting.

"What?"

Sean answered by pointing at the tiny emblem on the back of the box. "Does that seem out of place in Indonesia to you?"

Tommy's smile beamed. "It certainly does," he said with a satisfied nod. "And look at that," he pointed at the seams that ran alongside the outer edge of the box. "Looks like we're going to need the nail claw after all."

Sean rolled his eyes. "Yeah, I knew you were going to say that." He got down on his knees again and set the rucksack at the statue's base. His hand reached into the bag to retrieve the yellow nail claw and immediately went to work on prying the drawer from its slot.

At first, it wouldn't budge. The tip of the nail remover was almost too thick to fit into the tiny slit between the shelf and the rest of the box. Sean tried both sides and then the top. It took a few minutes, but he was finally able to get the drawer to move a few millimeters.

"It's in there tight," he said, grunting while he worked.

"Well, it's been there for a few thousand years, so you know..." Tommy's smart aleck response would have normally caused Sean to laugh if he wasn't in the middle of a painstaking effort.

The tool created a big enough gap that Sean was able to jam half the shaft inside and use the upper lip of the box to leverage it. He pushed hard, and the object slid out, stone grinding on stone as it moved. A short burst of musty air shot past their faces, tickling their hair. Sean sighed and took a long breath, straightening his back to stretch it.

Tommy drew close and got down on both knees. They stared at the drawer with shocked faces. Sean took a deep breath and let it out slowly, putting his hands on his hips. The two turned their heads toward each other and then back to the drawer.

It was empty. All that was inside were some characters chiseled hastily into the stone.

Tommy frowned and fished the paintbrush from the rucksack. He carefully dusted the bottom surface of the stone drawer, making the ancient characters a little easier to see.

"Is that Sudanese?" Sean asked. He thought he was correct in his assumption, but it was one of those rare languages like old Gaelic. Not many people spoke it or understood how to read it.

"I think so," Tommy said, pulling his phone out of a cargo pocket. He took a picture and tapped the screen a few times before putting it back. "But just to be safe, we'll let Tara and Alex have a look. Since neither of us can speak or read whatever this is, might be faster to just let them look it up."

"Good idea." Sean glanced over at the door, realizing they'd left it unwatched for more than a couple of minutes.

His feet started carrying him that way as Tommy continued to kneel by the base of the statue and gaze at the engraving. "I wonder why it's empty, though. I mean, this has to be the place, right?"

"Yeah," Sean said, only half hearing his friend's question.

"There wouldn't be a Davidic star on this drawer if it was the wrong place. You think someone stole it?"

Sean didn't answer this time. He reached the iron door and pulled it back a few inches. He leaned around the edge and peeked through the crack.

"Sean? I said, do you think someone stole it? I don't see any signs of robbery. Other than the few chips you just took off, it looks like the thing's been left intact ever since it was put here."

Out in the open on the temple roof, Sean's eyes darted from one stupa to the next, alert to a danger he wasn't sure was there. He swallowed and waited. If someone was out there, they weren't stupid. They were biding their time until the Americans came out.

There. Near the wall, he could see through the holes of a dome, someone crouching. The person was in casual, touristy clothes, but he was holding something typical tourists didn't: a gun.

Sean looked around the rest of the space, not expecting to see anyone else, more to give the effect that he'd not noticed the person hiding beyond one of the stupas. He eased the door closed and spun around quickly.

"We have to get out of here," he hissed urgently.

Tommy popped up from behind the statue, an expression of sudden concern on his face. "What? Why?"

Sean cast him a look that told him he should know better than to ask.

The realization hit Tommy a second later. "Right. Trouble. How many are there?"

"Don't know." Sean shook his head once. "I only saw one out there, but you can bet there are more."

Tommy's look of concern grew visibly worse. "How did they know we were here? No one knows we're here except the kids. And we know they didn't say anything to anyone."

"The fact is that someone followed us here." In his mind, Sean beat himself up for not seeing the tail. Over the years, people had become better and better at the art of tailing a target, often using two, three, and sometimes four decoys to throw off an alert driver. Things had changed rapidly over the last decade and were much more advanced than spycraft of the 1950s.

"How are we going to get out of here?" Tommy asked, realizing immediately after saying it that he wasn't being helpful.

Sean calmly, but swiftly, stepped to the front of the statue, knocking over a few of the candles. He picked up a heavy bronze vase and carried it back over to the door. He set it down and wedged the base of it between the bottom of the door and the threshold. A couple of firm kicks jammed it into place. Sean stood up and pulled on the door latch. It didn't budge.

He turned around and stalked back over to where Tommy was standing, watching his friend work.

"That's great, but it doesn't exactly help us get out of here."

"No," Sean agreed. "But it buys us some time."

"Time to do what?"

Sean bent over and grabbed the pistol out of his ankle holster. He checked the magazine again and made sure a round was in the chamber. Tommy copied his friend's procedure. They inched their way backward to the rear of the statue, keeping their eyes on the door.

When they were safely behind it, Tommy realized something that he'd blown off a few minutes ago.

"A draft," he said vaguely.

"What?" Sean held his weapon at the ready next to his chin.

"When you pulled out that drawer," Tommy pointed his barrel at the drawer sitting by the statue's base, "a draft of stale, cool air shot out from it. I can still feel a little of it right now." He crouched down and put his free hand out over the dark cavity beyond the dislodged drawer.

Sure enough, a stream of gentle, cool air trickled over his skin. He looked up at Sean, who was peering into the crevasse, then back down again. "Where do you think it goes?"

Sean stole a glance over at the door. "Doesn't matter. We don't have another option. In ten minutes, they could come through that door. They'll cut us down in no time. We were lucky in Israel. We got the drop on those guys. That's not going to happen here."

Tommy stood up. "Okay, but how do we get in there?"

Sean kneeled down on one knee and ran his finger along the bottom edge of the statue's platform. "This thing isn't built into the floor. It's just resting on top of it. We'll need to move it to be able to fit through the hole."

"Oh, I see. So we're just going to desecrate a place that Buddhists consider holy."

Sean caught his sarcasm but ignored it. "We're not going to hurt it. Just move it a little. Look, no disrespect to Buddhists, but it's just a representation of Buddha. It isn't actually him. Trust me, they'll be able to move it back."

"What if we break it?"

"We aren't going to break anything. Jeez." Sean was exasperated. He appreciated Tommy's love for history. Sean had similar feelings on the subject. But at the moment, survival took precedent over everything else. "Just help me move this thing."

Sean stood up behind the statue and started pushing on the back of the head and waist. Tommy joined him on the other side and mimicked his friend's efforts.

"Just so we're on the same page, we're trying to shimmy this thing back and forth until it slides over a bit. That sound about right?"

"Yep," Sean nodded.

The heavy statue barely moved at first, only sliding an inch along the ground as the two men pushed and pulled. Leaning against the heavy stone, the two tried rocking it back and forth, grunting harder with each moment's exertion. Their work gained momentum but not the way they'd planned. The bottom of the statue lifted higher and higher, first on the front, then on the back, and again on the other side. Each rocking motion created a loud thud that resonated off the domed walls.

"Sean," Tommy's voice filled with concern, "I don't think this is a good idea. It's going to fall over."

"Almost there," Sean said between breaths. "It'll be fine."

The two gave one last heave, and the statue slid forward but caught on the bottom front edge of the base. Gravity and momentum did the rest and the Buddha toppled over headfirst. It slammed into the floor with a loud crash. The sculpture's head snapped off and rolled over to the far wall. One of the arms broke free and lay on the floor amid a cloud of debris and dust.

"Not going to break it, huh?" Tommy gazed at the sight regretfully. "You think they're going to be able to just fix that?" He pointed with an outstretched hand.

Sean stared at the mess. "That was not what I had planned."

"You think?"

"Look, we'll write them a check or something. We have to move."

"That's a priceless piece of history we just destroyed." Tommy's hands were held out wide.

"I know, buddy. I promise. That wasn't what I had in mind but if we stick around here we're dead. Now please, help me move this base."

Tommy shook his head but did as requested. The two bent down, put their fingers under the lip of the stone box, and pulled hard, using their legs to do most of the lifting. The heavy object didn't put up as much of a fight as the statue, and toppled over after their first effort. It teetered over and stopped when the top hit the underside of the statue.

Where the box had been, a large hole opened up in the floor. The dank air wafted up into the chamber. Sean grabbed one of the two flashlights out of the rucksack and handed it to Tommy before taking the other for himself. The two flipped on the beams and pointed the lights down.

The area below was a dark passageway, surrounded on all sides by the stonework of the temple. Old cobwebs decorated the edges of the hole and corners of the corridor.

"The good news is that it's not a long drop down. Maybe eight feet at the most."

Sean's words did little to comfort Tommy, who was clearly reluctant about the idea. "You sure about this?"

Something struck the iron door on the other side of the room. It sounded like a bullet.

"They're testing the door's strength," Sean said. "Bullets won't get through it, but they'll get past my little wedge within five minutes. The tunnel is our only choice."

Tommy looked back over at the door and then back down into the hole.

"You know you've been in worse places, buddy," Sean said reassuringly.

"I hope you're right."

Tommy crouched down, grabbed the lip of the cavity, and lowered himself into the passageway.

Sean took one last glance over at the doorway. Something hit it hard. They were trying to barge through. In a few minutes, they would succeed. He just hoped the passageway didn't lead to a dead end, literally and figuratively.

He bent down, put the end of his flashlight in his mouth, and gripped it with his teeth.

Then he took hold of the edge of the hole and dropped into the darkness.

18
Yogyakarta

Tommy ran into the darkness at a cautious pace with Sean close behind. The light from their LED flashlights kept them from running into a wall, but there was no telling what the tunnel held in store. If they didn't pay attention, it would be easy to fall into another hole or roll an ankle on something. Right now, any kind of injury would be devastating if the men they were running from had ventured into the passageway.

Sean imagined they'd broken through his makeshift barricade by now and were circling around the statue of Buddha, discovering the cavity in the floor. The two Americans had been running for the last three minutes, giving them a significant head start. Three minutes might be an eternity but could be lost quickly if they weren't careful.

The corridor shot straight ahead for the first hundred feet, then it made an abrupt left for another twenty feet then shot right again. Sean and Tommy felt like they were being herded through a labyrinth with no way of knowing exactly where they were going. They reached the end of the flat passage and found a set of stairs that descended to a lower level. Tommy only hesitated for a second, knowing it was their only option. Going back wasn't a possibility.

He bounded down the stairs and reached the next floor. Eight steps later, they reached another right turn that presented a huge problem. The tunnel came to a T, shooting off to the right and left.

"Which way do you think?" Sean asked quietly, shining his light down one corridor and then the next. Even at a whisper, his voice sounded like the sounds of a roaring river bouncing off the stone walls.

"Was going to ask you the same thing."

Tommy tried to regain his bearings. "Our car should be out that way," he pointed left. Sean nodded. He'd been thinking the same thing.

"Fastest way between two points."

They took off again, padding along on the balls of their feet so as not to make as much noise. The two reached another turn in the tunnel. Tommy sped around it without thinking and ran face-first into a tangled mass of cobwebs. He grasped at his face and hair, panicking, nearly dropping his flashlight in the process. Fortunately, he didn't make a noise other than spitting the cobwebs out of his mouth.

Sean stepped by him, putting his hand out in front and pulling the remaining webs out of the way. "Come on," he whispered.

"I don't have one on me, do I?" Tommy asked. He swiped his hands around in panic-stricken paranoia.

"Dude, there are no spiders down here anymore. We have to move."

Tommy followed, though he still swiped at his neck and hair occasionally just to make sure Sean wasn't lying.

The tunnel stretched out another fifty yards in front of them and ended at another set of stairs. They flew down the steps, taking them two at a time until they reached the next landing. Yet another tunnel awaited.

"This thing goes on forever," Tommy said, gasping for air.

"We should be close."

Sean pressed on, going straight then following the passage to the right, keeping his hand out in front of his face to protect against more cobwebs. Tommy hurried after him, trying to keep up.

The two reached another fork in the corridor. This time, Tommy recommended they go right, suggesting that now the car was in that direction.

Sean nodded and kept moving. After making the right and then going around another corner that bent back to the left, they found themselves in a long stretch of tunnel that looked more than a few hundred yards long. The floor sloped downward at a slight angle, disappearing into the darkness beyond the end of their lights' reach.

Tommy frowned. "What's the matter? Keep going?"

"The floor goes down. We should already be at ground level. And from the length of it, this passage is longer than the length of the temple. It must extend beyond the exterior walls and end up somewhere on the grounds around the perimeter."

"Perimeter, parking lot, doesn't matter to me. So long as it gets us out of here alive, I'm good."

Tommy took off at a gallop. Sean scurried after him. Twenty seconds later, they realized that the floor was rising again. They picked up their pace and started to see a pale glow from the other end of the tunnel. It was a thin sliver at first, but as the two Americans drew closer, they saw that it was a narrow opening, about twenty inches wide and five feet tall.

They made it to the opening, and Sean took a quick look out. Thick stands of trees and emerald-green grass surrounded the exit. It was probably why the opening had gone unnoticed; at least he assumed it had largely gone unnoticed.

Sean went through first, easily slipping through the narrow space. Tommy, on the other hand, had a little more trouble, but he made it through right behind him, though his size didn't do him any favors.

"Remind me to drop a few pounds when we get back to the States," he said, trying to suck in his waistline as he squeezed through.

"I wasn't going to say anything."

Once on the other side, the two crept through the thicket of skinny, pale tree trunks.

Tommy couldn't let it go. "The fact that you weren't going to say something means you were thinking about saying something." His words came through clenched teeth as he tried to keep his voice down.

"Seriously? Right now we're having this conversation?"

"We weren't going to until you said you weren't going to say anything."

Sean stopped and stood up straight. He turned around and faced his friend. "We're not married. So please, let it go. If you want to get in shape, I encourage that."

He spun back around and started walking toward a clearing at the edge of the trees.

"You encourage that?" Tommy hissed, catching up. "Really? That's exactly what a husband would say. So now I'm the wife?"

"You're certainly not doing yourself any favors asking these kinds of questions. Now can you please just focus? We need to get out of here. In case you forgot, there are men, probably armed, trying to kill us."

The conversation ended abruptly as Tommy realized he was being overly dramatic.

The clearing was nothing more than a beaten-down, leaf-covered path that appeared to circle back around to the park surrounding the temple. Sean led the way, moving at a jog until they reached the edge of the tree line where a stretch of meadow ended in the parking area. They could see their car a few hundred yards away. Sean took a quick survey of the area to see if anyone stayed behind to watch their vehicle in case they were able to get past the siege outside the central stupa.

From what he could tell, there wasn't anyone suspicious, just unsuspecting tourists who were completely oblivious to the deadly game of cat and mouse that was going on right under their noses.

"Looks like the coast is clear," Sean said. "But they'll have guys up top keeping an eye on things. Going to be a race to get to the car before they do."

"You go first; I'll bring up the rear."

Tommy's offer had more to do with his being the slower of the two, but Sean declined.

"We go together. You ready?"

The journey through the tunnel had been a welcome respite from the heat and humidity of the Indonesian summer. Now they were back in the sun, and the damp air made their lungs heavy.

"Sure. No time like the present. Hopefully, anyone following us into the tunnel took a wrong turn."

Sean nodded then stared ahead across the meadow. "Go."

The two took off at a dead sprint. Fifty yards across the field, Tommy slowed noticeably, so Sean pulled back his pace a percentage to stay with his friend. His eyes shot over to the temple roof where there were two men in sunglasses standing at the edge. One had a phone to his ear. The second he noticed the two Americans running across the grassy span, he pointed. The other man with him disappeared, presumably heading for the steps leading back to ground level.

With a hundred yards to go, Tommy was struggling, taking in oxygen in huge, desperate gulps. But he didn't stop, though his pace was diminishing closer to a jog with every step.

"Not much farther, buddy," Sean encouraged him.

"You...get the...car...and meet me," Tommy managed to blurt out amid heaves.

"Not happening. Keep moving," he barked.

Sean looked to his left and saw the man who'd been at the top of the temple now running down the stairs. He'd already reached the second landing and would soon be on the ground and heading their way.

With twenty yards to go, Sean urged his friend to pick it up. "Here they come," he said, pointing at the guy descending the last set of stairs. Tommy found his second wind and pumped his legs harder.

Sean fished the keys out of his pocket and hit the unlock button on the keyless entry. The locks clicked as he reached the door. In two seconds, the door was open, and he was inside, shoving the keys in the ignition. Tommy skidded around the gravel and to the passenger side. He opened the door and slid in at the same time Sean revved the car to life.

Through the windshield, they could see the man from the rooftop sprinting their way with a black handgun held outstretched, pointed straight at them. As soon as the first shot was fired, Sean kicked the car into reverse and backed up, spinning the front tires and sending gravel flying into the grass. A second after the gunman squeezed the trigger, panic struck the tourists on the grounds. People screamed and started running for cover. The gunman fired again, now only thirty yards away but still too far to be accurate. His shots were out of desperation more than anything.

Sean spun the wheel, shifted the gears, and punched the accelerator. Before turning the car out of the parking lot, he saw two other men running at them from the woods they'd left moments ago.

The little car whipped out onto the cracked pavement and sped away, leaving the attackers to chase on foot.

Tommy was gasping for air in the passenger seat. Sean removed his rucksack and tossed it in the backseat before checking on his friend. "You okay?"

"Yeah. I really have to get on a workout regimen when we get back."

Sean diverted the conversation back to the issue at hand. "That's three times in three separate countries that someone has come after us. We need to know who they are, what they want, and why they're trying to kill us."

"Once we find out the answers to the first two questions, I'm pretty sure the third will answer itself."

"Good point," Sean nodded, shooting a quick glance out of the corner of his eye.

"The other questions I want answers to is where that relic went. Why was the box in the temple empty? And what did those engravings say?"

"I'm sure the kids will have an answer for us soon enough on the latter. But you're right. Why would someone go to all the trouble to hide something of extraordinary value in a highly secretive place just to put it somewhere else?"

The car hit one of the many potholes, but Sean kept it on course.

"You think it might be a decoy?" Tommy asked. His breathing had begun to slow. He looked nervously out the window into the rearview mirror.

"Maybe. Seems like an awful lot of trouble to go through to set up a decoy, though."

Sean swerved to miss another pothole, this time putting the right-side tires onto the edge of the lane. The rubber kicked up some debris, but a second later he was back in the middle again.

Tommy's phone beeped at the same time Sean felt his vibrate in his pants pocket. Tommy checked the screen. "It's from Tara." After tapping the device twice, he looked over at Sean and grinned. "We were right. It's Sudanese. And apparently, the message carved into that stone box says that we will find what we seek in the halls of the Tiger's Nest."

"Tiger's Nest?" Sean's eyes narrowed. He kept them facing forward, though, as he weaved around a slower-moving car.

"That's what she says." The phones beeped and vibrated again, signaling another message had arrived. "Now she says that there's a Buddhist monastery high up in the mountains of Bhutan called the *Tiger's Nest*. She thinks that might be our best bet."

Sean considered the information for a moment before speaking. "That would make sense, I suppose."

"Of course it would." Tommy spoke with renewed excitement, the exhaustion from the long sprint a distant memory. "With the proliferation of Islam in Indonesia, the Buddhist monks who were entrusted with the Hebrew relic must have known it would be in grave danger. According to the history of Borobudur, the monks abandoned it. They wouldn't have left something so precious behind."

"They would have thought to take it somewhere safe," Sean finished the thought.

"Exactly."

"Bhutan is a pretty mountainous country. If it's one of those monasteries that's up on a cliff, it would be about as safe a place as any to hide something like that." He spoke with confidence, but in his mind a twinge of nausea crept in. Sean had always been terrified of heights. On a trip to Machu Picchu, he'd barely been able to force himself up from a crawling position as he ascended some of the precipitous steps. The memory blurred his vision for a second, but he snapped himself back to the present. No sense in worrying about something until there was something to worry about. Maybe this *Tiger's Nest* wouldn't be as precariously placed on a mountain as the ancient Incan village.

Sean caught a glimpse of something move suddenly in the driver's side rearview. A silver sedan dove into the other lane, passing the car Sean had just blown by a minute before. His eyes shifted back and forth from the road ahead to the car behind them. He didn't want to alarm Tommy for no reason, but when he saw the man pop out of the passenger window, aiming a submachine gun at them, Sean figured it was time.

"Get your gun ready," he ordered without explanation.

Tommy looked at him, puzzled. "What?"

Sean's eyes flicked to the mirror. Tommy followed his gaze, and as soon as he saw what his friend was looking at, he sagged a little in the seat.

"We have company."

19
Yogyakarta

Sean stomped on the gas, getting all he could out of the weak four-cylinder engine. The motor resisted but eventually picked up speed as Sean deftly ducked the car in and out of the ever-increasing traffic heading into the city.

"If we go back into the city, they'll catch up to us, and we'll have nowhere to run," Tommy warned. He'd retrieved the gun from his holster and held it ready by the window.

"Yep. I'm aware of that." Sean jerked the wheel to the left, narrowly missing the back bumper of a delivery van. He hammered down on the gas, speeding the car directly at a flatbed truck in the other lane. "This is gonna be close," he almost yelled.

Tommy gripped the handle over the window until his knuckles went white. His entire face cinched into a grimace as if that would help the car somehow magically go faster.

At the last second, Sean pulled the wheel back toward the right lane. The flatbed rumbled by, its blaring horn accompanied by a loud, vibrating swoosh. They only missed the truck by a few inches.

The road ahead was mostly clear, but Sean knew that would change as soon as they reached the outskirts of the city. He glanced into the mirror again and saw the silver car zip easily around the delivery truck and fall in line behind them once more. The other vehicle was much faster and this time closed the gap between the two cars in mere seconds.

The man on the passenger side leaned out of the window again, brandishing his weapon. He opened fire, sending a barrage of bullets at the two Americans. The rear window cracked into spider webs as three rounds pierced the glass and went through the front windshield. Sean instinctively yanked the wheel to the left and back to the right in an attempt to throw off the shooter's aim, but that tactic would only be effective for a short time.

Tommy hit the button on the door and rolled down his window. He hung carefully out the side and fired off four shots before ducking back in and taking cover. The counterattack caused the other car's driver to weave out of the way, but he quickly resumed course, tucking in close behind. Sean looked back and saw the gunman leaning out the window again. Tommy was about to do the same, but Sean stopped him.

"Just hold on for a sec," he warned.

"What are you..."

Sean slammed his foot on the brake and pressed his head against the headrest, anticipating what was to come.

The car behind them couldn't react fast enough and plowed into the rear bumper. The gunman was hanging too far out the window, and the force of the jolt sent him flying out of the vehicle. His luck was beyond bad, and momentum carried his body through the air until his head struck a road sign. He fell to the ground, unmoving, and the chase went on.

Sean hit the gas again. Up ahead, he saw another sign pointing to the right. The road headed north and would take them around the city and back into the countryside. At least that's what he figured. Better to guess and be wrong than keep pressing on and know what would happen.

He barely padded the brakes and swung the car around the sharp turn and onto the new road. The tail end skidded, fishtailing into the other lane across the white paint marking the intersection. Sean stepped on the accelerator again, correcting the slide just before striking a motorcycle sitting at the stoplight. The rider's wide eyes were a cocktail of fear and disbelief under his clear visor, certain this moment would be his last.

Sean stole another look back and saw the silver sedan easily make the turn and fall in line close behind once more. This time, two men in the backseat popped their heads out but weren't going to make the same mistake the previous gunman made. They were more careful and only partially leaned out the window. The attackers' sedan closed the distance between the cars again. The men in the backseat fired their handguns, sending a hail of reckless hot metal at the Americans. Most of the bullets sailed by. A few thumped into the trunk.

Tommy poked his gun out the window again and launched a counter volley of five shots. All but one of the bullets missed as the silver sedan weaved and snaked clear. The lone shot that was on target merely struck a headlight. Tommy checked his magazine, taking a quick inventory of what he had left. "Three more shots," he informed Sean. "Got any other tricks up your sleeve?"

"Maybe," Sean said, jerking the wheel to the side to make them as difficult a target as possible.

The one-lane road opened up into two lanes in both directions and stretched out toward the mountains a few miles away. Sean reached down to his ankle and drew his weapon. He gripped it tight, holding it next to his leg. The car suddenly lurched violently forward, accompanied by a loud bang.

The silver sedan slowed down for a few seconds after ramming the rear of the Americans' car. They didn't wait to make their next move, though, and veered into the other lane to pull alongside.

Sean turned the wheel hard to the left, cutting off the maneuver. The sedan shifted lanes and accelerated again. The man in the backseat on the driver's side aimed his weapon again, but Tommy fired first, sending two of his three remaining rounds into the car's door. Aware of the danger, the driver hit the brakes immediately and resumed the chase just behind the Americans. He ducked back to the other side, putting two wheels on the shoulder, and inched closer to the back quarter panel.

It was a move Sean had seen before. Police were trained, in a chase situation, to ease up behind the car they were pursuing and turn into the back end just behind the rear wheel. The force would send the runaway car into a nearly inescapable spin and bring it to a stop. The silver sedan appeared poised to try just such a maneuver.

As the other driver got ready to strike, Sean slammed on the brakes again and yanked his steering wheel to the left. The other car was bigger, and his little compact rental vehicle shuddered on impact, but the maneuver did enough to wedge the sedan against the guardrail, sending a shower of sparks trailing behind it from the doors grinding on the metal.

The man in the back passenger seat had fallen over from the impact but had quickly regained his balance. He popped up and took aim to end the chase with a bullet to Sean's temple, but the American was faster. With one hand on the wheel and the other clutching his pistol, he flashed the gun out and extended it through the window. His trigger finger snapped like lightning, sending one hollow point after another through the open window of the sedan. One struck the gunman in the chest, sending him falling over backward; two other rounds found their mark in the driver's shoulder and the side of his head. Crimson splashed on the window with the latter, and the enemy vehicle instantly slowed. Sean mashed the gas pedal again and pulled away. He watched in the rear mirror as the last man alive in the backseat panicked, trying to reach over the seat to control the wheel. The sedan pulled hard to the right; its tires caught the rough asphalt, and physics took over. The vehicle flipped up into the air, dramatically at first, like a ballerina spinning in space. The next second, it crashed to the ground on its tires then rolled bottom over top for another thirty feet until it finished its deadly dance, coming to a stop on its roof.

Sean didn't let up. He kept the pedal to the floor and only glanced back in the rearview mirror at the smoking wreckage. Cars on the other side of the road were starting to slow down to get a better view of what happened. A few people got out and ran across the median to get a closer look or perhaps be a good Samaritan and lend a hand. Sean knew they needed to put distance between themselves and anyone else who might be following them. They'd only seen one car, but there could have been more reinforcements close behind. Sean and Tommy did not intend to stick around to find out.

Ahead, the thick, lush forests stretched into shadowy mountains. They were mere molehills compared to the mountains they would see in Bhutan. Sean stole another look back in the mirror just before their little car disappeared around a bend in the road.

Tommy looked back between the seats. There were still a few clear spots in the cracked rear window, but for the most part, it was completely destroyed. It was a miracle that any glass was still intact. He turned his focus to Sean, whose eyes were fixed on the road. "What about our stuff back in the hotel?"

Sean's answer was quick. "Call the front desk. Have them ship it back to Atlanta. They can take it out of the company credit card."

"Your company?" Tommy flashed a narrow grin with his eyes.

"Yours," Sean corrected, returning the wry smile with one of his own.

"That was a risky move you made. What if you'd missed or if they'd shot first?"

Sean didn't answer immediately. He steered the car around the curves leading up the mountain pass and slowed his speed a little, satisfied there were no other cars in pursuit.

"You weigh the risks and determine which has the best likely outcome. We couldn't outrun them in this car. And we certainly didn't have more weapons or ammunition. It was the only way we had a chance of getting away alive."

"And you just always do this, what, automatically?"

It was the first time Tommy had pushed the conversation before, in spite of them being friends for decades.

"Pretty much."

Tommy turned around and faced forward, easing back in his seat. He took several deep breaths, trying to calm his nerves. When he'd finally relaxed somewhat, he said, "Well, I apologize."

Sean's face became puzzled, and he looked over at his friend. "For what?"

"For always saying you were just lucky. I guess you really are that good."

"Better lucky than good."

Tommy smirked. "Like I always say, why not have both?"

20
Yogyakarta

Up ahead, the roads on the outskirts of the city were clogged with thousands of motorcycles, mopeds, compact cars, delivery vans, and rickshaws. Sharouf hadn't stuck around to watch the emergency crews arrive on the scene. He was certain they were working hard to clear the road of the wreckage by now. Both lanes would likely have been closed until the bodies were removed from the vehicle. Then a further delay until a tow truck could pull the sedan to the road's shoulder. Based on what he'd seen immediately following the incident, the first responders surely would have had to cut the bodies out of the sedan's twisted remains.

Memories of the event ripped through Sharouf's mind. The man in the backseat with him had been the first one to take a bullet. Exiting from the back of his guard's head, the round had flown precariously close, narrowly missing Sharouf's face and striking the window behind him. Blood and tissue had sprayed across Sharouf, and the body toppling backward had thrown him off balance.

He never saw the driver take the fatal bullet that caused him to lose control of the vehicle.

Sharouf hadn't been in a car accident before, but he wasn't afraid during the event.

When the vehicle started flipping, he found himself suspended in midair several times, his body striking the seat, the corpse of his assistant, and then the roof, over and over again. He'd balled up in a fetal position to protect his head when the driver's side backseat door flew open and he was miraculously deposited on the asphalt.

The second he felt the warm pavement against his skin, he looked up to see the car tumble to a standstill on its roof. A quick glance back revealed smoke, debris, and a few cars in the distance that were already beginning to slow, having seen the incident with a front row seat.

The top of Sharouf's skull started pounding. It must have struck several surfaces during the wreck. He winced and noticed his arm was also aching. He shook off the pain and forced himself to stand. The act was clumsy at first, like a newborn colt trying to get onto its hooves for the first time, but he was able to regain his balance after applying some focus.

Staggering toward the vehicle, Sharouf clutched his arm as he walked through the thin river of coolant, transmission fluid, and gasoline that leaked from the car and ran to the shoulder. He struggled around to the other side of the smoking vehicle and took a quick inventory.

The driver had a hole in the side of his head, and his neck was bent at an awkward angle. He didn't need to check the guy in the back. Sharouf already knew he was dead. Some of the man's blood still stuck to Sharouf's face. He took the bottom part of his shirt to remove what little he could of the thickening crimson liquid.

He stole a quick look to the right and saw a lone car, a five-door, rusted-out blue hatchback slowing down on the other side of the road. The driver stopped the vehicle and opened his door. He was a short, middle-aged man wearing a tan-colored windbreaker and generic blue jeans. He was clearly a local, and his lips spat out a flurry of words that Sharouf didn't understand.

The stranger crossed the median, still babbling loudly. It looked like he was coming to help. Sharouf looked back down to the ground and saw his pistol lying on the car's ceiling, next to his driver's foot. *Miracle number two.* He reached down and picked up the pistol, though the motion sent a fresh pain signal through his body. As the man approached, Sharouf stayed hunched over, half feigning misery until the good Samaritan was out of view from the approaching vehicles.

Satisfied the yammering man was out of sight, Sharouf aimed his weapon at him and motioned for his jacket. The stranger resisted at first, shaking his head and taking a step back. Sharouf insisted, jamming the barrel into the man's ribs.

"I need that," he said in heavily accented English.

Fear swept over the stranger's face, and he quickly obeyed, sliding the jacket off his body and handing it to the gunman.

Sharouf kept the weapon trained as he slipped into the snug windbreaker. The man was almost half his size, but he only needed the covering for a minute. As soon as he was gone, he could take it off.

He motioned for the man to sit down on the ground, which he did immediately. Sharouf briefly considered shooting him, but he could see the stranger was too afraid to do anything.

"You stay," Sharouf ordered. "Follow, and die. Understand?"

The man nodded, though the confusion mingling with fear in his eyes caused Sharouf to wonder. Still, he doubted the stranger would be any trouble.

He tucked the gun into his belt and started for the hatchback. As he approached, Sharouf could hear the dashboard dinging, signaling that the key was still inside. Off to his right, another few cars approached, only a half kilometer away. He waded through the grass in the median and back onto the asphalt before giving a tertiary check back at the wreckage to make sure the good Samaritan had stayed put. He could see the man's legs and feet sticking out from behind the trunk, telling him that the guy was still where he was supposed to be.

Sharouf hopped into the car and turned the key. The rickety engine coughed to life. He shifted it into gear and drove away, heading back toward the city.

Ten minutes later, Sharouf was sitting in traffic on the outskirts of Yogyakarta. He'd put the window down and attempted to look casual, donning a pair of cheap sunglasses the driver had left in the passenger seat. Seven minutes ago, two ambulances, a fire truck, and three police cars sped by on the other side of the road, heading to the scene. Back in the big city, it would be easy enough for him to ditch the vehicle and disappear. It was a routine Sharouf had gone through several times. He knew how to drop off the radar. Getting back to Dubai would be tricky, but he could manage. The bigger problem in his mind at the moment was the fact that he'd allowed Wyatt and his friend to escape.

After ten minutes of sitting in stop-and-go traffic, Sharouf reached a stoplight. His intentions were to turn right and head downtown, but as he pondered how to tell Mamoud what happened, another thought occurred to him.

When he and his men finally breached the iron door in the central stupa at Borobudur, they found it empty, save for the toppled statue of Buddha, some candles and urns, and a hole in the floor. He'd run around to the back wall to see how the Americans had been able to disappear and found the escape tunnel. In his rush to capture the two men, he'd sent two of his men down after them but hadn't paid much attention to the stone drawer that they'd left behind. Now, sitting at the red light, his memory recalled seeing something carved into the bottom of the drawer.

The light turned green, and he hesitated. The car behind him, a red compact two-door, started honking, urging him to hurry through the intersection.

Sharouf took a deep breath. There was still a chance to save the mission — and perhaps his life. While he'd been loyal to Mamoud for several years, his boss had no tolerance for failure. Sharouf feared no one, but he knew what could happen if he let down the wealthy young Arab.

The decision made, he pounded the gas and shot through the intersection just as the light turned red. Instead of turning right, though, he yanked the wheel to the left and headed back toward Borobudur.

If the Americans had found something there, they would have it with them, and there'd be no chance of recovering it. If, however, the stupa had been empty and only served to provide another clue, it could be that whatever was inscribed on that drawer could give him a hint as to their next destination.

He guided the car into the single lane and said a silent prayer to Allah that he still had time.

21
Atlanta

Emily stared at the computer screen, her mind fighting through a fog of fatigue. She'd spent the last several hours trying to dig up whatever she could on Mamoud Al Najaar but with few results. The young Arab didn't have a lot of dirt to dig up. Sure, he had a questionable lifestyle, especially considering his Muslim upbringing. Finding anything criminal, however, was another matter altogether. Emily was surprised to learn that Al Najaar had attended Western schools, though the more she read, the more she realized that was far more common than she was aware. Although she did know that the king of Jordan had been educated in the West and seemed to love Western culture.

The more she stared at the computer screen and flipped through pages of notes, the more confusing the issue with Al Najaar became.

Was he working for someone? A terrorist organization perhaps? Or was he just an arms dealer trying to make a few million?

The latter didn't make sense. The guy was beyond rich. The money he'd inherited from his father was more than some small countries had in their reserves. *No,* she thought. *It definitely wasn't for the money.*

Al Najaar didn't seem like the type to support a terrorist organization. Then again, a person really never could tell. She doubted that he was a middleman for another country. Unfortunately, there were more questions than answers at the moment — and the few answers she could muster simply didn't add up.

It was difficult to move large quantities of anything anymore, especially weapons. Al Najaar had been trying to relocate a volume of weapons that made the word *large* vastly inadequate. Every few days, Emily received reports from her agent on the scene. Al Najaar was moving guns, ammunition, standard military explosive devices, and even some heavy machinery. There were some things, however, that he'd not been able to access.

Emily was most curious about what Al Najaar was storing in the forty-foot shipping containers. Her asset had been unable to gain access up until that point. He'd even tried breaking into one of the containers by picking the lock. Each time he tried, though, another guard always seemed to rear his head at the most inopportune moments. Then there were the cameras constantly watching the area. Even if he could disguise his motives, it would only be a matter of time until he was discovered.

The agent had basically told her there was nothing else he could do except wait.

"What are you up to?" Emily said to the screen. She enlarged one of the images and cropped out the others to get better resolution on the one she wanted.

It was a surveillance photo of Al Najaar, taken just a few days ago from one of the neighboring homes. He was standing on his rooftop patio looking out over the gulf. He didn't have a care in the world, from the looks of it anyway, but that could have been a farce. Emily knew people like Al Najaar were snakes. They could sit there, hiding in the grass in plain sight, waiting for some unsuspecting person to come by, then suddenly snap and bite the intruder when they got too close to escape.

She stared at the screen a few seconds too long and was forced to pull back for a second, rubbing her burning eyes. When they felt better, she closed the image and opened another one. This particular photo featured Al Najaar speaking to one of his men, a guy named Sharouf Al Nasir. Finding information on Al Nasir had been somewhat difficult, even for a person in Emily's position. She'd pulled in a few extra resources to get the information she needed, and even then, details were sketchy. There were a few items regarding some mercenary work, but for the most part, the guy was a ghost. Two accounts mentioned that he was an expert assassin, used by several governments in the Middle East for missions that required a certain level of discretion. Again, there was little evidence as to what exactly happened.

Emily rubbed both sides of her face and leaned back again. She looked up at the ceiling. *What is this guy up to?* In less than a day, she could have MI6, the CIA, and half a dozen other resources on the scene in Dubai to take down Al Najaar and shut down whatever it was he was doing. She needed more evidence, though. The guns and other items weren't enough. Al Najaar could easily disavow all of it and pin it on one of his underlings. It was a game she'd seen play out more times than she cared to recall. Whenever the king was about to be taken, a pawn reared its head and took the fall.

With most of her resources exhausted, she picked up her cell phone and snapped a picture of the screen. She then sent a quick text message with the image attached. It was a short question, and one she doubted the recipient would have an answer for, but it was worth a shot.

She set the phone back down on the desk and resumed scanning the files. Someone had to have something on these guys.

22
Yogyakarta

Sharouf waited patiently for the other to arrive. He'd parked the stolen vehicle in the middle of a patch of tall grass in case the authorities happened to come by. There'd been little trouble getting back to the temple. Traffic was light at this time of day, as most of the tourists came during high visitation hours. The hotter the temperatures got, the more people retreated to cooler places.

He'd only been there for thirty minutes when he saw the black Mercedes SUV appear on the horizon. It was hardly an inconspicuous vehicle, especially considering the poverty that surrounded the city of Yogyakarta. In spite of that, their employer insisted on using luxury cars for transportation. Sharouf guessed it was to make some kind of a statement.

The SUV's driver saw Sharouf standing alone in the shade, leaning against a tree, and steered the vehicle into the parking lot. The tires crunched on the gravel and came to a sudden stop. Sharouf quickly stepped over to the passenger-side rear door and flung it open.

Nehem looked out at him with an expression of irritation. "Where are the rest of your men?" he asked.

Sharouf didn't appreciate the sarcasm and instantly responded, striking Nehem across the face with his palm.

The slap stung and sent a surge of anger through Nehem's body, but he restrained himself. These men could kill him in seconds, no matter how hard he struggled and fought.

A fire blazed in Sharouf's eyes. A dried trickle of blood stuck out on the side of his head, and the left side of his forehead had turned purple. Nehem thought better of mentioning whatever had happened to the man and instead asked as to the purpose of their little rendezvous.

"What am I doing here?"

Sharouf said nothing, instead grabbing the man by the wrist and yanking him out of the vehicle. The two men in the front seat got out as well and closed the doors, following the others toward the temple.

Nehem felt like a schoolboy being chastised by a teacher as Sharouf dragged him across the knoll. When they reached the stairs, the Arab continued up with Nehem in tow.

"Why are you taking me up there?" Nehem asked. There was a twinge of fear in his voice.

Sharouf motioned to his two men. One of them withdrew a pistol and shoved it into Nehem's back.

"Do not make me carry you up these stairs. I am not in the mood."

216

The cold, calculating tone of Sharouf's voice sent a chill through Nehem's spine. He nodded twice and obeyed, carefully making his way up the steps one at a time.

At the top, Nehem put his hand against one of the stupas and tried to catch his breath. Sharouf did not intend to let him do so. He grabbed the Israeli by the elbow again and pulled him along until they reached the central stupa. Sharouf gave a sweeping check of the area to make sure no one was looking before shoving Nehem into the big stupa's entryway. The door was as he'd left it less than an hour ago. In their hurry, Sharouf and his men had barely made an effort to close the door on the way out.

"We can't go in there," Nehem protested.

Sharouf answered by opening the door and pushing him inside. "Look at that. We *can* go in. Now walk around to the back of the statue's base."

Nehem saw the mess: the Buddha sculpture lying facedown with pieces broken off, candles and urns scattered on the floor. "What happened here?" He turned to face his captor, but the only answer he received was Sharouf pulling the weapon from his belt and pointing it at Nehem's face.

"I said go over there." He motioned with a nod of his head.

Nehem had been living in fear for the last several days. Having a gun pointed at him right now didn't change much of anything. It simply reinforced those fears. He kept his hands out to the side and slowly shuffled through the disarray. Sharouf followed closely, keeping the pistol trained on his prisoner. When Nehem arrived at the far wall, he stared down at the cavity next to the drawer.

His eyes widened. "You want me to go down there? Where does it go?"

"No." Sharouf shook his head. "Tell me what the inscription on the drawer says."

Nehem hadn't even noticed the engraving. His focus had been on the hole. Now that Sharouf mentioned it, he was surprised he'd missed it. He kneeled down on both knees and leaned over, bracing himself with one palm on the floor. He ran his index finger across the ancient lettering, slow and deliberate to make sure he was translating everything correctly. It didn't say much, but Nehem knew what it meant right away.

"What does it say, old man?" Sharouf pressed the barrel to the back of the Israeli's head.

Nehem took a long, slow breath. He dared not turn around. The slightest twitch could provoke this maniac. "It's Sudanese. It says that whatever was here before is gone."

"I know it's gone!" Sharouf shouted. "Where is it now?"

Nehem could see the man had become desperate. And desperate people did rash things. It wasn't beyond the realm of possibility that his captor would shoot him in the face and dump his body in the underground passage. Nehem swallowed hard. "It would appear that whoever took it relocated the relic to the mountains of Bhutan. To the Tiger's Nest."

Sharouf's right eye twitched a second before he squinted at the answer. "What do you mean, the tiger's nest?"

"There is a monastery in Bhutan. It's the only logical conclusion. This inscription says that the relic was taken to the Tiger's Nest. I know of no other place that goes by that name. Someone must have feared it would fall into the wrong hands and taken it to the monastery. It would surely be kept safe there."

"Why do you say that?"

"The Tiger's Nest is difficult to reach. It was built on the side of a steep cliff nearly five hundred years ago. The monks there are holy men. If someone entrusted them with a secret, it would be well kept and passed down through the centuries to a select few."

Sharouf pulled the weapon away from his prisoner's head for a moment and pondered the answer. "If you're lying to us, you will die."

Nehem laughed. He was beyond fear at this point. "We both know I'm going to die anyway, young man. It's only a question of when. My helping you will only extend my life so far. The moment we find what you're looking for is the moment you will kill me. I know this, so let's not pretend, shall we?"

Sharouf eyed him suspiciously. "Then why would you help us at all?"

Nehem drew in another deep breath and sighed. "Because I know that good will always triumph over evil. Whatever it is that you and your employer have planned will fail no matter what I do." He paused for a second then said, "Not to mention that I have dreamed all my life of seeing these artifacts. Would be a shame to come so close and not have that chance." Nehem didn't tell his captor that he hoped someone else would beat them to it, and that perhaps that someone could also be his savior.

Sharouf wasn't sure he believed the explanation, but it didn't matter. As long as the prisoner wasn't lying about the location, that was all he cared about. If the Americans had translated the inscription, they would be heading to the monastery as well. He relished the chance to face Wyatt again. This time, it would end differently. This time, he would be ready.

23
Paro, Bhutan

The drive west to Jakarta took nearly three hours. Sean only stopped once along the way to fill up the gas tank and check under the hood to make sure the little rental car hadn't taken on any damage during the chase that might strand them in the middle of nowhere. Bullet holes riddled the panels on the back and sides. The windows were basically destroyed, though they could still see through the severely cracked windshield.

Along the way, Tommy called the pilot to let him know there'd been a change of plans. Fortunately, the man had grown accustomed to the sudden changes his employer sometimes required. Tommy informed him they would need to fly to Bhutan, and based on a best guess from a quick Internet search, the city of Paro would probably be their best option as a port of entry. The pilot concurred.

Upon arriving at the airport, Sean glanced at his phone and saw he'd received a text message from Emily.

Tommy looked over as Sean was reading the screen. "Who's it from?" he asked as he opened his door and started to get out.

"Emily," Sean said, his voice distant.

He pressed his thumb and index finger against the screen and then pulled them apart, zooming in on an image. Emily had asked if he knew anything about the guy in the picture. She said his name was Sharouf Al Nasir, but nothing else. Emily's inability to get information on a target could only mean one thing: they were trying to keep their past a secret.

Odd thing was, the guy in the picture was one of the men in the car he'd just destroyed a few hours before.

His fingers flew across the screen until he found her name in his contact list. He tapped the phone symbol and waited. Six seconds later, Emily answered.

"Took you long enough. I was actually starting to worry."

He snorted. "Sorry, I don't like to text and drive. Why are you asking about that guy in the picture?"

"Do you know him?"

"No, but he and his goons did just try to kill me and Tommy. If you asked me to put money on it, I'd say he's dead now."

"Dead?"

"I'm not completely sure. They chased us from a temple here in Indonesia, tried to run us off the road, shot at us, the whole nine. It did not go well for them."

"Sean, I need to know, did you kill this man or not?"

He scratched his head for a moment and looked around the area. The sun shone brightly in the sky, making him thankful for his sunglasses. "I don't know, Em. Killed the guy's driver and one other gunman that was with them. He was on the other side of the car when it crashed."

"What do you mean, it crashed?"

A taxi honked, the driver behind the wheel frantically waving his hand at Tommy. He shook his head and motioned the driver on.

"I mean I shot the driver in the head and sped up. When I looked back, the car was flipping down the road. If I had to guess, everyone inside was dead, including the one in your photo. Where'd you get that anyway, and why are you watching him?"

Emily sighed. "I don't suppose there's any way you can find out if he was killed, could you?"

"Not a chance. Tommy and I are about to hop out of this country. We're chasing down a lead, and a very important Israeli's life is at stake. If you do a quick sniff around, you'll find out who was killed in the wreck." He thought for a second then added, "You still haven't answered my question."

She paused for a moment and then responded. "His name is Sharouf Al Nasir. We believe he works for a man out of Dubai by the name of Mamoud Al Najaar. Thing is, the guy's basically a ghost. Other than his name, we don't know much. Heck, even the name might be an alias of some kind. We aren't sure."

"What does this have to do with me?"

"Nothing…yet. I'll let you know if I need you, but from the sounds of it, you're already involved."

"So it would seem. A few days ago, someone tried to kill me and Tommy. They burned our houses down, thinking we were still inside. I barely got Tommy out. Now we know who did it. My question is: Why are they coming after us?"

"Axis has been running a sting on Al Najaar for a while now. Another agent is working on it. So far, he's found that Al Najaar seems to be importing a ton of weapons and ammunitions."

"What for?" Sean asked.

"That's just it. We don't know. Al Najaar can't be doing it for the money."

"So he's a sympathizer."

"Or an egomaniac," she offered.

"Could be both."

Tommy motioned that they needed to get going by waving his hand around in a circle.

"Em, I gotta let you go. I have a plane to catch. Let me know if you hear anything about Al Nasir. If you keep an eye on the news down in Yogyakarta, you should hear something any minute now."

"Will do. And be careful. If that guy isn't dead, he's not someone you want to run into a second time."

Sean grinned. "Neither am I."

He ended the call, grabbed his things, and followed Tommy into the terminal. Sean kept his phone in his hand as he moved through the swaths of travelers and sent a quick text message before putting it back in his pocket.

Getting through airport security had been a little more stressful than either Sean or Tommy had anticipated. Both men had grown accustomed to getting to where they needed to be without much fuss. There were, it appeared, still places that had plenty of red tape.

They were relieved to set foot inside the Gulfstream's cabin and kick up their feet. The events of the day had exhausted their adrenal glands, and now their bodies needed rest. Sean leaned his seat back and propped his feet on the footrest as the engines whined and the plane began moving down the runway.

It was the middle of the day, but they'd been in so many different time zones over the course of the last few days that both Tommy and Sean had trouble establishing what time they were really on.

By the time the plane left Indonesian soil, the two were in a deep sleep. The flight attendant elected not to bother them, instead letting them catch up on some shuteye. Neither man moved much until the plane entered Bhutan airspace in the late afternoon.

Paro's airport barely qualified as an international one. Only a few flights went in and out each day, and as the country was so small and remote, tucked away at the edge of the Himalayas, a massive hub wasn't necessary. A lone runway ran along the plain, nestled between barren foothills.

Because the trip to the Taktsang Trail was less than thirty minutes away, Sean and Tommy decided to pay a driver to take them up to the trailhead. Based on some quick research, they figured getting to the monastery and back would take about two hours, then figured in another hour for finding whatever it was they were looking for.

The two Americans stood outside the airport amid a short line of taxis.

"You don't happen to have a plan for finding this thing, do you?" Tommy asked.

Sean stretched his arms and yawned. He winked at his friend. "I figured we'd just ask the abbot where it is."

Tommy stared at him in annoyed disbelief. "Seriously? That's your plan?"

"From what I understand, a lot of these Buddhist monks are very honest and friendly. They're usually more than happy to share information with people when asked."

"True...except in this case they've been entrusted with hiding a priceless relic that's over three thousand years old."

"Well, there's that. But if you forego the details, I'm pretty sure they'll be happy to help us."

Tommy rolled his eyes and shook his head. "Just in case, I'll be trying to think of an actual plan."

"Knock yourself out. Last I checked, I didn't see any other clues in that Indonesian temple."

"We left in a hurry. There may have been something else there."

Sean was dubious. "I don't think so. If there were more clues, we would have seen them in that drawer or at the base of the statue. There was nothing else. That means we can spend several hours traipsing around a temple high up in the mountains of Bhutan, or we can ask the monk in charge to show us where it is."

"And you think that's going to work?" It was Tommy's turn to look doubtful.

"I'm just saying, we're probably the first people in over two thousand years to ask for it."

"Technically, this particular monastery is only around five hundred years old."

"You know what I mean." Sean shot his friend a narrow-eyed glare.

A red four-door car pulled up to the curb and stopped at their feet. The car looked only a year or two old and was made by one of the Chinese automotive companies.

The driver was a young man, short with a boyish face and a shaggy head of black hair. He got out and smiled broadly at the two Americans. "You are Mr. Wyatt and Mr. Shultz, yes?" His English was good, which was a mild concern when Tommy had made the arrangements.

"That's us," Tommy answered.

The driver motioned with his hand that he wanted to take the bags, which both men refused.

"We're okay, thank you."

"Is this all you have?" The driver appeared perplexed.

"We like to travel light," Sean answered.

"Ah, clever. No pesky bag fees." He clearly didn't know they'd flown on a private jet. "My name is Pak. I will be your driver. I understand you want to see Tiger's Nest."

His English was solid, and better than good enough to understand simple directions.

"That is correct, Pak," Tommy said.

"You want to go there today?"

The two visitors nodded.

"We must hurry then. Sun will go down in four hours. It take two hours for most people to go up and down. If you want to see the sights, you will not have much time."

"Let's do it," Sean said.

Pak scurried around to the driver's side door and hopped in while the Americans got in the back. As soon as the doors were closed, Pak jammed the gas pedal and zipped the car out onto the road.

Sean and Tommy were jostled but stabilized themselves with the handgrip above the windows.

"It only take twenty minutes to get to the Taktsang Trail from here. You two look like you are in good shape, so maybe it not take as long for you to reach the monastery."

Sean thought about making a wisecrack about Tommy's lack of fitness, but a knowing glare from the other side of the backseat kept him in check. "We'll be fine," he said instead.

Pak guided the car out onto the main road and then off again onto a winding side road that twisted its way up through the hills and into the dramatic mountains. The landscape reminded the visitors of Colorado. Flatlands erupted into jagged hills, covered in evergreen trees and outcroppings of massive rocks. At certain curves in the road, the views were absolutely stunning. A river flowed through the valley off in the distance near a small town.

"I never hear anyone talk about visiting this place. I'm not sure why. This countryside is gorgeous." Sean said.

Pak answered, clearly eavesdropping. "Bhutan is one of the best kept secrets in the world. We like to keep it that way."

"Makes sense," Tommy said, looking out the window at the mountain range. "Heaven knows we've screwed up enough of our pretty country by overpopulating and overselling tourism."

Pak nodded. "Some visitors good. Like you two." His smile beamed in the rearview mirror. "But too many make mess."

Sean kept his thoughts to himself, hoping that the same mess that happened in Israel and Indonesia didn't happen here. Just in case things got sticky, he and Tommy had replenished their ammunition supply before getting off the plane. They usually traveled with extra magazines and a spare weapon each, just in case. More often than not, they weren't needed on ventures with the IAA. Lately, though, things had been different.

About twenty minutes after leaving the airport, the vehicle came to a stop in a small, shaded parking area surrounded by a ranch-style wooden fence. Pak put the car in park and stepped out to open the door for Tommy.

He was a second too late, as his passenger was already exiting and had one foot on the gravel. The air was much cooler in the mountains and smelled of spruce, hemlock, and pine. The forests were thick and kept most of the ground in a cool shade throughout the day.

The men surveyed the area, tracing the outline of the fencing until they found where it opened into a high wooden archway at the trailhead. Words were written in various languages, including Chinese characters and English, describing the Taktsang Trail. In a clearing just beyond the fence, a dozen ponies and four donkeys loitered near the edge of the forest. All of the animals were saddled and ready to transport any late arriving visitors to the top of the trail. The smell of horsehair mingled with the scent of the forest.

Sean's eyes lingered on a faded white five-door hatchback on the far side of the parking area. It sat in the shadows, keeping the car's interior dark. He was sure a woman sat behind the wheel, but it was difficult to make out her face.

"You can take one of the pack animals if you prefer. They move pretty slow, though." Pak pointed at the ponies as he spoke.

"We'll be fine walking, Pak. Thank you," Sean said, removing his gaze from the white vehicle.

Tommy handed the driver a fold of cash and asked, "Are you going to wait here, or should we let you know when we are heading back down?"

Pak graciously accepted the tip with his trademark grin. "I wait for you to come back. No mobile phone service up here."

The two Americans looked at each other and shrugged. "Perfect."

"Your phones might work on top. Not down here, though."

"Well, there's that," Tommy said. "We'll plan on seeing you when we get back down here. I think we should only be at the monastery for an hour."

"Okay. When it start to get dark, the park close. So you hurry."

The visitors nodded and walked away toward the trail.

The archway and fencing surrounding the trailhead were covered in a wild array of colorful flags and pennants. Some of the cloth had things written in Chinese: prayers, words honoring ancestors, and blessings of various kinds.

Sean led the way up the short slope and over the rolling hill. The narrow trail cut through the evergreen forest, disappearing at times as it weaved back and forth among the trees. The two friends kept on full alert, watching every possible angle. The thick forest

233

provided an excellent place for trouble to hide, and even with their diligent observation skills, someone could easily sneak up on them.

The trail flattened out at first then sloped up dramatically. It swung right and left, zigzagging its way up the mountain, making the journey a little more bearable. After twenty minutes of hiking, the altitude and the steep incline began to take its toll on both men, particularly Tommy. He breathed heavily as he walked in line behind Sean, laboring to keep up the pace.

Sean's legs burned, but he knew that they needed to hurry. The slower they went, the less time they'd have to look for the relic upon reaching the top. So he pressed on, forcing himself to keep going.

The two passed a few other visitors who were on their way down. They were older folk, a man and a woman with fanny packs attached to their belts. When the two were out of earshot, Tommy cast a quick look back and then said to Sean, "How in the world did they make it to the top of this mountain alive?"

Sean shook his head in disbelief at his friend. "When we get back, you're going to a gym every day."

The two kept pushing on up the winding trail. They had to stop more than a few times to let Tommy catch his breath before pressing on. Every once in a while, Sean thought he heard something in the woods behind them, but when he turned around he saw nothing. It was probably just a chipmunk or a bird scrounging around in the pine needles and leaves. He sighed. Maybe he was a little *too* high strung.

The journey up the mountain had taken much longer than expected when they reached an observation spot on the trail. The monastery and the cafeteria below it were both visible, as if the people who designed the trail had put it there as a carrot to keep people going just a little farther.

The two Americans soon learned that the observation point was more like a mirage. The final length of the journey took another twenty hard minutes of walking before they reached the cafeteria. People were beginning their descent in earnest now, clearing out of the visitor's center and eating area in droves. The sun had already retreated to the west of the mountain, leaving the monastery in the cool shade of approaching twilight.

"We'll have less than an hour here if we want to get back to the parking area before dark," Sean said.

Tommy was still struggling to catch his breath, but he nodded and pointed at a bridge that crossed over from a steep staircase to a landing at the foot of the monastery. "Looks like we have to go down some steps and then back up those over there to reach the bridge."

Sean's heart sank. He swallowed hard as his mind began to run wild with the fear that had corrupted his courage since he was a boy. Tommy meandered over to where the descending staircase began and took a step down. He turned around and looked back at Sean with tired but determined eyes. "Come on, man; like you said, gotta hurry."

Sean's feet involuntarily shuffled across the ground, carrying him closer to the point where it looked like the earth dropped off into an eternal abyss. He told himself with each step that it wouldn't be as bad as he thought, that there would be a slight drop with a staircase complete with a walled-in guardrail to keep him safe. Upon reaching the edge, he realized it was the complete opposite.

The ancient stone steps dropped dramatically down almost a hundred feet before reaching a narrow plot of ground. A thin trail stretched over to a similar set of stairs that reached up to the bridge. There were no guardrails. No safety wall. Just an agonizingly long drop to a sudden stop at the bottom.

24
Paro

Tommy passed his friend a disparaging glance. "You know, for an international man of mystery, you sure do have a problem with heights. What's the deal with that anyway? You can dodge bullets, but a cliff terrifies you. I would have thought you'd be over that by now." He was already down five steps and didn't seem at all bothered by the precipice. "Were you dropped on your head as a child or something?"

Sean crouched down low and moved his first foot over the edge, carefully placing it on the step. "Mom pushed me out of a swing," Sean snapped. "And yes, I fell on my head."

"Really? That's why you're so scared of heights?"

"It's the only conclusion I can come to." He pressed his hands to the top ledge and put the other foot down to the second step.

"Are you seriously going to take this long to go down the stairs? 'Cause there's, like, two hundred of them, and that's just on this side."

Sean motioned with his hand. "Go on ahead. I'll catch up."

"Not at that speed you won't." Tommy snickered at his own joke.

"Go up to the monastery, and find the abbot. Tell him what we're here for. See if he can help us. I'll be there in a bit."

"If by a bit you mean tomorrow, then yeah." Tommy shook his head and took off at what Sean considered a reckless pace, almost bounding down the stairs.

Sean kept his body as low as he could as he descended the steps one after another. He kept his eyes on the next step and nothing else, desperately trying not to see the vast distance to the bottom. His hands shook violently, mirroring his head's gyrating movement. As he crept ever closer to the base of the stairs, he picked up his pace ever so slightly, getting into a sloth-like rhythm overlapping one foot and then the other. Halfway down, he began to feel more comfortable and stole a glance over at Tommy who'd already begun ascending the other staircase. What Sean lacked in speed due to fear, Tommy would lack in fitness as he climbed the other steps.

Sean's pace quickened when he was twenty feet from the bottom, the terror of falling no longer an issue. He sped up until he reached the floor. When his feet landed on solid ground, he took a deep breath. There was still another cliff to the right, but the wall on the left made him feel at least a little safer. He took off at a jog and hurried over to the other staircase. Tommy's speed had slowed significantly, as Sean knew it would, but he'd reached the top and disappeared over the upper ledge.

When Sean arrived at the base of the next set of stairs, he swallowed hard. The momentary respite of being on safe ground vanished in an instant, and his deeply rooted fear returned.

"Just look at the next step above you," he said to himself. He repeated the mantra as he put his foot on the first stone ledge then the next.

He made it to the top of the stairs ten minutes later, a journey that should have only taken four. He was proud that he'd been able to conquer the climb, but his hands still trembled even as he reached the upper landing and stepped away. The next obstacle was the bridge. Just when he thought his battle was over, the bridge crossed over a crevasse that dropped several hundred feet down to the jagged rocks below. "This place is a nightmare," he said again in a low tone.

A young couple walked leisurely across the bridge, stopping midway to lean over the railing. The move made Sean queasy. At least there was something he could hold onto. He shuffled over to the crossing and grabbed the rail nearest the mountain wall then started across. In the case of the bridge, he found that moving as fast as possible was the way to do it, sort of like ripping off a Band-Aid. The couple in the middle smiled at him and seemed as if they might start up a conversation, but Sean was in no mood to talk and kept his eyes focused on the bridge as he made his way across.

With his feet on solid ground again, he bent over and grabbed his knees. He took several deep breaths and started to relax again. His eyes wandered to his surroundings, taking in the extraordinary vistas and the dangerous placement of the monastery. Tommy appeared in a doorway up another shorter set of stairs. He was followed closely by a man in dark-orange robes. His head was shaved clean over a pair of narrow eyes. Lines stretched out from his nose and underneath his eyes, showing his advanced years of age even from fifty feet away.

Tommy waved, motioning for Sean to join them.

A few minutes later, within the temple's confines, Sean finished telling his story to the abbot. "So you see, that is why we have come to your place of worship," he said.

He and Tommy sat across from the old abbot and a younger monk who translated Sean's message. They'd been brought into a small room with cream-colored walls supported by dark wooden beams. Candles burned on shelves and sconces, casting an eerie, flickering yellow light on the four men. The travelers had been offered tea, which they accepted as a show of good faith. Sean took another sip from the bone cup and set it down on the matching dish placed in front of him.

Tommy had already given him a rough idea of what they were there for, but Sean tried to clarify since the abbot was still somewhat uncertain as to their purpose. Once he had heard Sean's explanation, the abbot's face took on a grave expression.

He spoke deliberately so that the translator didn't miss any details.

"We have been entrusted with the protection of this relic for centuries. Before that, our monks guarded it for thousands of years at Borobudur. Not once, in all that time, has it been reported that a visitor requested to see the relic. You are the first."

Sean and Tommy shot each other a quick glance and then returned their gaze to the old man.

"However, just because you are the first to inquire about its existence here does not entitle you to receive it. Only someone who knows the heart of the one who protected it can receive its power."

This last bit caused concern for the two Americans.

"What do you mean?" Sean asked.

The translator passed along the question, and the abbot nodded. He stared through Sean and then Tommy.

"This relic is very powerful. In the wrong hands, it could cause much pain throughout the world. You must pass the test if you are to receive it."

"Test?" Tommy looked worried. "What test?"

When the abbot heard the question, he stood up and motioned for the three to follow him.

The two friends looked at each other questioningly, wondering where the monks were taking them. They shrugged and followed the young interpreter and his master into a narrow hallway. More candles burned atop brass sconces along the walls. The little flames danced in the darkness as the monks passed by.

The corridor went straight for thirty feet, passing by dormitories and prayer rooms. It abruptly shot off to the left, back to the right, and then up one flight of stairs to a dark wooden door. The abbot turned and said something to the interpreter. His voice was almost inaudible. When the young apprentice translated, he too kept his voice low.

"We must not interrupt the evening prayers," he said. "Be very quiet."

Sean and Tommy nodded. They'd removed their shoes before entering the monastery, something they assumed the monks would appreciate. Now they clutched their shoes tighter, wary of dropping them.

The door swung open silently, revealing another hallway on the other side. The four stepped in and padded quietly along the ancient wooden floor. The wall to the right had several small windows that looked through into a vast chamber with twenty-foot ceilings. Red tassels hung from the walls every five feet. Circular pillars, painted red, supported the dropped ceilings before they vaulted to the top. The Americans noted the strong smell of incense and located the smoking censer in the front of the room on top of a platform. Surrounding the platform, dozens of men in matching robes chanted in unison. Their bodies swayed back and forth in rhythm as their ghostly prayers echoed through the chamber.

The group pressed on, and soon the corridor took another sharp turn to the left. From what the visitors could tell, they were heading toward the mountain. Sure enough, the walled corridor ended and gave way to another door. It was marked with an emblem that had been burned into its center. The symbol was out of place in such a remote

Eastern country. It was the Davidic star of Israel.

The abbot reached into the folds of his robe and removed a key, hanging around his neck on a piece of string. He looped it up over his head and inserted it into the door. The older man said something to the young monk and then turned the key carefully; the old lock clicked. The man put the key back over his head and reverently pushed the door. Unlike the previous one, this door creaked loudly. It clearly hadn't been used in a long time. The abbot's apprentice grabbed a candle from the wall and handed it to his master then repeated the action to give each of the visitors their own source of light.

"He says this door hasn't been opened in nearly five hundred years."

Musty, damp air wafted out through the opening as the four moved forward into the tunnel. The jagged rock looked as if it had been hewn in a hurry. Sean imagined that whoever did it worked quickly to get the relic hidden in case someone had followed it from Indonesia. Water dripped down a strip on the left side, splattering on the rock below. He wasn't sure where it flowed to, probably an underground river. He shook away the random thoughts and looked ahead. The abbot walked into a large circular room. The light from his candle barely reached the edge of the wall. He stopped in the center where a three-foot-high stone platform stood. On top of it, three golden boxes shimmered in the flickering candlelight.

Sean and Tommy stepped close, standing at the abbot's side. They gazed in wonder at the three containers.

"What are these?" Sean whispered.

The interpreter didn't need to ask the abbot. He already knew the answer. "This is your test." He held out his hand, palm up, as if displaying the three objects. "You must choose the correct box. Only one holds the relic you seek. The other two offer death."

Tommy frowned. "Death? What do you mean, death?"

Sean stared at the boxes. They were each about two feet long and a foot wide. He figured they were made of wood, probably cedar, and layered in a thin coating of gold. A six-pointed star had been engraved into each one. The three containers also featured a gem inlaid into the removable top. Each precious stone was different: one ruby, one white stone, and one onyx. Sean figured the white to be quartz, but he wasn't sure. The gems were cut and smoothed into ovals then inserted just above the high priest's symbol.

The abbot and his apprentice withdrew, stepping back into the recess of the tunnel.

They offered no further instruction or assistance.

"How are we supposed to know which one of these is the right one?" Tommy hissed, trying to keep his voice low enough so the abbot wouldn't hear his doubts.

"I'm working on it," Sean said through clenched teeth. "It has to have something to do with the gems on the tops."

"I was thinking the same thing, but what's the difference?"

"One line of thought suggests the red one. The white one and black one are at opposite ends of the spectrum, while the ruby is different than both."

Tommy nodded. "Right. So the one with the ruby." He started to reach out, but Sean grabbed his wrist and pulled him back.

"Not so fast."

Tommy looked at him like a frightened child who'd just been chastised for reaching for a forbidden cookie.

"There are other things to consider, though. Think about it. The white and black stones look like the Urim and the Thummim, the same gems that were said to go with the breastplate. In the Jewish histories, it didn't say anything about a ruby being used with the Hoshen."

"Good point. So not the red one?"

Sean shook his head. "Probably not."

Tommy swallowed hard as he gazed at the two potential boxes. "Both the white and the black were used to get answers from God. Some of the legends suggest that the stones moved, while others say they lit up. But in both cases, the stones reacted most often to direct yes or no questions."

"And which one was the gem that represented the yes?"

Both sets of eyes drifted to the box on the end with the white stone set in its top.

"The white one," Tommy said.

"Right."

They continued to gaze at the gilded container. Doubts lingered in their hearts. If they were wrong, the abbot said that death awaited. Neither man knew what that meant, nor did they want to find out. Tommy twisted his head, risking a peek over his shoulder. The abbot and his apprentice had vanished. The light from their candles was gone, leaving Sean and Tommy alone in the chamber.

"Where did they go?" he asked, turning around to look once more at the box.

"I imagine if we choose the wrong box they will lock us in here," Sean said. "It's unlikely there's something in the other two that would kill us. These things have been here too long."

"Unless they're booby trapped."

"True, but I don't think so. I'm thinking they'd go a little more in the direction of Poe's story, 'The Cask of Amontillado.'"

"Wall us up and let us starve to death in here?"

"Yep."

Tommy shivered at the thought. "Okay, so we're sure it's the box with the white stone?"

Sean nodded. "Has to be."

He took a step to the side and drew closer to the box. He set his candle down on the rock plinth next to the object. His hands reached out and touched the smooth edges of the top. The seam between the main part of the container and its closure was extremely thin. Whoever had built it was extremely precise with their craftsmanship.

Tommy hovered behind Sean, looking closely over his shoulder.

Sean grasped the top from both sides and started to lift it up. There would be no turning back now.

25
Paro

Sean's fingers remained steady as he pulled up on the lid. He winced slightly as wild thoughts of acid spray shooting out from the box ran through his imagination. When the top came free, nothing escaped the container. Instead, they were greeted by something glittering in the yellow candlelight. Sean let out a long breath and completely removed the lid, setting it aside on the end of the altar.

Inside the box was an artifact that hadn't been seen in nearly three thousand years. Twelve precious stones were set into the metal breastplate. Golden chains were attached to the end of one side via a matching gold clasp. Two more were connected to the sides and wrapped underneath the piece.

The two Americans blinked rapidly, their eyes not fully believing what they saw.

"It's beautiful," Tommy said. "This is one of the holiest holy relics in all of Judaism. Only the high priest of Israel was allowed to wear it. That means only a handful of people ever put this thing on in the history of the world."

"It's pretty incredible," Sean said. "We need to get it out of here if we're going to save your friend."

"Right." Tommy's face contorted. "Toting this thing down the mountain won't exactly be inconspicuous."

"We can stuff it in this bag," Sean offered.

"That will not be necessary."

The voice came from the darkness near the entrance. Sean and Tommy spun around, each instantly drawing their weapons and retreating from the light. Though their reactions were fast due to years of experience and training, they were undeniably in a bad situation.

A match flared to life in the tunnel. It moved to the left, touching the wick of a candle. Once more, the candle's illumination lit up the area around it, casting a pale corona onto the faces of the two monks. It also revealed another face, one that the Americans instantly recognized.

Sharouf Al Nasir.

Sean kept his pistol trained at the man's head, but the darkness made it difficult to be sure of his aim. If he missed, Sean would hit one of the monks that Sharouf was using as human shields.

"You're not going to need those weapons," Sharouf said. "Put them down, and bring me the Hoshen."

Sean and Tommy simultaneously inched their way behind the stone platform and met in the middle, using the altar and the golden boxes as cover.

"Why don't you come over and get it yourself, Sharouf?" Sean sneered.

The Arab clicked his tongue and shook his head. "No. I do not think so. We do not have time for your games, American. I do not feel like sitting around and waiting out a stalemate with you. Here is what will happen. I am going to send this young man over to collect the breastplate. I will keep the old man with me. You will allow the young monk to bring the Hoshen back to me, and in return, I will let all of you live."

Sean knew there was a catch to what Sharouf was offering, and he didn't want to think about it. Unfortunately, he didn't have an ounce of leverage at the moment.

"What's the play?" Tommy whispered. "If we give him the relic, he'll either kill us or lock us in here."

"Either way, we're dead. No one's going to check for us in here. You heard the abbot. That door hasn't been opened in five hundred years."

"Do we have a deal?" Sharouf pressed the issue.

They were out of time.

"Okay," Sean said. "Fine. Send the boy over. But if you screw around, I'm putting a hollow point between your eyes."

"That is a big risk to take, American. I doubt you will do something that stupid. And if you do, my men will cut you down." He paused for a second and pushed the young monk forward. "Here comes the boy. Give him the breastplate, and we will be on our way."

The interpreter stumbled forward. When they'd first met him, Sean and Tommy figured the monk was young, but now that his life was on the line, he looked much younger.

"Just take it easy, kid," Sean said, keeping his pistol pointed at Sharouf's head. You're going to get out of this just fine. We all are. Isn't that right, Sharouf?"

"You're in no position to question me," the Arab answered. "But I will let all of you live, yes."

The apprentice made it to the box and hesitated for a second. His eyes lowered and took in the sight of the glittering breastplate.

"Pick it up, and take it to him," Sean ordered.

The monk's eyes leveled with Sean's. He swallowed and reached into the box. His thin fingers wrapped around the edges of the breastplate, and he lifted it out easily. Sean thought it might have been a little heavier.

"Bring it to me," Sharouf said. His voice boomed through the circular chamber.

The young monk turned around slowly, holding the relic across his forearms and shuffled his way back across the floor to the tunnel. When he reached Sharouf's position, he held out his arms, and the Arab reached out and snatched the breastplate. Sean and Tommy watched the whole thing play out, looking for a crack, a moment where they could seize the advantage. That moment never came.

"Good," Sharouf said. He passed the relic back to one of his men and returned his focus to the two monks.

He put a hand on the abbot's shoulder and pulled him back toward the door. Another hand reached out and tugged on the interpreter.

"Where's he going?" Tommy asked, though there was a sinking feeling in his tone.

"Not sure," Sean answered quietly.

The candle disappeared from view. Six seconds later, the door slammed shut, and they heard the lock click into place. Sean jumped up, placed a foot on the stone platform, and launched himself toward the door with his weapon fully extended.

"Sharouf!" he yelled as he hit the ground and sprinted forward.

"He's gone," a familiar and frightened voice said from the other end of the passage.

Sean's heart jumped into his throat. The interpreter and the abbot reappeared at the edge of the room. The light from the

Americans' candles brushed across their worried faces. Sean lowered his weapon. Tommy did the same and stepped around the plinth.

"You two okay?" Sean asked.

The interpreter nodded, but the abbot's face showed deep concern. He began speaking rapidly while the younger monk listened. When the abbot was finished, the boy translated.

"He says that the world is in grave danger, and there is no one to stop them. No one will come to get us out because visiting this part of the monastery is forbidden. Only he is permitted to go to the door, and no one has ever been in here. Even if someone knew about it, the only key that can open the door was taken by those men."

Tommy sighed and shoved his pistol back into its holster. He turned away and kicked the air. "Well isn't this just perfect!" he shouted. His voice echoed off the walls somewhat louder than he expected.

"Relax," Sean said calmly. He put his weapon back into its holster as well. "Help is on the way."

"Help?" Tommy asked incredulous. "What help? No one knows we're in here. You just heard the man say that no one is permitted in this part of the monastery. And the only key that can open the door is gone."

He pulled out his cell phone in the desperate hope that he could somehow get service. So deep in the mountain, though, there was no chance. "Of course."

"We're underneath, like, eighty feet of rock. No chance that thing's going to work in here."

Sean's comment didn't help, but Tommy couldn't understand how he was staying so calm.

"What's wrong with you?" Tommy asked. "We're going to die in here."

Sean walked back over to the platform and moved the empty box over to the side. He sat down and crossed a leg over one knee. "We're not going to die. Help is on the way."

The two monks listened closely as the two friends went back and forth, watching with keen interest.

"Why do you keep saying that? Who knows we're in here?"

Sean folded his hands and placed them on top of a leg. "Who's the best person you could think of to pick that lock and open the door?"

Tommy was exasperated. His hands shot out to both sides and then dropped, smacking his thighs. "I don't know. A locksmith?"

Sean flicked an eyebrow at the obvious answer and then cocked his head to the side. "I was thinking more along the lines of a thief."

"A thief? What thief..." he stopped himself before he could finish the sentence. "Wait a minute. How?"

"I texted her before we left Indonesia. She was closer to Bhutan than we were. I texted her again when we started our hike."

"But how do you know those men didn't see her?"

Sean shot him a glance that expressed what he said. "Really? I'm pretty sure she knows how to stay out of sight. She waited at the base of the mountain in the parking lot. I assume she followed those men when they started up the trail."

"You assume? You assume?" He asked the question twice, somewhat more troubled the second time. "How will she know how to find this cave? Even if Adriana did follow those guys up the mountain, how would she be able to follow them and us through all those passages without being noticed?"

"Tommy, you need to trust me." Sean turned to the two monks. "Don't worry. We're going to get out of here. And that breastplate is useless without the other relics. If they don't get the two stones that go with it, it will just be a shiny decoration on their walls."

The interpreter looked dubious, but he translated for the abbot. The old man nodded. He took a seat on the hard floor and leaned his back against the wall. The apprentice did the same.

Sean kept talking. "According to what Tara and Alex came up with, the Urim and the Thummim were taken into Babylon by Daniel the prophet. He was entrusted with watching over them until he died."

Tommy broke away from his frustration and tried to focus on what Sean was saying. At least that way he could try to be productive instead of freaking out, which helped no one. "Okay. So if he kept it until he died, do you think he gave it to someone else?"

Sean shook his head. "Based on my knowledge of the life of Daniel, I don't think he would do that. He seemed like a loner. His three best friends were already dead when he met his end. Since they were gone, I doubt he would have trusted anyone else, especially the Persians when they took over."

"So you think the stones are buried with him?"

"Maybe. What do you know about Daniel's burial place?"

Tommy thought about it for a minute. He scratched the stubble on his right cheek as he considered the question. "I know a lot of biblical history but am a little shady on that. The city of Susa in Iran comes to mind. From what I recall, the supposed burial site is pretty elaborate."

"Then that's where we'll go. It's our only lead." Sean's face was determined as he stared at the floor, rocking back and forth on his makeshift seat.

Tommy shook his head. "That's assuming we can get out of this death chamber."

The sound of metal on metal squeaked from the other end of the corridor. There was another noise, something moving inside the mechanical part of the door, then a click and the creaking hinges as the portal swung open. A bright-white LED light shone into the passage and approached slowly. Sean stood up and peered into the light. Tommy reached for his gun, but Sean kept his arms to his side. The two monks stood up off to the right of the tunnel opening and took a step back.

When the person with the light reached the chamber threshold, they lowered the cell phone with the light on the front. The glow from the candles stretched over and revealed the face of their new visitor: Adriana Villa.

26
Paro

Adriana smiled mischievously. When she spoke, her Spanish accent made her words sound as sweet as honey. "Are you okay, Tommy? You look like you've seen a ghost."

His mouth was wide open, and his eyes matched the expression.

Sean stepped over and wrapped his arms around her. He pressed his lips against hers and kissed her hard for a moment. He hated to let go, but now wasn't the time for catching up on missed time. Nehem was still in trouble.

"I've missed you," he said.

"I can tell," she answered, still grinning.

"We need to hurry. They have the Hoshen, and they'll likely be going after the two stones next. We can't let them get there before us."

Tommy was still bewildered. "How did you find us? I mean...how were you able to follow them undetected?"

"You really don't have much faith in me, do you Thomas?"

He blushed. And whenever she called him that, it made it worse.

"We'll talk about that later," Sean said. He turned his attention to the abbot and bowed low. "Thank you. We're sorry for the..." he motioned with his hand, "however you say all of what just happened."

The young monk didn't interpret this time. Instead he just said, "Go, and stop them."

"Will do."

The two Americans led the way back out the tunnel and through the secret passageway, with Adriana close behind. They kept their conversation to a minimum until they reached fresh air and the waning daylight.

When they were outside, Sean spoke up first as he put on his shoes. "I saw you in your car on the other side of the parking lot."

"Yes. I stayed in the car and watched. Soon after you two started up the trail, I noticed those men follow you. Once I was satisfied none of them lingered behind, I got on their tail. It was a little trickier to go unnoticed once we were out of the woods, but they were so focused on catching up to you two, I didn't have too much trouble."

Tommy slid into his second shoe and stood up. "I wonder how they were able find out that we were coming here."

"I was wondering the same thing," Sean said as he stood. "And I guess this answers the question as to whether or not Sharouf survived the crash."

"Where are you going next?" she asked as she stepped down onto the path leading to the bridge.

"Susa, Iran," Tommy answered. "It's the supposed burial place of Daniel the prophet."

"The fact that they were willing to lock you two in that cave means they probably know where they're going next."

Sean nodded. "Yeah. Which means Nehem is probably still alive. I doubt Mamoud and his henchmen would have figured any of this out."

"It's why they needed him in the first place," Tommy added. "I wonder if he had anything to do with them showing up here in Bhutan."

"Could be. But we'll have to wait for those answers. For now, we have to get back to the car."

A sinking feeling crept into Sean's chest. His eyes drifted over to the bridge and the nightmarish staircase. *Not again,* he thought.

Having made it over the difficult obstacle less than an hour before helped give Sean enough confidence to make it down the steps and up the other side faster than the first time around, but it still took much longer than his two companions. When he reached the top of the steps near the cafeteria, Tommy and Adriana were already standing by a tree. Tommy's chest was heaving as he tried to catch his breath, while Adriana seemed to be unaffected by the climb.

"Sorry, guys. Went as fast as I could," Sean offered.

"Don't worry about it, bud. We'll catch up to them." Tommy tried to grin through his labored breaths.

"Good job," Adriana said without an ounce of sarcasm. She knew how difficult it was for Sean to deal with heights.

"No time for a snack," Sean said, changing the subject. "We'll need to hurry. We're at least twenty to thirty minutes behind them now."

The three took off down the mountain at a gallop. At certain points on the trail, they had to slow to a jog, eventually barely moving faster than a brisk walk. Still, they pressed on, trying to keep pace with the group they were tracking. Getting down to the trailhead took almost half the time it took to go up. Along the way, they passed a straggler or two who had almost lingered too long at the information center up top.

By the time they made it to the bottom, there was barely any sunlight left. The sky radiated with bright oranges, pinks, and purples. They slowed down just before going over the last crest that led to the parking area. If they'd somehow caught up to Mamoud's men, they could find themselves running into an ambush. They moved in tandem, keeping to the tree line, moving laterally at first and then down, from behind one tree trunk to another to keep visibility at a minimum. Once they were close enough, Sean surveyed the parking area and saw that only a few cars remained. Adriana's was off to the far side,

Sean and Tommy's was a little closer, and three other vehicles sat empty, parked in random places along the edge of the forest. One probably belonged to whoever was closing the cafeteria at the top. The other two were likely the stragglers they passed on the way down. Whatever the case, Sharouf and his men were gone.

Relieved wasn't exactly how Sean would have expressed his feelings. He was glad not to be walking into a trap. Then again, the men who'd stolen the Hoshen believed the Americans were still on top of the mountain, trapped in a forbidden cave with no way out.

Even though he was happy to put off a shootout, he knew that now Mamoud's cronies had the advantage. And they also had a head start.

He peered into the window of their rental and saw Pak's outline. He was lying in the driver's seat motionless. Sean's heart started pounding a little quicker.

They hurried down the hill to the car. Sean got there first and started to bang on the door when Pak shot up from the seat with wide eyes.

He unlocked the doors and got out quickly. "Hey. You made it back before dark. I sorry. I started to take nap. Get very tired when I sit for long time."

Tommy patted him on the shoulder. "It's no problem, Pak. Glad you're okay."

The man's eyes questioned the statement. "Why I not be okay?"

"No reason," Sean stepped in. "Just happy to see you. Mind taking us back to the airport?"

The driver's face beamed its perpetual beam. "Of course," he exclaimed. "You find what you looking for?"

"Sort of. Still have some work to do in another place."

Adriana started for her vehicle. She turned to Sean and asked, "Mind if I catch a ride on your airplane?" Her grin creased the corner of her right cheek.

"Absolutely."

She spun around and ran over to her car while the two Americans hopped in their rental.

Tommy sat in the front seat with Pak. He looked over at the driver as he started to back the car out. "Hey, Pak, how fast can you get us back to the airport?"

A sly grin creased the driver's face. "You ask right question."

27
Dubai

Mamoud stared in disgust at the Israeli archaeologist. His men had put the prisoner back in his cell as soon as he arrived back at the mansion from the Indonesian flight. Once Sharouf knew where to find the breastplate, he sent two of his men back to Dubai with Nehem. It was a risky move but a calculated one. Sharouf reasoned the older man would slow them down. Even though he'd come in handy with his ability to decipher the clue in the temple at Borobudur, Sharouf's plan for the monastery in Bhutan hadn't required any such expertise.

His trap had worked perfectly. With only so many flights coming into Paro on any given day, it was easy to pick out the one with the Americans on it. Sharouf and his men watched from a distance as Wyatt and Schultz got in their car and made their way up to the base of the mountain trail.

They followed the two men up the winding trail, careful to stay far enough behind to not be seen, and keeping close to the trees that lined the path in case they needed to duck for cover. Once, one of his men stepped on a twig, snapping it loudly. Fortunately, he and his men reacted quickly, ducking out of sight in the nick of time. It had been painful to watch how slowly Wyatt made his way across the ravine. It was an extended period of time Sharouf had not counted on, not that it mattered. The plan had worked brilliantly.

Wyatt and his friend had convinced the monastery's abbot to take them to the hidden cavern, which turned out better than Sharouf could have hoped. The targets were boxed in with no way to escape. He'd wondered if he did the right thing by leaving them there to die, but what choice did he have? If they engaged in a shootout, someone would hear. The other monks would discover the passageway and seal it off. Then everyone would be trapped. By locking Wyatt inside, no one would know what happened, and no one could get in to save them. There was the off chance that someone would notice the abbot was missing and go looking for him, but by the time that happened and they were able to unlock the door, Sharouf and his men would already be back in Dubai.

Now he stood in the doorway of Nehem's cell, watching his employer extract the final piece of the puzzle. A fresh scar from the car accident in Indonesia still marked his face.

"Where are the stones?" Mamoud asked. "We're not going through this cat and mouse game again, Doctor. Tell me where we need to go. If you play nice, I'll even let you see the power the ancient relics possess before I kill you."

"I will never lead you to the stones. I do not know how you were able to get the Hoshen, but the stones will remain hidden for all eternity."

Mamoud slowly closed and reopened his eyes then shook his head. When he spoke, he wagged a warning finger. "I thought you might say something like that, which is why I figured you might need a little extra motivation." He motioned to Sharouf who, in turn, waved his hand to one of the other bodyguards.

Three seconds later, a stocky, broad-shouldered young Arab with a shaved head wrestled a woman in white pants and a white blouse through the door. She was probably in her midtwenties. Her black hair hung down past her shoulders. The handkerchief clenched between her teeth kept her from screaming, but that didn't stop her from making as much noise as she could. When her eyes locked with her father's, she froze for a moment.

"Raizel?" Nehem started to stand, but Mamoud pressed down on his shoulder with remarkable strength, forcing him back into the seat. The Israeli's eyes shifted instantly to his captor's. "Let her go, you monster. She's innocent."

"None of you are innocent!" Mamoud boomed. "I'm tired of your games, Nehem.

Tell me where the stones are, or I will cut your daughter to pieces before your eyes."

Tears streamed down Nehem's face, mirroring those of his daughter. She was full of confusion and fear as she gazed at her father. He knew she didn't understand why any of this was happening. No matter what their insane captor believed, she was truly innocent. Raizel had her whole life ahead of her. As he stared at her tear-stained face, Nehem weighed the consequences of his decision. If he gave up the location of the stones, Mamoud would be unchallenged by any world government, any army. He would always be a step ahead. *Was that future really certain, though?* There was always the chance that someone could stop him, even if the odds were low. All that mattered right now was his daughter. The lives of millions of people didn't matter to Nehem at this moment. Only one did.

"Susa." He blurted out the word amid choking back tears.

Mamoud tilted his head sideways and narrowed his eyes. "What did you say?"

"I said the stones are in Susa."

"In Iran?"

"Yes, in Iran at the tomb of Daniel the prophet." Nehem spat out the words quickly so he couldn't change his mind.

"You're certain of this?"

Nehem looked up into the young Arab's dark eyes. "I swear it."

Mamoud thought for a second before responding. "You know what will happen..."

"Yes, I know!" Nehem shouted. "Now let my daughter go. You have what you asked for. Let her go in peace. Do whatever you want with me."

"No. We will need to keep you both a little longer, my hasty friend. If I let her go now and find out you're lying to me, we'll have to go through the trouble of finding her again. She might even do something stupid like go to the police and tell them what happened. While the authorities are comfortably in my pocket, I don't need the extra hassle right now. I have much to tend to, after all."

"So you're going to keep us here while you go to Iran?"

Mamoud shook his head. "No. I'm going to need you once we get there. If what you say is true and the tomb of Daniel is the location of the stones, I will release you both from there." He leaned close and lowered his voice. "Just so you know; I do not believe you are lying about the tomb. I believe you. It's just that if we come across something like in Indonesia and your expertise is needed, it will be nice to know you're close by."

It took every ounce of Nehem's energy to keep him in his seat. His mind ran wild with visions of launching himself at the man, wrapping his arms around his throat and strangling him until the last gasp of air escaped his lungs. Instead, Nehem snorted loudly and attempted to slow his breathing.

"You want to kill me, don't you?" Mamoud asked, still leaning close.

Nehem locked eyes with his captor and said nothing.

"I know you do. I would too if I were in your position. Understand, it isn't personal. It is my mission. And soon, the entire world will behold the fruits of my labors."

28
Buka, Azerbaijan

Sean ended the call with Emily and set the device back on the tray to his right. He was frustrated. After telling her everything that happened in Indonesia and Bhutan, she was still stuck amid a bunch of red tape. She wanted to go after Al Najaar and his crew, but the CIA had somehow learned of what Axis was up to. They'd stepped in, and now the entire mission was in danger. She asked for the go-ahead from President Dawkins, but he was stalling. He knew that going after an Emirate national could be political suicide, and as he put it, "You don't piss in your friend's backyard."

That meant Emily was in a holding pattern and couldn't do anything until there was more proof that Al Najaar was up to something. Sean knew that calling her and asking her to kick in the man's door was a shot in the dark. It was hopeful at best. And the president was right: They shouldn't go in without evidence of some wrongdoing. Just because one of his men had tried to kill Sean was no reason to start World War III. It was worth the shot, though. If Emily could marshal a strike team to go into Mamoud's compound — or even better, see what he'd been doing with all those shipments — it would not only buy Sean some time, it might just end this whole charade much quicker.

Since that plan was out of the question, he pondered another. She needed proof. Maybe he could give it to her.

Of all the resources Emily had at her disposal, one of her weaknesses was technology. Axis had a codebreaker and electronics security officer available at all hours of the day. Neither one, however, was capable of doing what Tara and Alex could do. The irony wasn't lost on him.

Sean remembered Tommy telling him about how they were able to hack into nearly any database in the world. Although heavily encrypted databases slowed them down, it didn't stop them gaining access. However, there were a few doors they knew not to knock on, such as the Pentagon's mainframe; that was a hack that could see them spend the next fifty years behind bars.

The thought kept poking at Sean's mind. If the kids could break into Mamoud's databases and find out what he'd been shipping and importing, they might be able to find enough proof to warrant sending in the cavalry. It was worth a shot.

He looked over at Tommy in the seat across from him. "You said Tara and Alex were accomplished at hacking into things, right?"

Tommy nodded. "Yeah. I mean, they've toyed around with a few things from time to time. Nothing illegal. Well, maybe it was illegal, but they didn't steal anything. It was just to snoop around."

"That's exactly what we need them to do right now. Give them a call, and see if they can pull any information on Mamoud Al Najaar: big transactions, shipments, manifests, anything they can find. He's up to something. We need to tell Emily exactly what it is so she can do her thing."

Tommy nodded and picked up his phone. Sean directed his attention to Adriana, who was sitting next to him. "What about your father?" he asked. "He's a part of the intelligence community. Does he know anything about this guy or what he might be up to?"

She stared at the floor for a moment. It was a second of vulnerability. He'd struck a nerve with his question, though he wasn't sure why.

"No," she answered. "He's gone under."

Sean frowned. "Under? Why?"

"It's complicated. I'll tell you all about it at some point. But he won't be able to help us."

Sean nodded, letting the issue go. "Okay." He paused and looked out the window at the sea below before speaking up again. "Have you ever been to Iran?"

"Yes. Only for a short visit. It is an interesting culture. I'll need to hide my face while we're there."

"Actually, you really don't have to, though it might be better that way."

She raised an eyebrow. "Excuse me?" She jabbed him in the ribs.

He winced and laughed. "I didn't mean it like that. What I meant was, it would keep you disguised. Most women don't hide their faces in that country. But doing so might be useful. And there's something else I need you to do. I have a plan."

She listened closely as he laid out the details. When he was finished, she nodded slowly. "I like it. Of course, it all hinges on getting there before Al Najaar and his men."

"I have to believe we will. And even if we don't, I have a backup plan."

"Do I get to hear it?"

He shook off the question. "No. And I don't think you'd want to."

Tommy ended his conversation with the kids and looked with satisfaction across the row at the other two passengers. "They're on it. They said it may take a few hours, but given the volume he's been working with, it will be hard for Al Najaar to keep everything hidden." He looked as if he had another question. "So that takes care of that end, but what about our end? How's this going to play out?"

The plane started its descent, and the engines whined as the turbines slowed.

"Al Najaar will be there in Susa."

"How do you know that?"

"It's his style. He wants other people to do the dirty work. Then he wants to show up and take all the glory. More than that, though, he'll want to try out his newfound toys."

"He'll attempt to use the relics," Adriana said.

"Right. Which is why your role is so important."

"I'll take care of it."

Tommy looked befuddled. "Her role? What about mine?"

The other two smiled. "You'll be with me. Did you remember to tell your man to bring extra ammunition? I have a bad feeling we're going to need it."

"I talked to our contacts on the ground before we left Bhutan, and they said it would be ready to go."

To say getting into Iran would be tricky would be a monstrous understatement. Relations between Iran and the United States had never been solid, but over the years, things had deteriorated to a point where it seemed reconciliation would never be possible. The Iranian leader was seen on all the major media outlets, basically taunting the American president, daring him to make a move. While President Dawkins wouldn't be goaded, he made subtle statements that let Iran know the U.S. wouldn't be pushed around.

At the center of the debacle was Iran's desperate effort to become a nuclear power. They were years, maybe decades away from achieving anything threatening, but the act they were trying was concerning in itself.

Sean wished that, for a day, things between the two countries were a little more amicable. It would make entering the country so much easier. As it was, they had to come up with an alternative plan for getting in illegally.

Tommy knew a smuggler who worked out of Baku in Azerbaijan, an Iranian neighbor to the northwest. Since getting into Azerbaijan was far less complicated, it made perfect sense to land there, drive south down the coast of the Caspian Sea, and cross the border via boat.

Tommy's connection, a guy named Mick, smuggled all kinds of goods into Iran on a biweekly basis, taking everything from liquor to blue jeans to his distributors in the major cities. From what Tommy said, Mick had quite the elaborate operation, which was perfect since getting caught might mean never seeing the light of day again.

The plan was to board Mick's boat about fifteen miles north of the Iranian border and take it thirty miles south to a point he'd used frequently. It was little more than a beachhead with no cities or residential areas nearby, but it provided exactly what they needed as a clean entry point.

Turkmenistan was closer in proximity to their rendezvous point in Iran, but Sean and Tommy's contacts there were basically nonexistent. They may have been able to pull something together, but it would have taken longer, and time wasn't something they had to spare.

Sean looked out the window again at the Caspian Sea below. The city of Baku exploded from the flat plains and merged with the sea. Baku was thriving. Tourism had picked up over the last decade, and Europeans were flocking to the area to enjoy the culture and climate. The city was impeccably clean and well run by the local government, which kept things safe for visitors. It also provided an excellent base of operations for smugglers like Mick.

The plane continued its descent into the city, circling over the city's sprawling growth of concrete and steel.

Adriana retreated to the rear of the plane to try on her burkha. She wouldn't need it in Azerbaijan but making sure it fit properly wasn't something she wanted to do on a small watercraft as they tried to sneak into Iran illegally.

A few minutes later, she reappeared, covered head to toe with the jet-black outfit. "I don't know how women wear these things all the time," she complained. "It's difficult to see clearly out of it."

Tommy laughed. "You know, Iran is kind of progressive now. You could have worn jeans and a light jacket to go with that headpiece."

Her eyes flung daggers at him, but from behind the veil, he barely noticed.

"I'm just saying. But better safe than sari, right...get it...sari...never mind."

Sean shook his head. "That's India, man."

"I know. I just thought...whatever. Sari I brought it up."

Adriana had been raised just outside of Madrid on her father's estate. Part of being European was a general tendency to be a little more on the liberal side of things. Adriana's schooling and friendships had cemented that belief system along the way.

Tommy left the conversation about her outfit and got back to business. "We'll be meeting with our contact in fifty minutes in an old textile warehouse about three miles from the airport. Mick will pick us up and take us to the rendezvous point in Tehran. Our support is going to be sneaking across the border by land. Once we've been outfitted, we'll probably be on our own."

Sean agreed. "We'll be fine. It'll be easier to move around with just the three of us."

"Like a bull in a china shop," Tommy quipped.

"Yeah, and for the first hour we're there, we need to keep things quiet."

"You think this man, Al Najaar, knows where we're headed?"

"Probably not Azerbaijan. But I'd say it's a safe bet he knows we're going to Susa. If he's ahead, he'll take precautions."

"And if he's behind?"

A familiar sly grin crept onto Sean's face.

"I've got a plan for that too."

29
Tehran

Mick was a stout, red-haired grunt of man. From the second Sean laid eyes on him, he knew they'd called on the right guy. Everything about the smuggler told Sean the man knew what he was doing. And Mick was a stickler for details.

From the second the three walked into the empty textile warehouse, Mick made sure they understood everything about what was about to happen. They'd wait until sunset to make the drive to the boat and board it under the cover of darkness. Crossing the border on the water would take less than an hour. When they made land, Mick's man on the other side would take them into the city to meet their contacts at the predetermined rendezvous point.

The drive down the coast took longer than Sean would have liked but was truly the quickest route. It didn't help that they were sitting in the back of a delivery truck. This clearly wasn't the first time Mick had smuggled people. A small air conditioning unit was attached to the wall to vent cool air into the boxy cargo area. Without it, the temperature inside would have been unbearable.

Boxes were stacked here and there, though they hardly took up the majority of space. This was an additional run, Mick had explained in the warehouse, so he wouldn't have a full truck. He figured if he was making the run he might as well take a few extra things along. The man was all about efficiency.

The occupants felt the truck slow and lean to the right. They were turning left. The smooth ride on the asphalt immediately turned bumpy. Though he couldn't see outside, Sean figured they'd turned onto an access road of some kind.

Ten minutes of jostling went by before the truck finally came to a stop. The slide door on the back went up, and the scent of salty air rushed into the cargo area. The new moon shone down on the beach with just enough light for the travelers to see the small boat anchored a few hundred feet out. Two wooden dinghies were beached nearby, and one of Mick's men was already busy getting them ready to head out to the boat.

"Go ahead, and grab a few boxes on your way to the dinghies, if you don't mind," Mick ordered.

None of the three complained and happily helped unload the cargo and carry it over to the dinghies. The process took less than five minutes, and soon, they were bobbing through the waves courtesy of a single outboard motor.

Arriving at the boat, they had been greeted by a toothy older man with bronze, wrinkled skin. He wore a stained yellow tunic and linen pants. He politely helped Adriana aboard while leaving Tommy and Sean to heft themselves up the small ladder on the starboard side. Mick and his rider quickly loaded the boxes aboard the larger vessel. He tied one of the dinghies to the back of the boat, and once everything was aboard, waved off his assistant. The man steered his dinghy away and guided it back to land.

"This is Aman," Mick said, introducing the three to the boat's captain. "He'll be taking us across the border. He doesn't say much, but he's a good man and a great smuggler." Aman nodded, still grinning broadly.

"We appreciate your help," Tommy said, exchanging a nod with him.

"You can have a seat up there," Mick pointed to the front of the boat where some wooden benches jutted out from the hull. "We should be there in about fifty minutes."

Aman stepped into the wheelhouse and started the engine. A moment later, the vessel was gliding across the calm water, headed south.

Fifteen minutes into the journey, Mick made his way to where his guests were sitting and pointed toward the dark shore. An outcropping of light illuminated the sky in the distance, and several more dotted the coast where homes and fishing compounds occupied the land.

"We're in Iranian waters now," he said. "Just passed the border."

A chill went through Tommy's spine.

For Sean, it was just another day at the office. He'd done several clandestine entries like this before although never with people he cared about on a personal level.

"Thanks, Mick," Sean said with a nod. "We'll be ready to make for land at your word."

Mick nodded and went back inside the flimsy structure.

The salty air blew over Sean's face and hair. For a minute, he was back in Destin, inhaling deeply. The next minute, he looked off the starboard bow at the Iranian coastline. Buildings were sparse in this region, which is why Mick had chosen it for their entry point. Half an hour later, Aman veered the boat toward a dark patch of land well out of sight from any man-made lights. The boat slowed to a coasting stop. It bobbed in the gentle Caspian waves as the three stood up and grabbed their few belongings.

"We need to move fast," Mick said. "Help me get those boxes on the dinghy, and we'll be gone." He turned his attention to Aman. "You know the drill. If I'm not back in twenty minutes..." he trailed off, and the boat's captain nodded.

Sean grabbed the rope and started pulling the smaller craft to starboard while the others hurriedly picked up the boxes and got them ready for transfer. Once the dinghy was tied off on the side, they placed the cargo carefully on the little vessel's bottom. The process didn't take long, and a few minutes later, the nose of the small craft was digging into the beach. The outline of a few palm trees stretched out against the dark backdrop of the starry night sky.

Mick pulled a flashlight out of an old gear bag and hit the switch a few times. Two headlights repeated the gesture from farther inland. It was hard to tell what kind of vehicle from their vantage point. The driver had done a good job making it invisible from the water.

Everyone grabbed the cargo one last time and hauled it across the rocky sand in the direction the lights had flashed. Once they were closer, they could see it was a moving van, similar to the delivery truck they'd ridden in earlier.

The driver had a thick, black beard and matching curly hair. He stepped down out of the cab and grabbed the box Adriana was carrying. He offered her a smile and hustled around to the rear of the truck and slid it inside. He did the same with the boxes

Tommy and Sean were carrying and then ran down to the boat to get the remaining cargo.

"Only one more down there, Farjad."

The driver nodded without turning around. They'd clearly been doing this together for a while.

Mick turned to the three. "It's a few hours to Tehran from here." He jumped up into the cargo hold and pulled up a false floor panel. "If you hear Farjad bang on the cab twice, you'll need to hide in these. Security checkpoints are pretty random, but it's possible you could go through one. They typically aren't very thorough since the borders are so secure, but you never know. Usually, a quick glance inside is all they want."

Sean raised an eyebrow. "And if they want more?"

"Then you never met me. I hear the key to surviving in an Iranian prison is developing a strong stomach." He winked, showing the first sign of a sense of humor since they'd met the man.

Farjad returned a moment later with the last box and loaded it onto the truck. Mick took an envelope out of a shirt pocket and handed to him. "Good work as always, my friend. You know where to take them?"

Farjad nodded. "I know the place." He turned to his passengers. "Don't let him worry you. I will get you there safely. Did he say something about the checkpoints?"

Tommy nodded.

"I assure you. I can get around them easily enough."

Tommy hoped he was right. They all did.

"Try to get some rest," Farjad said. "Trust me. I know what I'm doing."

"He does," Mick added. "He's the best at this sort of thing. That's why I hired him."

Sean extended his hand. "We appreciate all the help, Mick."

The man took shook his hand firmly and grinned. "And we appreciate your business."

The ride into Tehran was surprisingly uneventful and one of the most uncomfortable the Americans and Spaniard had ever taken. Not only was it bumpy and warm, but every time the truck stopped, the occupants in the back had to listen carefully in case Farjad gave the signal to hide. The knocks never came, though, and soon the truck was moving again.

None of the three travelers were able to rest during the journey. They were all on full alert the entire time. The minutes ticked by like weeks, and the tension in the back of the van was thick as cold molasses. And every little noise made them twitch their heads to the rear gate, waiting for it to open.

When they finally arrived in Tehran, they heard Farjad turn off the engine and close the cab door. He opened the back, and they were greeted with the city's dry early morning air and a smile from the driver.

"See? I told you it would be no trouble. This is your stop for the night. It's one of Mick's safe houses." He motioned to a nondescript one-story concrete building twenty yards away across an empty parking lot. There were two metal doors on the front and from what Sean could tell, a deadbolt above the latch. The façade of the building was about twenty feet across and looked like it was abandoned.

"You have a key for us?" Tommy asked.

"Right here," Farjad said and placed it in Tommy's hand. "There should be everything you need inside: a few beds, toilets, two showers. No food, but it's a little late in the night to be eating. You're meeting someone tomorrow, right?"

Sean nodded. "In the morning, yes."

"Very good. I'll have a car here for you before sunlight. It's yours as long as you need it."

Sean was starting to wonder how much Tommy had paid this guy. "I appreciate it, Farjad. Thanks for all your help."

"My pleasure." He grabbed the nylon strap attached to the sliding door and brought it down quietly. He locked the latch and ran around to the front of the truck, hopped in, and sped away.

The three took in their surroundings for a moment. Tall apartment buildings and twenty-story developments clogged the horizon. They were on the outskirts of the city. The bright lights of the Iranian capital illuminated the black sky above. The unnatural whitish hue blurred out all but the brightest stars.

"I don't know about you two," Tommy interrupted the silent moment, "but I need to get a few hours' sleep."

30
Tehran

The rest of the night dragged by, each second adding more anxiety than the last. The three friends tried to get a little sleep, but calming their minds proved extremely difficult. Only after extreme fatigue took over were they able to doze off for a few hours.

Sean woke first, slipped on his shoes, and floated over to the door. He'd taken a shower the night before so he wouldn't be in a rush when it was time to go. He also thought it might help him relax. That part he was wrong about.

He took a quick glance through the peephole to make sure no one was standing outside and then opened the door. The muggy morning air washed over him, and he blinked a few times to adjust to the early sunlight.

A common misconception in the United States is that Iran is nothing but desert. The far edges of Tehran would be considered high desert, with the heart of the city sitting at around three thousand, nine hundred feet in elevation. The metropolitan area is situated at the base of the Alborz Mountain Range and experiences a drastic change in temperature and weather from summer to winter. During the latter, huge ski resorts provide steady revenue and entertainment for the region's population. Sean had seen pictures taken during winter and wanted to make a visit to test out the local powder. Snowboarding was something of a guilty pleasure he'd not had the opportunity to partake in for more than two years. If they got out of this relic hunt alive, he might have to make it a point to come back to Tehran. Although preferably through legal channels, if possible.

Sean heard the sound of a vehicle approaching. His first instinct was to shut and lock the door, but he reminded himself that someone was supposed to be coming with a car. He wondered who the drop-off person might be, when a white, four-door Toyota pulled into the parking lot and squeaked to a stop. Sean looked through the windshield, and his curious expression changed to a broad smile as a familiar face got out of the driver's seat.

"You're late," he said.

The driver shut the door and crossed his arms, pretending to be offended. "Hey, do you want a ride or not?"

The man's bushy beard had got thicker since Sean had last seen him. His skin had darkened to a deep bronze, a result of spending weeks on end in the sunshine. His hair was scraggly and reached the tops of his ears, longer than it had ever been in the time the two knew each other. Whether it was intentional or not, the new look made for good cover in this foreign land.

"I had no idea you were the one picking us up, Mac."

The other man beamed and stepped forward, wrapping both arms around Sean and clapping him on the back. "It's good to see you again, my friend. Been too long."

Mac let go and noticed Tommy stumble to the safe house doorway, looking around like a lost chicken. He'd never been able to wake quickly. "Tommy, look who's here," he said, still keeping his voice as low as possible.

Tommy rubbed his eyes and grinned. "There you are. I was starting to worry we'd missed you." He rushed over and gave Mac a quick hug.

"You weren't even starting to wake up," Mac joked.

"And you remember Adriana," Sean said, pointing at the Spaniard as she approached. Unlike Tommy, she appeared ready to take on the day.

"You are certainly a sight for weary eyes," Mac said. "I trust you're doing well."

She nodded and bowed graciously. "Good to see you again too, Mac."

Joe McElroy had worked for the parks service in the state of Georgia for years. He'd got bored with it and had been looking for a change. It just so happened that with Sean's retirement, Tommy's organization needed a man like him. When Joe, whom everyone called Mac, found out about his wife's secret past as a certified government badass, the two decided it was time for a change. They signed up immediately and never regretted a second of it. All-expenses-paid travel around the globe gave them a chance to get closer and see some things they'd always dreamed of seeing. Sure, the work was hard at times, especially when they were on a dig, but it was worth it. So far, they'd not come across too much trouble along the way, which was something Sean and Tommy seemed to always find in spades.

"Is Helen here?" Adriana asked, taking a step closer.

Joe's eyes squinted into little narrow beads. "Who do you think your quartermaster is?"

He motioned with his hand for them to follow him.

"We might be followed to the warehouse. We need to drop Adriana at the market before we get there. I'll pick her up on our way back through."

Tommy hadn't heard that part of the plan and expressed his concern. "Wait. We're dropping her off at the market? Why? So she can get some fresh fruit or something?"

She shook her head and glared balls of fire at him.

"Funny. And no. She's going to pick up a little surprise for our friend Al Najaar. Just in case."

Joe interrupted. "The market is about ten minutes from here. If we drop her off, she's going to be followed. One of those four men will probably break off and tail her."

She passed him a warning glare. "I can handle myself, Mac."

"Oh, I know that." His eyes passed over the surroundings. "Just thought you should be aware." Mac turned his attention back to the guys. "The drive from here to Susa is close to eight hours. That will put you there in the late afternoon. You should still have several hours of daylight. But if you were planning on doing any sightseeing before you initiated your search, you should probably curtail that notion." He winked.

"That's a shame," Sean said. "I really wanted to take in some of the restaurants and tea houses. Maybe next time."

"Well, we best get a move on. You're on a tight schedule, after all."

The group grabbed their belongings and loaded into the car. Seven minutes later, they were thrust into the early morning rush of downtown Tehran traffic. Cars moved slowly, in and out of empty spaces, in a futile attempt to get ahead. Pedestrians walked along the sidewalks in tightly packed clumps.

"I don't mean to be rude, but it might save us all some time if you got out here and went ahead on foot," Mac suggested, pointing at the chaos on the street. "I know a side road where we can get out of this mess and over to the warehouse. I mean, if you don't mind. It's only a few more blocks from here."

She opened the door and stepped out. "I'll meet you in an hour. Don't worry about coming back here. I can get a ride. Just send me the address." She closed the door and scurried away, pulling the mask up over her face to make sure she stayed incognito.

Mac glanced back into the mirror. "You don't think I upset her, do you?"

Sean smirked. "Nope. That was her way of saying your idea was a good one. Now get us out of here. She won't let you hear the end of it if she somehow beats us to the rendezvous point."

Working his magic, Joe deftly dodged in and out of the seemingly endless bumper-to-bumper traffic and finally found the side street he was looking for. After nearly running over a man selling hats, they found their way out of the rush and onto a quieter, less-occupied street.

"I heard you were in Copenhagen," Mac said to Sean as he sped up, heading away from the city's heart.

"I heard the same about you."

Mac laughed. "Must have just missed you. The missus and I were there checking out some interesting Viking stuff. We had a good time. The weather there this time of year is amazing."

"Yeah, it's one of my favorite cities in the world. I'll have to go back sometime soon. Hopefully, I'll be able to enjoy the visit."

"You didn't enjoy working with Tommy on an expedition?"

"He wasn't working with me," Tommy corrected. "He was helping a friend."

Joe pursed his lips and nodded. "You tend to do a lot of that sort of thing, don't you?"

Sean looked out the window at the passing buildings. Their architecture was like a mix between Communist 1960s and modern art deco. It was a confusing thing to behold. "I guess I do," he said in a distant tone.

When they pulled into the warehouse parking lot twenty minutes later, they found it to be empty. The dilapidated building looked like it hadn't housed business for several years. Rusted corrugated sliding doors hung loosely against the gray cinderblock walls. A bland metal entry door stood off to the side of the larger entrance. Joe stopped the car in front of the hangar-like doors and got out. When he opened his door, the three could still hear the sounds of the city around them. Cars and buses, motorcycles, horns, truck brakes, and construction tools all mingled into a cacophony of mayhem.

Joe pulled the sliding door to the side, revealing a vast, hollowed-out interior. He got back in and drove the car forward, parking it next to a gray van. He shut off the ignition and got out. His passengers did the same, and Sean made himself useful by offering to close the big doorway.

Once it was shut, the giant warehouse fell into shadow. Beams of sunlight pierced the dusty darkness along the eastern wall, the yellow lasers enhanced by billions of dust particles floating in the air. Rusty steel beams shot up from the dirty floor to support girders above.

The van door opened and closed. A second later, a fortysomething woman with curly auburn hair stepped around the hood. Her bright smile pierced through the shadows.

"Good to see you again, Helen." Sean said. He reached out and wrapped his arms around her, hugging her tight.

"Likewise, boys." She let go of him and repeated the greeting with Tommy.

"Hi, Helen," Tommy said as he embraced her.

She turned and opened up the side of the van. The seats had been removed to make room for cargo. In this case, the cargo was five baby bed mattresses.

She put her hands on her hips. "I understand you boys need some guns."

"Indeed we do," Sean said with a smile. "I've got to ask, though—"

"The guns are hidden in the mattresses," she answered before he could finish.

"Actually, I was going to ask how you got the weapons here and what you were doing in the area to begin with, but that was going to be my second question."

Joe answered for her. "We were on a dig on the border when Tommy called. Since we had a security team with us, it was easy enough to get the weapons. All we had to do was find a place to hide them. Getting in was tricky. Their borders are locked down pretty tight, especially for Americans. We had to find another way in. Took a bit of doing, but our Iranian friend was quite helpful."

"We were able to acquire most of what you asked for. You'll have to settle for 9-mm pistols, though. None of the guys had forties on hand. Plenty of ammo, though." Helen finished her sentence by reaching over and pulling the top off the closest mattress. She ripped away a thin layer of cotton and revealed a row of handguns, submachine guns, and corresponding magazines.

"Nice," Sean said, admiring their resourcefulness. "Were you able to get some knives for Adriana? You know how much she likes those."

"Sure did," Mac said, pulling back the cover on another mattress. Five four-inch throwing daggers were sheathed in a utility belt. A tactical knife was concealed in a longer housing at one end of the belt. There was something else included with the other blades that Tommy and Sean hadn't expected.

"Is that a tomahawk?" Tommy asked. He took a step closer and lifted the weapon. Its black steel was perfectly balanced, the beard sharpened to a fine, lethal point. The edge of the blade was razor thin.

"Yeah, one of the guys said if she liked knives she might like to give this a try. He has a line on them from back in the States. Said a guy in Tennessee runs a company called RMJ Tactical that manufactures them for the military. Apparently, he also makes custom historical tomahawks. You know, the ones with like a peace pipe on one end and such."

Tommy swung the weapon around in a reckless fashion. From the look on his face, he was highly intrigued by the weapon.

Sean stuck his hand out and grabbed Tommy by the wrist, halting his movements. "Why don't we let her play with that toy? Grab yourself a few guns, and let's get ready to move. When Adriana gets back, we'll need to leave immediately."

Tommy looked like a child who had been punished for misbehaving, but he did as suggested and laid the weapon back in the faux mattress.

Sean turned back to Helen and Mac. "This will do nicely. Mind if we take those duffle bags?" He pointed at two black bags sitting behind the passenger seat on the floor.

"They're yours," Helen said. "We had a feeling you might need something to carry all this."

He gave an appreciative nod and set to work loading the bags. He checked each weapon, making sure no rounds were chambered and to see if all of them functioned the way they should. Sean was judicious in what he chose to bring. He knew Adriana would want a Heckler & Koch to go along with her knives, tomahawk, and pistol, but concealing the submachine gun might prove to be problematic. Sean preferred to travel a little lighter, taking a pair of handguns and a stack of fully loaded magazines. He stuffed the ammunition into a vest he felt he could conceal with a jacket, and continued stocking the bags.

"So when Adriana gets here, I guess y'all will be buzzin' out of here, huh?" Joe was unable to hide the disappointment in his voice.

"Pretty much, Mac. I wish we could hang out longer. When we get back to the States, we'll look you up and grab dinner."

Joe and Helen smiled at the offer. Helen looked perplexed. "Where did you say she had to go?"

Sean's eyes shifted mischievously from one person to the other.

"He didn't." Joe answered for him.

31
Tehran

Adriana slithered through the flowing mass of people like a snake through a debris-filled river, colliding with people on more than one occasion. One man, with a thick beard that stretched nearly to his eyes, stopped and stared at her. The look was one of surprise more than irritation. He probably couldn't believe a woman could take a bump to the shoulder like that and keep her balance. What he didn't know was that beneath the black robes and veil was one of the world's most agile thieves.

Not bogged down with the need to make money, Adriana had pursued a life of adventure. For the past several years, she had spent most of her time researching and tracking down stolen artwork from World War II. Adolf Hitler, it seems, was a sucker for collecting, and he had amassed a priceless fortune in art from various sources in Europe.

A portion of that collection was discovered in a cave near his countryside estate by the fabled unit known as the Monuments Men. Movies and books were written about the men and their search for the lost masterpieces. While their mission had been largely successful, so many other works of art were still missing. She made it her personal obsession to find out where they might be, steal them back, and return them to either their rightful owners, or the appropriate museums.

With a hobby like that, staying fit and nimble were obvious prerequisites.

Her eyes remained narrow as she navigated the pedestrian chaos until she arrived at the market. Fabric awnings and tents lined the streets. Even at this early hour, vendors were in peak performance, shouting out offers and deals to any passersby whose ears they could bend. She glanced up at the strips of cloudless, blue sky hovering over the canyon of buildings and tents. For a second, her mind drifted, and she wondered how women could wear these dark outfits in the blazing heat of summer. She shook the thought from her head and refocused. She was looking for a specific type of vendor, one she'd seen in this area before. Maybe the seller had moved or was out of business. For what Sean needed her to buy, it was likely that someone else would have the requisite items, assuming they were somewhat common.

She weaved through the potential buyers of spices, fruits, meats, and vegetables and finally arrived at the stall she remembered from a previous visit. Adriana couldn't remember if the seller was the same person, but it didn't matter. The old man in the turban with squinty black eyes, a gray beard, and three missing teeth would do just as well as any. She looked down at the rows of bracelets, necklaces, earrings, and stones.

Adriana pointed at two items and asked in Farsi, "How much?"

The man responded with a price that was cheaper than she'd thought he'd give. She reached into the folds of her robe and produced several bills. She quickly counted it and pressed the money into his palm. He turned away to get change as she'd given him too much money, but when he spun slowly back around, she'd vanished into the seething mass of people.

As she moved through the street, Adriana secured her purchase in a small leather pouch that she'd taken from the stall. She didn't consider it stealing. After all, she'd given the man almost double what he asked for. He wouldn't miss a little bag. But it was what Sean had said they needed, and she trusted him. Underneath her robe, Adriana wore a pair of gray capri pants and quickly tucked the pouch in her back pocket for safekeeping.

Thirty yards away, she could see the opening where the side street intersected the main road. From there, she would go across to where another street led out of town. She could hail a taxi and give the driver the address once she was safely in the car. Her little side mission was easier than she'd imagined.

Just as the thought entered her mind, Adriana felt a firm hand slap down on her shoulder. She stopped instantly but didn't turn around. Strong fingers dug into the soft tissue between her clavicle and her neck, sending a sharp pain through her nerves. She squinted into the sunlight and waited for a moment. If her assailant were armed, it would be unlikely that he would use a gun in this mob. Discharging a firearm would cause a panic. And it would also lead to his arrest, more than likely.

Sure enough, the man's voice filled her in on the missing detail. "If you try to run, I will stick my knife in your kidneys. If you try to scream for help, I will stick it through the back of your neck to silence you."

Adriana spoke enough Farsi to know what he was saying, though she was better with Arabic. She assumed he was holding the blade close without actually pressing it against her since she didn't feel the point.

"What do you want?" she asked in the man's preferred tongue.

"You are to come with me. My employer has requested your presence."

"Oh? And he only sent *you* to bring me in? He should have sent more men."

The man snorted and then grunted a quick laugh. "And why is that?"

She dropped suddenly and spun into the arm that held her. In the same motion, her hand grabbed his wrist and pulled back as she jammed her palm into his elbow. The opposing force snapped the joint in an excruciating angle, and the man yelled out in pain.

Adriana was a spinning vortex of black death in her flowing robes. Using the shock of the newly broken arm against him, she dropped again and swept her leg at his heels. The blow flipped him onto his back. Amid his panicked fall, the man let go of his knife in a desperate attempt to brace himself. She saw the flash of metal, snatched the seven-inch blade out of the air, and brought it down into his throat at the exact moment his body struck the concrete.

Several people looked on in horror at what had just happened. Adriana stood over the shaking body. The man's lone good hand grasped in vain at the handle of the weapon that killed him, his own knife. Her eyes narrowed again as she locked gazes with some of the witnesses.

"I am another man's wife. He touched me." Her words struck home with the circle that had gathered around the scene. No one said anything, and none made a move to subdue her.

A moment later, the crowd began to disperse. It was only a matter of minutes before someone would call the police. None of the witnesses would dare bother her directly, so if she were to escape, it had to be now.

She took off at a sprint, heading toward the main street. The immediate throng in front of her parted like the Red Sea, not wanting to incite the wrath they'd just beheld. Ten yards in, though, she had to bump and nudge her way through until she reached the line of cars backed up along the road. Free of the pedestrian traffic, she darted across the street, sliding through the narrow spaces between bumpers until she reached the other crowded sidewalk.

Adriana paused for a second and looked back to see if anyone else was following. As far as she could tell, there was no one. Satisfied she was alone, she took off down the almost vacant alley and ran toward the next street. If someone was following her, she didn't intend to let them keep up easily.

Halfway down the side street, she ducked behind a garbage bin and removed the black robes. Speed was more important than concealment now, though she kept the veil and scarf around her face and neck. Her skin tingled for a second, exposed to the fresh air by her black short-sleeved shirt. She reached into the pockets of the robe and removed her remaining currency before lifting the lid of the garbage bin and stuffing the linen clothing inside. After another cautious glance down the street, she pushed off the bin like an Olympic sprinter, heading for the finish line fifty yards away.

Sirens sounded in the distance, a faint whine at first that began to gradually draw closer. Someone had called the police. They would be at a disadvantage in the rush hour traffic, which would give her the edge she needed.

Adriana slowed to a brisk walk as she arrived at the next intersection and found herself facing a hotel and several apartment buildings. To her right, several older men were sipping on their morning tea. To her left, a couple of college-aged girls munched on light sandwiches as they chatted and laughed. In front of the hotel, she found her salvation. A taxi driver leaned against the door, waiting for his next customer. She waved at him, getting his attention, and jogged across the street. He opened the rear door for her, and she nearly dove in.

Somewhat befuddled, the driver closed the door and got behind the wheel. "Where to?" he asked.

She pulled the phone out of her front pocket and tapped the screen. It contained one new text message from Sean, giving the warehouse address. "Here," she ordered.

The man nodded, turned the lever on the meter, and stepped on the gas.

32
Atlanta,

"This is Emily Starks." She'd been expecting the call, though she had to admit to herself, not so soon.

Emily walked over and closed her office door. Even though the staff at Axis headquarters was minimal, she'd rather not have any of her team hearing her secret discussions with people outside the agency.

"Hey, Miss Starks. This is Tara with IAA. Sean and Tommy gave me your number."

"You can call me Emily, Tara. Were you and Alex able to find anything?"

"Actually, we found a lot. Neither of us is even sure what some of it means, but we were able to pull the purchase orders and records off Al Najaar's database. It took a bit of doing. We've never seen a non-government database so heavily encrypted before. From the looks of it, this guy poured a ton of money into whatever he's doing."

"Can you send me the files?"

"They're already on their way. You may have to check your spam folder. Most email systems put big files there, and these are gargantuan."

Emily watched her computer monitor until the new message notification popped up. She clicked the button to allow her computer to view the large file and started scanning through it.

The numbers in the columns were astronomical. Many of the items were valued in the tens of millions of dollars, and a few were in the hundreds of millions.

"This doesn't make any sense," she said, staring at the screen.

"What do you mean?"

Emily continued to scroll through the page. "If Al Najaar was buying weapons from an illegal arms dealer, I'd say he overpaid. Guns and ammunition, ordinance, rockets, none of that costs this much. This looks like a shopping list for an army."

"That's what we thought. Keep scrolling down until you see the images."

Emily rolled down the screen until an image passed by and disappeared through the top of the monitor. She stopped and brought it back into view. When she did, everything became as clear as a Swarovski crystal. "Oh no!"

"Yep. If I had to guess, based on the numbers from that spreadsheet, he's amassed several hundred of those."

A million thoughts raced through Emily's head, but one kept popping up. "If he's loading these onto freighters, that means he's planning on taking them somewhere and launching them."

"That's what we thought too. If a lot of those other items are missiles or bombs, those things could cause chaos in several major cities."

"Tens of thousands, maybe hundreds of thousands of people would die." Emily's voice trailed off.

"So this guy is bad news."

"Yeah." Emily swallowed and forced herself to move forward. "Thanks for your help with this, Tara. And be sure to thank Alex for me. I don't think I need to tell you that this information needs to remain completely secret."

"I understand." She paused and then asked, "Do I need to be worried?"

"No," Emily answered quickly. "We'll take care of it. This is what we do. I'll let you know if we need anything else."

She ended the call and set her phone down. It was definitely risky using outside help for something so sensitive. But getting one of the other agencies to use their resources would have taken too long, and based on what she was seeing, they didn't have that kind of time. Al Najaar's plans were becoming clearer now.

Emily stared at the screen. The image of the long, smooth, winged object was one she'd seen before at demonstrations or in propaganda videos. Now it was much more threatening. A fully armed drone could knock out an entire city block, maybe two depending on the warheads it carried.

And Al Najaar had one thousand drones.

She scrolled through the files again, clicking each one to see what other information was available. Most of them were more shipping manifests or accounting documents. One was marked with a strange sequence of numbers and letters. None of the other files appeared to be identified in that manner. She clicked on the link, and a new set of images flashed onto the screen. Her breath quickened, and her heart pounded faster. She rolled the images down until she reached the bottom.

Each picture was an overhead view of four major cities: Hong Kong, Mumbai, Tokyo, New York. Several places were circled within the cities, including one place on each that was a few miles outside the downtown areas. Emily zoomed in on the latter and found that the terrain was mostly flat, yet still close enough to the water that transportation could be fast and efficient.

"He's chosen densely populated targets," she whispered to herself. "And other than New York, I doubt any of those governments would be on their toes for it." She checked the locations again and confirmed what she feared. Getting into port in any of these places would be easy enough for a massive shipping vessel. Customs officials and coast guards would usher them in unwittingly.

Another thought occurred to her. If Al Najaar was successful, these kinds of attacks could not only incite mass chaos, but something far bigger.

War on a global scale.

33
Susa, Iran

Sean's cell phone started vibrating in his pocket. He removed it, checked the caller ID, and answered. "What's up, Em?"

She spoke fast and direct. "Al Najaar is planning a massive attack on four major cities. I'm putting a team together right now to take him down, but my eyes on his compound told me that he's gone, probably left the country. No one knows where."

Sean pushed aside his instincts for a sarcastic response due to the severity of the situation. "What kind of attack?"

"Tommy's kids were able to pull up shipping manifests, orders, inventories, the whole nine yards. He's been buying attack drones by the hundreds. By my count, he has a thousand of them, all fully equipped with a devastating arsenal."

"Bioweapons?"

"We don't think so." She didn't sound certain. "But we can't rule it out. Even if there aren't bios, he's got enough firepower to kill tens, maybe hundreds of thousands of people."

Sean stepped farther away from the others and retreated to a dusty corner of the warehouse. "If he's got all that, why hasn't he gone forward with the attacks?"

"I don't know. It might have something to do with whatever he's looking for." Her tone became grave. "Sean, we're going to attempt to blockade his ships from leaving Dubai, but we don't have much time. If you find Al Najaar, you have to take him out. Or at the very least, slow him down."

He nodded. "I was planning on the first option." He looked back over at his friends standing by the van. "How much time do you think we have?"

"Maybe twenty-four hours. Maybe less. I don't really have an answer for that either."

"You're just full of helpful information."

She ignored the barb. "I'm going to oversee the mission from Atlanta. I have eyes and ears on the ground in Dubai with the strike team. The president preferred I sit this one out. I told him a fighter jet could have me there in a few hours, but he refused. Let me know if you're able to take down Al Najaar. It might make things on our end go a little more smoothly."

"Will do."

He ended the call and walked back to the others.

They looked at him expectantly, but Tommy was the first to speak up. "What was that about? Looked serious."

"It is. Like that's any different."

"True."

"That was Emily. She said the guy we're after has amassed some kind of arsenal and is planning an attack on several major cities. Sounds like she knows which ones and more importantly, where the weapons are stashed."

"So she has a handle on it," Joe said.

"I think so. She's putting together a team right now to take the ships Al Najaar is using to move the weapons, which by the way, are a thousand drones."

"Drones?" Tommy asked. "Where did he get those?"

"She didn't say, but she did say we only have about a twenty-four hour window. I'll assume it's half that."

"So you two need to get a move on," Helen advised.

"Right," Sean agreed. "Let's get everything packed in the car and ready to go so we can get out of here fast."

Adriana arrived at the warehouse five minutes later. She spoke briefly about the man who'd tried to abduct her. Sean was relieved she was okay. He knew she could handle herself, but it still didn't bring him a great deal of comfort to know she put herself in harm's way so often.

Joe made an off-the-cuff joke about the guy not knowing who he was messing with that eased the momentary tension.

Adriana opened one of the gear bags and was beyond satisfied with the weapons they'd provided. She was equally intrigued by the tomahawk, which she accepted graciously after flipping it around in her hand a few times.

Helen informed them that she and Joe had set up a contact person for them in Susa, a man by the name of Muhammad Bin Jarad. Being local to the area, he would know a great deal about Daniel's tomb and could expedite their search. Bin Jarad was someone Helen and Joe trusted. They'd worked with him before when doing some research in one of the areas nearby and had established a loose friendship.

With their supplies packed in the little Toyota, the friends said their goodbyes and took off on the long road to Susa. The eight-hour drive was brutally boring, with only the occasional town or rock formation to change up the flat, barren land. Now and then, a series of mountains or hills would appear in the distance, but for the most part, it was one of the less scenic drives the visitors had ever encountered. Eventually, the flatlands gave way to rolling, green plains and then canyons, larger hills, and the city of Susa.

The town was like an oasis of life, springing up out of a dead dust bowl. Lush green trees were scattered everywhere. Farms rich with a burgeoning harvest stretched out for thousands of acres around the outskirts of the city. Architecture in the city was fairly dated, unlike many of the more modern buildings featured in Tehran. An ancient fortress looked down over the city from a high hilltop, ruins from a time long ago.

One of the most famous ziggurats in the world, Chogha Zanbil wasn't far from the metropolitan area. It was a historic site both Sean and Tommy had seen before on a previous research trip. The enormous structure still stood as a lasting tribute to the incredible power and influence of ancient Babylon.

Sean steered the car through the sparse traffic on the edge of town and into the more densely populated downtown area. They'd been instructed to meet their contact in a place known as the Red Tea House just outside the bazaar. Sean found a parking spot in front of an old hotel. They decided not to risk leaving the weapons bags in the car, so each grabbed one and slung it over their shoulders.

Susa was a little more old school than Tehran when it came to the general view of women, and Adriana had to make sure to keep her face, skin and hair covered. A light, linen blouse covering her top and a darker skirt draped over her leggings, along with the headpiece, ensured she didn't draw too much attention.

Sean looked up the street and saw the sign for the rendezvous location. He was glad that they'd found a place to meet that wasn't too close to the tomb. Getting a plan in place before they got to the location would make things safer and their search much faster. According to Joe, the man they were meeting had maps of the place that were unavailable to the public. The fact that there were secret tunnels and underground thoroughfares only served to increase the likelihood that they were in the right place. Not that he doubted it, but there was always the chance. Deep down, he hoped that the relics hadn't been moved like they had been from Borobudur.

The three walked casually through a gaggle of people strolling along the sidewalk. Susa's bazaar was much smaller than others they'd visited in larger cities, like Marrakech or Istanbul. White tents hung over the modest collection of stalls along the walkway. Some of the sellers were closing down for the day, the afternoon rush ending more than an hour ago. A few others hung around hoping to make a little extra money before dark.

Ahead on the left, a red fabric hung over an open doorway, propped up at two points by poles set into divots in the sidewalk. The words painted onto the stucco wall told the visitors they were in the right place: *The Red Tea House*. Sean let the other two enter first, giving one last look around before he stepped across the threshold.

Inside, they found a cantina-style tea room. It was long and narrow, with a bar set against the back wall and tables lining the rest of the room's perimeter. Men ranging in age from forty to seventy sat quietly sipping their hot beverages. In this part of the world, tea was almost considered a privilege, as was being a man. A quick survey of the room told the group that Adriana wasn't welcome. Every eye widened simultaneously as the men stared in disbelief at the woman who had the nerve to enter their fortress of masculinity.

She turned around and faced Sean. A concerned looked filled her eyes. He sighed and ticked his head to the right, motioning for her to wait outside. She shook her head but complied.

"I'll keep a lookout for trouble," she whispered as she passed.

"Sorry," he said.

Once she was gone, the room came alive again, filled with quiet conversation among the patrons. They probably figured the two Americans didn't speak Farsi, which was a mistaken assumption. Three men nearby mentioned how they couldn't believe a woman would presume she could just walk in here.

Another at the bar turned around and said something about stupid Westerners.

In the far left corner, a man in a white T-shirt and khakis stood up and walked toward the two visitors. He looked young, probably in his early thirties, with thick black hair and a matching mustache. He smiled as he approached.

"Don't let them bother you. They don't know you speak Farsi," the man said loud enough for everyone to hear. He cocked his head to the side. "Perhaps they should speak some other dialect." His English was perfect and carried the slightest twinge of a British accent.

The man stuck out his hand, which Sean shook firmly. "Muhammad, I presume?"

"At your service," he bowed dramatically before shaking Tommy's hand. "I have a table over here. Please, join me. I presume your female friend will be fine staying outside for a moment?"

Muhammad's eyes were tucked behind a few sun-stroked wrinkles appeared young, like a man in his twenties, but the lines across his cheeks and the leathery skin looked like he'd been around four to five decades. Sean figured it was somewhere in the middle, probably closer to his own age. According to a quick briefing from Joe, Muhammad was Muslim, raised and educated in England, and tolerant of all religions. He'd forged a relationship with Joe and Helen with a mutual love of adventure and archaeology. Somehow, Sean figured there was a little more to that story than he'd been told, but he decided to leave it alone for now.

Sean smirked and tilted his head back for a fraction of a second. "Yeah, she'll be okay."

Muhammad couldn't tell if he was being serious or not, based on the sarcastic sound of his voice, but he sat down anyway and motioned for the other two to sit as well. He stuck his hand down into a brown canvas satchel and pulled out several sheets of paper. The rolled up sheets were old, frayed on the edges, and the writings and drawings had faded over time. The papers that may have been white or pale cream when they were new had turned to an almost brownish color.

He spread them out flat on the table and pushed away the nearly empty teacup. "Don't want to spill anything on these. They're over two hundred years old."

Sean and Tommy passed each other an impressed glance and then focused on the drawings.

"This," Muhammad pointed at the map's center, "is where Daniel's tomb is. These lines indicate tunnels that go in and around the surrounding area. There is one passage, however, that is not on this map. We'll have to take this one," he tapped on the paper, "to reach the secret entrance."

"Secret entrance?" Tommy asked, throwing a suspicious look at Sean.

"Yes. I have spent a great amount of time studying about the prophet Daniel. While there are many historians who debate this as the true location of his tomb, I believe it is. But," he raised a finger to emphasize his point, "I believe that the one the tourists see is merely a diversion for where the prophet is actually buried."

Sean nodded. "Okay, I'm intrigued. How long will it take us to get there?"

Muhammad shook his head. "Not long. Five minutes to the entrance. Another ten to the secret tunnel. After that, I'm not sure."

"Wait," Tommy held up his hand. "What do you mean you're not sure? Haven't you been in this tunnel?"

Their host looked up from the papers and shook his head as if the answer was obvious. "No. No one has. It's still sealed. I only recently excavated enough dirt to be able to see it."

"How are we going to get through if it's still sealed?"

Muhammad smiled. "I left all the necessary tools at the location. I doubt anyone would have seen them or stolen them."

Sean leaned over the table and peered through Muhammad's eyes. "Time isn't a luxury we have here. If we don't get to that tomb, a lot of people are going to die. A madman by the name of Mamoud Al Najaar is trying to beat us to the tomb, and if he succeeds, it's going to be very bad for all of us."

Muhammad nodded slowly. "I see. I have heard of this man, Al Najaar. He's very wealthy. There are some in dark circles who have said he is looking to wage a war on the West."

"You've heard that?"

He shrugged. "Only in whispers. But it's the whispers you need to listen to the hardest. Men like Al Najaar give good Muslims like me a bad name. I don't know what beef he has with the West. But I, for one, wish men like him would get over it."

Sean and Tommy both grinned at the response.

"We all do, brother," Sean said. Then, "We best get going before my girlfriend starts to wonder what we're doing in here."

Muhammad rolled up the maps and stuffed them into protective tubes before returning them to his bag. Back outside, they found Adriana standing with her arms crossed, turning her head from side to side as she watched the thinning crowd of pedestrians.

"Where to next?" she asked as the men appeared from the tea house.

"We follow him." Sean answered, pointing at Muhammad.

"Sorry for the unwelcome reception you had in there. Old customs, you know."

"Don't worry about it," she said.

He smiled and bowed. "Thank you for understanding. Now, since time is of the essence, I suggest we hurry."

Muhammad took off at a brisk pace, crossing the street without looking and floating down the sidewalk as if he was on a rapid people mover. The others rushed after him, heading toward the center of town. Rising above the apartments and businesses, a white, spiraling cone stood out in the cloudless blue sky: the shrine sitting atop the tomb of Daniel.

34
Susa

The entrance to the tunnels wasn't exactly well hidden. It was, however, well protected. An iron gate covered the arched portal and was locked with a heavy, rusted padlock. A shallow stream of murky water trickled out and into a concrete duct leading away from the tunnel, disappearing into another, smaller hole in a wall thirty feet away.

Muhammad had acquired a key, though Sean and the others decided it would be best not to ask why. They locked the gate once they were inside and hurried through the passage.

"This doesn't seem like such a secret," Tommy commented as he pointed his flashlight around. The beam danced on the curved walls and stretched out ahead of the group as they progressed.

"Most people think it's a sewage drain," Muhammad explained. "That keeps many curious eyes away. Only a few people come down here, usually engineers or city planners, and those are few and far between. No one has any reason to try to find this secret entrance." He made a sharp right and continued down the damp corridor. A rat scurried away, keeping close to the wall as it retreated from the intruders.

"Was it difficult to get dig permits for this?" Tommy asked. He slipped on a wet patch of concrete and nearly fell but caught his balance with an elbow against the wall.

Muhammad laughed. "Permit? This city has so many other things going on, I seriously doubt anyone in the local government would even know where to begin with giving out an excavation permit."

Sean raised an eyebrow and glanced over at his friend. "So how are you keeping the site secure?"

The group rounded a corner and arrived at another intersection where the paths came to a T. Warning signs hung on the wall to the left. They surrounded a plastic drop cloth hanging from the wall. Some of the signs read in Arabic, Farsi, and English, *Danger, keep out*; others warned of lethal chemicals, and still more had skulls and crossbones.

Sean nodded, seeing the answer to his question.

"Not exactly subtle," Adriana said, admiring the handiwork.

"But effective." Muhammad grinned over his shoulder and pulled back the plastic.

He pointed his flashlight inside the cavity. The light revealed a small generator, floodlights, shovels, picks, brushes, sifting trays, baskets, and several other tools of the archaeological trade.

"Okay," Tommy said, "I'm impressed."

They followed their guide into the dig site and closed the drop cloth behind. Muhammad led the way over to the far wall. The visitors' eyes came to rest upon an incredible find. Aramaic characters were carved into the ancient rock in neat lines from right to left and stretched four feet across in the wall's center. In the corners above the far edges of the script was a sequence of characters separated by an inch or two of space and barely noticeable seams. As Sean drew closer, he noticed thin lines surrounding the words. Each one was a separate piece of stone cut into the wall.

"They are names," Muhammad said, answering the unasked question. "Names of Hebrew leaders, priests, prophets, and kings. There are twenty-eight names on those squares."

"Why are they there?" Tommy asked.

"I assume because Daniel wanted to honor those who had gone before him."

"How did you find this?" Sean asked, turning to face their guide.

Muhammad shrugged. "I've always wondered what was underneath the tomb. Outside the shrine, visitors can stop to pray or pay their respects to the great prophet, but no one is allowed inside. As far as I know, no one has ever seen the actual remains. It would be difficult to determine if it is actually Daniel or not, and I have no intention of doing such research. I simply wanted to know what else was down here and why it was so secretive."

"Curiosity can be dangerous," Sean said as he ran his fingers across the letters carved into the smooth stone.

Their guide smiled and lowered his head a moment. He raised it again and said, "I do not believe I have made many enemies in this world."

"It's not your enemies you should be worried about. It's the enemies of your friends you need to be aware of."

"Speaking of enemies," Tommy interrupted, "could we hurry this along? Ours could be arriving at any moment."

"Right," Sean nodded.

He continued moving his finger across the stone until he felt the thinnest of gaps. He worked his fingernail into it and slid it up and down, confirming what he thought. "We're going to have to wedge this thing out, which means the wall will be damaged." He turned to Muhammad. "You okay with that?"

The Iranian took a step back and grabbed a sledgehammer and a metal wedge. He flipped on the generator and hit the start button. The floodlights flickered to life and cast a bright glow throughout the entire area. "I've been waiting long enough to see what's behind this door."

The other three picked up some crowbars that were leaning against the wall and went to work. They shimmied the sharp edges into the narrow space between the center stone and the wall around it. The work was painstaking and difficult. Every time it seemed they had made progress and the rectangular stone started to slide out a little, it slipped back into place. After twenty minutes of hard effort, the heat and humidity of the space started to take its toll. Beads of sweat rolled down the sides of every face.

Sean took a step back, breathing hard. "Take a break for a second."

Tommy was the first to obey, grateful for a breather. He slogged over to his gear bag, unzipped it, and pulled out a bottle of cool water. Half of the contents were gone in a matter of seconds as he poured the liquid down his throat.

Adriana leaned her tool against the wall and stared at the engravings.

"It's an account of the Babylonian captivity the Hebrews endured," Muhammad informed her. He stood nearby and gazed upon the wall.

Sean eyed the peculiar corners with the names cut into individual squares. He lowered his gaze to the floor and took to a knee near the wall. His fingertips ran across the smooth stone. It was similar to the way the walls had been cut, hewn smooth with a laser-like precision. Something stood out about the floor. Actually, it wasn't what stood out. It was what was missing.

"This door wasn't meant to come out this way," he blurted.

Tommy finished the last drops of his water and tossed the bottle back into the gear bag. "What do you mean? You saying we should push it?"

Sean shook his head. "No. This would have been put here just a shade over two thousand years ago." He jerked his thumb at the wall. "If whoever put it here slid it into place, we would see signs of scraping on the floor. There might even be some big gouges."

"Maybe they didn't slide it across the stone. They could have used mats or some kind of buffer."

"I don't think so," Sean disagreed. "Look at how perfectly flush these seams are. If this is a door, it was cut from the wall itself."

Muhammad listened to the conversation and jumped in. "How do you think it works then?"

Sean turned to Tommy. "Do you remember studying the layout of the ancient temple in Jerusalem?"

Tommy blinked and rolled his shoulders, nodding. "Yeah. Which part in particular?"

"History suggests that the designers of Solomon's temple built in safety measures to protect the Ark of the Covenant from falling into the wrong hands."

The light went on in Tommy's eyes. "Right. The widely held belief is that there were two pillars standing next to the entrance to the most holy place, a location which only the high priest was allowed to visit once a year."

"Exactly. From what I remember, those two columns would sink into the ground in the event that the city came under attack. It worked with counterweights and sand."

"Yeah, but how does that apply to this situation?"

Sean stood and stepped close to the wall once more. He reached up and ran a fingernail under the edge of one of the squares with a name on it. His Aramaic was rusty. He thought he knew what the name was, but he motioned for Adriana to take a look at it. Tommy moved closer as well.

"What does this name say?"

"Isaiah," she answered.

"Most likely the great prophet of Israel," Muhammad added.

"And this one?" Sean pointed at the next name in line.

"Samuel," Tommy answered quickly. He clearly didn't want to be outdone.

"Aaron. David. Solomon. Shadrach. Josiah." Adriana called out the next five.

Before she could say the next name, Sean stopped her. "Wait. The one before Josiah. Did you say Shadrach?"

"Yes," she answered, confused by the question. "Why?"

He pressed his finger to the center of the square in question. "Keep going."

She called out several more names. When she said, "Meshach," he stopped her again.

"Tommy, put your finger on that one."

His friend smiled and obeyed, realizing the method to Sean's madness. "It's the names of Daniel's friends."

"Looks that way. Adriana, see if the name of Abednego is over there on the other side." She grinned and stepped over to the other corner.

She traced a line across the first row and into the second row before she found the one she was looking for. "Got it," she said, putting her finger on the square.

"I'm sorry," Muhammad asked, "but I don't understand what is going on."

"These names," Sean tapped the square with renewed excitement, "don't fit with all the others. Priests, kings, prophets—Daniel's friends weren't any of those. They were just students who were taken to Babylon to study the ways of the empire."

"Okay," Tommy spoke up. "Thanks for the refresher. But what exactly are we doing here?"

Sean picked up the crowbar he'd set aside and stepped over to where Adriana was keeping her finger pressed firmly against the stone square. He flipped the tool around to use the shorter end. "You can move your finger," he said to her with a smile. She raised an eyebrow and stepped back.

He worked the tool's point into the tiny seam between the squares. When he was satisfied with the depth, he took a deep breath and leveraged the bar forward. The square came out easier than he expected, extending out of the wall by three inches. Everyone in the room stared at the object in disbelief. It was a cubical rod. Sean grabbed onto the end, careful not to break it off, and tugged on it gently, sliding the rod out of the wall until it came free. The long, cubed shaft was about two feet long.

"Amazing," Muhammad said, breaking the near silence.

"Wait," Sean held up his hand, stopping their guide from saying anything else. Everyone in the room listened but heard nothing.

"What are we listening for?" Tommy asked.

Sean shrugged off the question and set the rod to the side. "Quick. Do the same with the other two."

Tommy did as instructed and reached down to grab his own crowbar. He replicated the process while Sean found the remaining cube and went to work. Tommy's came free fairly easily, only taking a minute or two of careful effort. The third rod was somewhat more temperamental, but Sean was able to shimmy it free. With the three rods for each of Daniel's friends lying against the wall, the four explorers listened again. Once more, the only sound they could discern was the faint trickle of water coming from the drainage tunnels.

They stared at the wall with heightened anticipation, but nothing happened. Sean scratched his head. His mouth was agape, and he couldn't help but feel a little frustrated.

"Shouldn't something be moving now?" Tommy asked sincerely.

Sean nodded. "Yeah."

"This place is very old," Muhammad offered. "Maybe the contraption doesn't work anymore."

Adriana shook her head. "That would be true if they used ropes or any type of component that decays quickly. Whoever designed this knew that it could be a long time before anyone found it. Like they said," she motioned at Sean, "the temple's anti-theft system could have endured thousands of years."

Muhammad seemed satisfied with the explanation, but that still didn't answer the question as to why the contraption wasn't moving. Sean inched closer to the stone wall.

"We're missing something," Tommy said, taking a step back. He scanned the squares until he found an anomaly. "These columns all have the names of Daniel's friends on the surface."

Sean nodded his agreement.

"So maybe there's a friend we missed." Tommy moved forward again, this time slowly running his index finger across the squares, examining each name with the greatest of care.

He completed one side of the wall and sidestepped over to the other corner. He repeated the process, checking each square before moving on to the next. Suddenly, he stopped on one unusually long name.

"What?" Sean asked, almost begging it out of him.

Tommy tapped on the stone. "This name doesn't fit. He wasn't a king of Judah, a priest, or even Hebrew."

Sean raised an eyebrow as the answer came to him. "Of course. The king of Babylon befriended Daniel and after that, the king of the Medes, Darius became his friend as well. According to the biblical account, Darius reluctantly threw Daniel into a pit of lions, which the prophet miraculously survived. After that occurrence, Daniel became one of the most trusted advisers to the new Persian rulers. But it was Nebuchadnezzar who set Daniel up in the government before everything went down."

Tommy smiled. "Bingo."

Adriana moved closer and hefted the crowbar. She moved Tommy aside without saying a word and wedged the sharp edge of the metal between the slits next to one of the most famous names in ancient history.

Nebuchadnezzar.

35
Susa

Adriana pried the cube loose, and soon she was able to slide the entire column out from its place. The second the rod was completely free of the wall, a new sound entered the antechamber. It was difficult to make out exactly what it was, but after ten seconds a deep rumble replaced the noise. The floor and walls vibrated like a small magnitude earthquake. Light danced around, gyrating across the surfaces, and dust particles flew freely in the air.

Suddenly, the engraved wall began to move downward, slowly, inch by inch. The gap at the top was just a slit at first, but the mechanism gained momentum, and soon it was a foot, then two. A blast of stale air shot out from the darkness on the other side, mingling with air from the outside world for the first time in thousands of years.

The visitors exchanged ecstatic glances while Muhammad simply stared forward into the opening darkness, eyes wide with disbelief and wonder.

When the stone completed its journey, the top was flush with the ground, almost seamlessly. The group waited a moment, gazing into the beyond, wondering what might await. Sean didn't pause long. He turned around, grabbed a flashlight from his gear bag, and started forward. Muhammad grabbed his shoulder, stopping him.

"You must be careful. There could be measures left by the people who built this place."

"I've seen my share of booby traps, Muhammad." Sean grinned and winked. "I'll be careful."

He spun around and pointed his light into the abyss. The LED beam pierced the darkness and stopped on a point forty feet away. It was a wall not dissimilar to those surrounding them. Sean redirected the light to the floor just beyond the portal's threshold and took a wary step forward. The others tucked in close behind him, wielding their own lights to keep the path illuminated.

The dusty air tickled their noses, and a few rebellious particles found their way into Tommy's lungs, causing him to cough violently for a moment. He raised the collar of his T-shirt over his nose as a filter and pressed on.

In the bluish light, the four realized they were in a perfectly circular room, carved immaculately from the bedrock beneath the city. The walls stopped at about eight feet, where the domed ceiling rose to a point thirty feet high in its center.

Muhammad, ironically, was puzzled by the room's design. Even in the darkness, his face visibly contorted into a questioning expression. "I don't understand," he said, his head turning quickly back and forth as he examined the architecture. "This room is a Muslim design. I don't understand. Daniel was a Hebrew prophet."

Adriana nodded her agreement, though she ignored his confused looks and walked slowly toward the middle of the room. Sean was right next to her, moving in tandem. A stone sarcophagus, eight feet in length, was the target of their prowl.

"Actually," Tommy said, still eyeing the walls and ceiling, "it would make perfect sense. When the Babylonians were captured, many of their priests, military minds, and leaders were put to death. Nebuchadnezzar was already dead, and his successors largely failed. Belshazzar, a drunken fool, was left in his place to run things while his father, another weak ruler, ran off to Palestine to establish a colony. According to the story, Daniel foretold the empire's demise after a strange hand appeared in the throne room and wrote it on the wall."

"Which is where the term, 'writing on the wall,' came from." Sean added. As he stepped closer to the long box, his eyes remained locked on an object that sat on its top.

Tommy stopped what he was doing and moved toward the stunning alabaster sarcophagus as well. "Right. Anyway, the Medes and Persians were led by Cyrus, a Persian. He allowed Daniel to live and brought him into his council. If one of the Persian kings designed this burial chamber for Daniel, that would explain why it appears to be an early Muslim design."

Muhammad nodded. "Fascinating."

"Yeah, and a little long. Try to shorten it next time," Sean joked. His voice bounced off the walls and ceiling.

"Hilarious," Tommy said, nearing the box.

Sean reached out to the object atop the creamy-white sarcophagus. It was a small cube, and its yellowish color was unmistakable. The little container was made of pure gold. It was grimy and dusty from centuries underground, but it was nonetheless remarkable.

"What is that?" Tommy asked, the whites of his eyes gleaming in the flashlight's pale glow.

Sean took a deep breath. "I think it's what we've been looking for."

The cube had a lid pressed firmly into the main portion, and it took a few seconds before he could wriggle it free.

Muhammad came close and stared along with the others as Sean opened the cube. They all held their breath, uncertain of what would be within. As the lid came free, their beams fell upon an incredible, and at the same time, unspectacular sight. Two stones, one white and one black, lay within the cube.

"The Urim and the Thummim," Adriana said reverently, her voice barely a whisper.

Sean reached a hand in and picked up the stones. Suddenly, an unfamiliar voice stopped him cold.

"Put the stones back in the box, please." The accent was faintly Middle Eastern, but the English was perfectly clear.

Sean froze in place for a second while the other three spun round. Tommy instinctively reached for his gun but realized that would be a mistake. Seven gunmen, dressed in black and wearing scarves over their faces and headlamps on their foreheads, had pistols aimed in their direction. Adriana sensed the danger and twisted her head around slowly to assess the situation. Muhammad put his hands up instantly, obviously unaccustomed to being in such a spot.

"Don't make me ask you again." The man in the center of the gunmen was the one giving the orders. He was dressed similarly to the others but wore nothing across his face. His tanned skin, dark hair, and facial structure belied his Arab descent. He held his weapon, identical to the other six, down at his waist with hands crossed.

Sean let out a sigh and did as he was told. The stones clanked at the bottom of the metal cube.

"Thank you," the man said. "Now all of you move away from the sarcophagus. Over there to the left will be fine." He pointed in the direction he wanted the group to go.

"No sudden movements," one of the gunmen ordered.

Sean knew the second speaker must have been Sharouf, the second in command.

"I had a feeling you'd follow us here, Mamoud," Sean said as he and the others inched their way over to the wall. "I have to say, I was starting to wonder if you'd got lost."

"Always the cocky American, even when you stand in the face of death and failure." Mamoud's expression remained stoically unimpressed.

"It seems to have worked for me so far."

Tommy and Adriana kept their eyes narrowed, watching the situation develop.

Mamoud turned around and jerked an older man forward. The prisoner was dressed in a white linen shirt and light cream-colored linen pants. "You wanted to see those stones so badly," Mamoud said. "Let's go take a look at your life's work before I bring it to an end."

The older man snorted, but his eyes were full of fear. He looked like he'd not slept for days, and his clothes were wrinkled and dirty.

Sean gave a slow nod to the prisoner, trying to convey that everything would be okay. Nehem's return expression was one of bewilderment, clearly wondering how that was possible.

Mamoud raised his weapon and jammed it in the archaeologist's back, forcing him forward. "Please, I don't have all day. We have a war to start, and the sooner the better."

The two padded across the floor to the sarcophagus bathed in the light from the gunmen's headlamps and the flashlights the other four still held.

"That's far enough, Nehem," Mamoud said. He shoved the older man aside and pointed his headlamp into the golden box. A sickly smile stretched across his face, and his eyes grew wide as they beheld the two stones. He reached in and picked them up, holding them close to his face to give a closer examination. "Now the power of Israel is in the hands of Abraham's true heir," he nearly whispered the sentence. He turned so that his prisoner could see the stones. "With these, I will always be a step ahead of my enemies."

Nehem didn't say a word as he gazed upon the precious stones. Every instinct within him said to snatch them and make a break for the door, a move that would be certain suicide. Mamoud must have sensed his thoughts as he withdrew a half step.

"Go stand over there with the others," Mamoud ordered.

Nehem hesitated but obeyed, slinking over to where Sean and the others were huddled by the wall.

"What now, Mamoud?" Sean asked. "I mean, what exactly is your plan? You said you wanted a war. War with whom?"

In the residual light of his headlamp, Mamoud's face took on a sinister expression. "You shouldn't worry about such things, Sean Wyatt. You and your friends will be dead, buried in this tomb along with the Hebrew heretic within this box." He tapped on the sarcophagus.

"Maybe. But I've always had a curious nature."

Mamoud considered the question for a minute. He looked down at the stones in his hand and then at the floor. Distant, painful memories seeped into his mind. "When I was in college, during the aftermath of the 9/11 attacks, my mother was visiting a friend in one of the towns on the outskirts of Baghdad. She was there on a mission, helping to give food to homeless people. She was kindhearted and always helped others. On day three of the invasion, a drone mistakenly dropped a bomb on the compound where she was working." A twinge of distant pain scratched his voice.

"My mother was one of thousands of innocent people the United States and its friends have murdered. You sit there in your cozy living rooms watching CNN coverage of the devastation like it was a video game, never thinking that every building your army destroys has an innocent janitor, a security guard, an ordinary person just trying to make an honest living. It is time that America and its allies face the same fate. You want to know with whom I will wage war?" He paused for a moment and rubbed the stones with his thumb. "I will wage it with the world. You think your people, your media, your governments know terror? You think they know pain?" He lifted his head and stared through Sean's eyes. "You haven't seen anything yet."

36
Susa

Mamoud motioned to one of his men carrying a black duffle bag. "Bring me the Hoshen," he barked.

The gunman obeyed and hurried over to where his employer stood. He set the bag on top of the sarcophagus and awaited further orders. Mamoud motioned for him to join the others. Once the minion was back in position, Mamoud spun around and unzipped the bag. He stuffed his gun into his belt and reached in with both hands, pulling out the golden breastplate with the twelve stones imbedded in the front. He held it up, admiring it as the shiny metal glimmered in the glow of the artificial light.

"It's an impressive piece," he said. His voice reverberated off the walls. "And it will bring about the downfall of the infidels." He laid it gently on the flat stone and placed the Urim and the Thummim at the top edge of the breastplate.

Sharouf's eyes flicked back and forth between his targets and his employer while the gun in his hands remained trained on the five huddled by the wall.

Mamoud gazed at the relics as if wondering what to do next.

Sean snorted a laugh. "Don't know how it works, do you?"

Mamoud's eyes barely lifted, peering under the lids at the American. "Oh, I know how it works. I was just considering what question to ask first. And now I believe I have one."

He put his hands out wide with palms up and tilted his head toward the ceiling with eyes closed. "Mighty Allah, show me your will. Will I kill these infidels this day?" He waited for a moment and then looked back down at the relics. The silence crushed him as he waited. But nothing happened.

He raised his hands higher and prayed again. "Great Allah, will I kill these infidels this day for your glory?" His voice boomed through the chamber this time.

Sean could feel the weight of his gun hanging over his shoulder. Every instinct inside him wanted to draw down on the villain and end this right here and now. To do so would get him and the others cut down instantly, though. So he waited and used his sense of humor instead.

"I'm guessing right now is when something is supposed to happen, right?"

Mamoud looked down again. Still, the relics showed no signs of changing. The look on his face switched in seconds to one of terrible concern. His eyes widened in disbelief. "It should have worked. Why is it not working?"

Sean shrugged. "It happens to every guy sooner or later. You know, one in three have trouble performing—"

"Shut up!" Mamoud commanded.

Sean stopped talking but offered a sheepish grin to top off the insult.

"You," he pointed at Nehem. "What is wrong with this? Why isn't it answering me?"

Nehem shrugged. He truly didn't know the answer, but he offered one nonetheless. "Perhaps all the stories about those objects were merely legends, myths created by the priesthood in Israel to keep the people under control. Or maybe it doesn't work for someone like you, a man of evil intentions."

Flames roared through Mamoud's eyes. He looked back down at the objects and picked up the white stone. He examined it closely for several seconds and then threw it on the ground. The piece shattered into hundreds of pieces. His hand went to his gun, and he jerked it out of his belt, pointing it at Sean. Nehem desperately stuck out his hand as if doing so would somehow piece the broken stone back together.

"Very clever, Sean. You swapped out the stones." He put out his other hand and motioned with his fingers for the American to come forward. "Bring them to me, slowly."

Sean's eyes were slits. "Suppose I don't?"

"I can always just kill you and take them from you."

"You're going to kill us anyway. So what's the difference?"

Mamoud pursed his lips and nodded. "That's true. But you will have to watch your friends die first. I think I'll start with the girl." He steered the barrel to where Adriana was standing defiantly to the right of Tommy and the others. She had the same look on her face that Sean did, the look of a snake waiting to strike when the moment presented itself.

"Okay, take it easy. I'll give them to you." He held his hands up slowly, palms facing forward. "I have to reach in my pocket to get them."

"I know you're armed. Take out your gun first, set it on the ground, and move away."

"Just now thinking of that?" Tommy snipped.

"Tommy, relax," Sean said in a half-joking tone. "Remember, he's not a professional. I'm guessing Mr. Al Najaar here is new to the kidnapping, hostage-taking, world terror game. Cut him some slack."

"Shut up!" Mamoud's voice shook with urgency. "All of you, remove your weapons, and put them on the ground. If anyone tries to be a cowboy, my men and I will kill you where you stand."

Sean nodded and did as he was told. He pulled his pistol out and laid it on the ground. His companions did the same as Muhammad and Nehem watched out of the corners of their eyes.

"Good," Mamoud said when he was satisfied they were unarmed. "All of you take two steps toward my men over there." The group obeyed again, putting themselves several feet away from the guns on the floor.

"Now bring me the stones," Mamoud beckoned, motioning with his fingers.

Sean kept his hands out and moved cautiously toward the sarcophagus. He stopped at the head of the heavy stone box and waited to see what Mamoud would say next.

"Put them on the lid," he motioned with a tilt of the head.

Sean bit his lower lip and let out a sigh. He lowered his right hand and shoved it into the pocket where he'd deposited the stones a few minutes before. He felt the smooth, rounded pieces and withdrew his hand once he had both. They had an odd warmth that he'd not noticed before. He stretched out his fist and opened his fingers to set them on the sarcophagus. Everyone's eyes locked in on the eerie sight as Sean placed the items on the surface. The black stone emanated a strange, purplish glow that lit up the immediate area.

Mamoud's breath came quick and heavy, but he didn't falter. "Move away from the stones. Now!" He waved his weapon, motioning for Sean to return to the side. His eyes kept drifting back to the strange objects.

Sean hesitated for a second, also mesmerized by the odd light. "You know," he said, taking a wary step back, "the black one means the answer to your question was no."

Mamoud's nostrils flared. His face twisted in a frown, and his head snapped to the side for a second. "What? What do you mean?"

"You asked if you would kill us today. I'm guessing you figured it was a given. According to those relics, looks like it isn't." Sean nodded at the stones as he took another step away.

The young Arab cocked his head to the side. "Oh?" he said and raised the weapon, taking aim at Sean's head. "I assure you. It is."

A flicker of light passed across the room as a shadow moved through the floodlights in the antechamber. Mamoud turned his head to see what caused the anomaly, but it was already too late. The sound of a silenced pistol popped through the room, the bullet ripping through the forehead of his gunman on the right-hand side of the doorway. Another weapon fired from a different position, but it had the same result, its round piercing through the right cheek of another gunman. The remaining four henchmen reacted quickly, immediately realizing the danger. They spun around in unison and opened fire, choosing to shoot first and aim second. The mystery attackers landed one more round in the shoulder of a third gunman before retreating to cover on either side of the entrance. Tommy wasn't sure, but he thought he recognized the silhouettes.

The distraction was the opening Sean had been waiting for. He took two quick steps and launched himself across the remaining six feet. His shoulder planted into Mamoud's right arm. It jolted the weapon from his hand. The gun clacked on the floor just before the two bodies crashed into the hard stone a few feet away. Mamoud shrieked from the sudden impact and subsequent sharp pain in his shoulder. Sean's momentum sent him rolling off his target, but he was quick to get back on his feet and resume the assault. He swung his boot at Mamoud's face. The Arab winced but found enough strength to raise both hands to block the strike. He shifted his weight and grabbed Sean's foot and then twisted it hard, using Sean's inertia against him. With his boot jerked at an awkward angle, Sean's body spun in midair, doing a complete three-sixty before he fell to the ground with a thud. His hands and elbows struck the surface first.

Adriana's reaction to the strangers' ambush was instantaneous. She'd managed to keep the tomahawk out of sight during their capture.

She grabbed it from its belt holster and rushed the nearest gunman while he was preoccupied with the shooters. His back was exposed, a fact she took immediate advantage of. Adriana felt the perfectly balanced weight of the tomahawk in her hand as she darted forward and swung the deadly weapon's sharp edge at the villain's back. The blade sank deep into his tissue and stuck into the shoulder blade. He yelped in agony and slouched forward. She wasn't done yet. Her hands worked quickly, yanking the tomahawk out of the bloody target. She whipped it up, spun the man around, and struck hard with the spike, driving the black steel straight into the man's heart. His eyes flared in shock before the body fell limp to the floor in a heap. Adriana bent down on one knee, worked her weapon free, and scooped the fallen gunman's pistol from his fingers just as Tommy charged by, a whoosh of air following him.

The man he was targeting had sensed danger when his partner screamed a few moments before. He'd already turned around, but his reaction was too slow. Tommy leaped at him with a flying sidekick, his boot heel striking the man in the chest. The blow sent the gunman crashing into the wall, momentarily stunned. Tommy used the moment to his advantage and threw a haymaker of an uppercut, landing it right under the gunman's jaw. The target's head snapped back accompanied by a sickening smacking sound. The unconscious gunman slumped against the wall, his knees buckling under the dead weight.

"Heads up!" Adriana shouted.

The two remaining henchmen on the other side of the room realized the imminent threat and turned their attention to Tommy and Adriana. Tommy was the first target they acquired and drew down on. With no cover, nowhere to run, and no weapon at the ready, Tommy had to think fast. He ducked down, grabbed the unconscious henchman, and spun the body around to use as a human shield.

His move wasn't a second too soon. The gunmen opened fire, peppering the body with a spray of deadly metal. One bullet ripped through the man's arm and clipped Tommy's shoulder, but he held tight until the popping sounds turned to clicks, their magazines empty.

Adriana stole the moment and stepped forward, firing on the two exposed killers and taking one out at the knee and chest. The other one took two rounds in the gut before a bullet pierced his forehead, sending a red splash onto the wall behind him.

Sean pushed himself off the floor, though his elbows throbbed painfully. Mamoud regained his balance and saw Sean regrouping. The Arab's eyes flashed toward his gun on the floor. Sean caught the glance and knew what the man would do next. The two dove simultaneously for the gun, both hands hitting it and sending it sliding away.

The popping sounds from the gunfight had ceased. Through his peripheral vision, Sean saw that Adriana and Tommy were okay, which meant they'd taken out the rest of Mamoud's men.

He grappled with his opponent, their hands swatting and swinging at each other as they rolled on the floor, each trying to stretch out for the weapon they believed was their salvation. Sean grabbed Mamoud's wrists and pulled him close, but the madman gained the advantage and rolled over on top of him. He punched Sean on the cheek, opening a fresh cut on his face. He attempted a second, but Sean forced up a forearm and blocked it. Sean grabbed the other arm and pulled Mamoud close, head butting him in the nose.

The Arab leaned back, but Sean didn't let go, bashing the man's nose against his head again and sending a fresh surge of pain through his opponent's face. Blood oozed from the broken appendage, and tears poured from his eyes.

Adriana watched with her weapon drawn. Mamoud managed to wriggle free and lean back. She had a clear shot and pulled the trigger. The gun clicked. "Crap." She tossed the weapon aside and picked up the tomahawk again.

Mamoud swung his arms wildly, landing a blow against the side of Sean's head and another on his jaw, followed by some striking him in the ribs and gut, most blocked by the American's forearms. The brute ferocity of the attack signaled Mamoud's desperation.

Sean shifted his weight and whipped his legs around, a move that threw his opponent clear and sent him rolling to a sudden stop against the sarcophagus. Sean popped up and assumed a crouching martial arts position, ready to finish the fight. He realized that Mamoud had stopped only a few feet away from one of his pistols. Unarmed, Sean would be an easy target, and there was no way he could beat him to it this time.

"Sean," Adriana shouted. He glanced left. She tossed the tomahawk in a dramatic arc.

Sean snatched it out of the air and whirled around instantly, flinging the deadly weapon at his crawling target. The blade rolled through the air in a blur and struck Mamoud at the base of his neck. He grunted and collapsed, grasping at the foreign object protruding from his body. He rolled onto his back and clutched the weapon by the handle, debating on whether or not to remove it. Mamoud knew the grim truth. The blade was dripping with blood, but the second he took it out, his life would spew forth and end in seconds.

Sean and the others moved quickly over to where the dying man lay. He looked up at them with enraged disdain. His eyes flashed rage, but he was helpless. A sickly laugh escaped his lips even as his body trembled. "Killing me won't stop the war from coming. My ships are already on their way." He coughed. Blood from the broken nose covered his face, and he spat his words. "My drones will rain death on the Western empire, and no one will be able to stop it. You lose, American."

"I don't think so, Mamoud. We know about your ships. At this very moment, a coordinated effort among global agencies is making sure your drones are safely grounded." Sean crossed his arms. His ribs ached, and he winced from the shot he took on the jaw, but he was okay. He stared at the dying man with his usual sly grin. "It's over, Mamoud. *You* lose."

Mamoud's eyes widened. Tears filled them, and he grimaced. "That is impossible."

"Actually," Tommy jumped in, "this is kind of what we do. Foil the plans of evil masterminds and such."

Mamoud struggled to breathe. Blood was oozing down his neck at a steady pace now. He knew there was only one thing left to do. "May Allah have his vengeance on you."

He closed his eyes and yanked the tomahawk out of his neck. His eyes shot open again as blood spurted out onto the floor and the side of the sarcophagus, fast at first, but as the seconds went by, it slowed, eventually to a steady trickle. Finally, Mamoud's head drooped to the side, and his body went limp.

A shuffling sound came from the entryway, and the group spun around as two silhouettes entered, surrounded by the bright light from the antechamber. As they drew closer, the faces were revealed from the shadows.

"Cut it a little close there, Mac," Sean said, grinning.

"You're welcome," Joe said, returning the smile.

Helen holstered her weapon and stepped over to Sean. "We hung back to make sure they didn't know we were around. Looks like they didn't figure on you having us follow them while they were following you." She put a finger to his cheek. "You're going to need to put some ice or a steak on that. Don't want it to swell."

Sean chuckled. "I'll get around to it."

Joe and Helen looked down at the dead madman. "Was that true what you said about global agencies taking down his ships?"

Sean nodded. "I hope so. Emily is on it. Knowing her, that means it's probably done. From the sounds of it, she put a ton of resources into the operation." He sighed, just now starting to catch his breath. "Their little scheme is done."

Muhammad's confusion was written all over his face. "I don't understand," he said, pointing at Joe and Helen. "You had them follow you? Don't get me wrong, Mac, I'm glad to see you. Very glad. And you as well, Helen." He changed his expression to one of gratitude and bowed low to both.

"Yeah," Joe said, "Sean knew where they were headed, but he also knew Mamoud and his friends probably had no idea where to go once they got to Susa. If they were left to their own devices, they'd have been rummaging around the tourist site above us." He motioned to the ceiling with a flick of the head.

Nehem listened to the conversation, standing behind the others. He turned his eyes to the mysterious stones resting on the sarcophagus and moved closer. He noticed for the first time a thin engraving on the lid. The others noticed he'd turned his attention to the box and watched as he ran a finger along the lettering. "Here lies Daniel, a servant of the one true God," he read aloud.

Sean and Tommy passed each other a knowing smile.

The Israeli archaeologist turned his attention to the breastplate. He picked it up with the greatest of reverence and stared at it for a long moment. No one said a word, letting him have the time he wanted with a relic he'd chased for so long. A tear trickled down the side of Nehem's face. He quickly wiped it away and turned to Sean. "Thank you, all of you, for this."

Sean gave a single nod; his satisfied grin said enough.

Then Nehem turned to Muhammad. "Long ago, our people were brothers. We came from the same father. You are my brother. I thank you."

Muhammad bowed his head low. "The side of good does not choose religions, races, or countries. It only chooses good. These men had evil intentions. It is a shame the few discredit the many. But I thank you for your gratitude."

The two smiled at each other for a second, and then Tommy interrupted. "So, not to put a damper on this tender moment, but we're surrounded by a bunch of dead bodies. Any chance we could take this party somewhere else?"

Adriana shook her head and punched him in the good shoulder.

"What?" he genuinely looked offended. "I'm just saying."

Helen interjected. "And there's the matter of the young woman we found in their vehicle. She was unconscious but alive. They'd left her in the back, not sure why. We put her in our van for safekeeping. It's warm in there, but she'll be fine."

Nehem's eyes perked up. "A young woman? What did she look like? You said she's alive?"

Joe nodded. "Yep. You think you know her?"

Tears welled in the corners of Nehem's eyes. His voice trembled. "My daughter."

37
Jerusalem
Two Months Later

"That's a remarkable contraption," Sean said. He stared at a case made from three-inch thick glass. Inside, the Hoshen gleamed in the yellowish gallery light. On the opposite side of the room, the two stones sat on a pedestal in a similar case.

"Thank you," Nehem said, beaming with pride. "They were both designed to lower the artifacts to one of two locations. Same as the Isaiah scroll, there is a safe level, and then there is a research level, all deep below ground. The three pieces we found are still undergoing evaluation and analysis."

Following the events in Susa, Nehem had extracted the artifacts in secret. He wasn't about to let the Iranian government get their hands on what he believed rightfully belonged to the people of Israel. He knew that if that happened, the relics would be put in a basement somewhere, or worse. Based on the interaction of the stones with the breastplate, there was something mysterious and potentially dangerous going on.

Once the group left the country, Muhammad set about sealing up the entrance to the tomb. He reasoned that anyone who wanted to pay homage to Daniel could do it in the tourist spot above ground. No one needed to know about the actual crypt. Sean and the others agreed. Within a week, the entire antechamber was blocked off with cinder blocks and concrete.

At the new display's opening ceremony, Tommy was standing nearby, next to Adriana. He raised a suspicious eyebrow. "I hope your scientists aren't trying to figure out a way to replicate it and put it to military use."

Nehem shrugged, stretching out the cream-colored suit he'd chosen for the opening ceremony. "I honestly do not know. I can only speak for my research team. We want to know how it works. We've never seen anything like it."

"Neither have we," Sean interjected.

"Right," Nehem agreed. "And we owe it to ourselves to at least ask the questions. Don't we?"

"Doctor," Adriana said, "those relics are in their rightful place. We trust that you and your government won't do anything foolish."

Tommy seemed irritated, but he pushed those feelings aside. "Well, either way, Israel is an American ally, so I guess at least we're on the right side."

Nehem raised a playful eyebrow and nodded. "Indeed." His eyes drifted over to the opposite side of the room. His daughter stood by the wall, talking to a pair of the honored guests. Her bright smile charming everyone within fifteen feet.

Sean spent the next half hour shaking hands with diplomats, archaeologists, researchers, and curious visitors. Gradually, he let himself slip through the mob and out the door. The late afternoon sun splashed onto his face and instantly warmed his skin. He realized how cool the inside of the museum was kept, probably more for the protection of ancient artifacts than the comfort of the visitors.

He put on his sunglasses and strolled leisurely over to a railing that looked out over the city. White apartments and office buildings towered in the distance among the sprawl of smaller, similarly colored dwellings. Dark-green cypress trees waved in the breeze nearby. Sean stopped at the polished steel railing and rested his hands on it. Behind him, the bright-white stone of the museum reflected the sunlight in the corners of his sunglasses.

He'd only been standing alone for a minute before he realized someone was behind him.

"That's good work you did, taking down all of those shipping vessels." He didn't turn around as he spoke. He didn't need to. Sean knew who was standing behind him. Partly because Emily always wore the same perfume. She'd worn it for years.

She didn't bother asking how he knew it was her. She just assumed he was good. "I appreciate the compliment."

"It's why you're the director."

She drew in a deep breath and then sighed. "Take a few weeks off, Sean. Enjoy some time with your lady friend. Relax. See the Holy Land or something."

"I've seen it." He stared out at the setting. "Seems like every time I try to kick off my shoes and relax, something happens. Adriana said she needs to check in on her father. Apparently, he got a troubling text message from someone."

Emily's face scrunched in concern as she leaned over and rested her elbows on the rail. "Troubling?"

"Yeah. She didn't elaborate much. But she'll be on the next flight out of here to meet him."

"Isn't he in Ecuador or something?"

Sean shook his head. "Not anymore. From the sound of it, he's on the move."

"You going to help her?"

"I offered." He shook his head again. "But she wants to take care of it herself. I try to respect her wishes. Adriana can handle herself."

Silence fell over the conversation, filled only with the sound of the wind rustling through the trees and washing over the hillside amid the distant noise of vehicular traffic.

"I don't suppose you have a job for me?" he blurted.

She snorted a laugh and bowed her head. "No. Not right now. We're busy cleaning up all the fallout from this one." She paused for a minute before saying, "You know, you saved a lot of lives. Possibly millions. We found enough munitions and explosives to take out entire sections of major cities. By the time the air forces responded, a lot of people would have died."

"Yeah. That's what bothers me," he said.

She patted him on the back and started to head back into the museum. "It's why we're here, Sean. It's why you came back. It's why I always knew you'd come back."

"And why you bugged me all those years." He smirked as he said it.

"Yep."

"Well, you know you can call me when you're in a pinch." He stood up straight and faced her. "Hopefully, that isn't too often. No offense. The less I hear from you, the better. Means the world isn't going crazy."

She smiled and reached out both arms, wrapping them around his strong shoulders. He returned the gesture and hugged her back. A moment later, Emily was walking away, her heels clicking on the concrete as she approached the museum.

Adriana and Tommy passed her as they exited the building, shaking her hand and bidding her goodbye before joining Sean. Adriana wore a tight black dress with matching heels and a silver belt hanging just below her hips. She looked ravishing as the two walked toward Sean. Tommy less so, with his plaid button-up shirt nearly untucked and mismatched with the standard tweed blazer he seemed to wear at all formal occasions.

Adriana spoke first. "I have to go see about my father." Her dark eyes mesmerized him like a chocolate whirlpool sucking him down into a delicious death.

"I know," he forced a smile. "I understand. Go take care of him. I know you will. Call me if you need me." He offered the last bit even though he knew she was too proud to do such a thing.

Her eyes narrowed, and a narrow grin crossed her lips like a lion about to devour its prey. "Oh, I need you. But that will have to wait."

"Thank goodness," Tommy cut in as the two moved closer together, lips brushing each other.

Both heads twisted in his direction simultaneously. "Do you mind?" Sean asked. He didn't wait for an answer, instead turning back to her and pressing his lips firmly against hers. Ten seconds went by that felt like an hour to Tommy. Finally, they let go, and Adriana left, winding her way down the path and back to where the cars were parked.

Sean watched her until she disappeared behind a row of shrubs and small trees. Tommy stepped closer to him and clapped his hand on his friend's shoulder.

"You're a lucky man."

Sean chuckled. "I would be if I could keep her around for more than a few days at a time."

The two stared after her even though she was gone from sight.

"You knew the situation when you got involved. She's not the settling down type. Not yet anyway."

"I know."

"But you're hoping that someday she might be."

"Maybe."

Tommy's head turned, and he eyed his friend suspiciously. "You know, Sean, you're not the settling down type either."

Sean's lips parted in a grin, and he looked over at Tommy. "I know. But I'm hoping someday I might be."

Did you enjoy this book?

If so, swing by Amazon, Kobo, iTunes, or Barnes and Noble, and leave a review. Reviews really help people decide whether or not a book is right for them. Authors also depend on reviews to help keep things rolling so more stories can be written for years to come.

Thanks again for reading this novel.

Don't worry, Sean, Tommy, and Adriana will return...

GET FREE BOOKS
Grab the Ernest Dempsey Starter Library
for FREE.
A full length novel and two novellas, just for
joining the free VIP reader group.
Find out more here: ernestdempsey.net

OTHER BOOKS BY ERNEST DEMPSEY

SEAN WYATT THRILERS:

THE SECRET OF THE STONES (GET IT FREE)
THE CLERIC'S VAULT
THE LAST CHAMBER
THE GRECIAN MANIFESTO
THE NORSE DIRECTIVE
GAME OF SHADOWS
WAR OF THIEVES TRILOGY: AN ADRIANA VILLA THRILLER

SCIENCE FICTION/FANTASY:

THE DREAM RIDER
THE DREAM RIDER 2: RETRIBUTION

373

DEDICATION

For my great friend, Jacob "FedEx" Stout. Thanks for always talking things through with me and being there to push me forward.

SPECIAL THANKS

As always, I have to thank my terrific editors, Anne Storer and Jason Whited, for their tireless and precise work to make my books the best they can be. I'd also like to thank the members of my launch team. Their resilient support and encouragement never ceases to make me smile. In addition, a huge thank you goes out to Frank Paine for his consulting on international affairs and travel.

Author Notes
Fact vs. Fiction

Readers seem to enjoy finding out which things are fact and which things are created from an author's imagination. I know I like to do the same as a reader.

In this book there are many places where fiction and fact are intertwined closely. This makes discerning what is real and fake a difficult thing to do.

All of the characters are fictional, created in my imagination, with one exception. Daniel was a very real person. Not only is his existence documented in several Scriptures but Cuneiform tablets have been discovered in ancient Babylon that state he was to be the king of the entire empire should the king and his son be killed. This is an amazing piece of evidence to the incredible rise to power Daniel experienced.

He was a student in Jerusalem, taken as a captive to a foreign land, and then made such impressions on the leadership that he was made the third most powerful person in the known world at the time. Pretty cool stuff!

The relics known as the Hoshen, Urim, and Thummim have been a fascinating study for me for the last decade. While archaeologists, treasure hunters, and many others search desperately for the Ark of the Covenant, I was always just as interested in these holy relics that seemed to disappear at about the same time as the Ark.

Though no one is certain where the three objects are, there is no question to their mysterious powers that were documented in the Bible's Old Testament. As to how the devices/relics worked, that is left to speculation. Was it moved by the power of a deity or were quantum physics at play? We may never know in this lifetime.

The tomb of the high priest in Jerusalem is a little fact and a little fiction. I changed the exact location and the name of the priest but recently, researchers have discovered a high priest's tomb from around the time of the Babylonian era. The details within the tomb were a figment of my imagination.

The great temple in Yogyakarta is believed to be one of the oldest in Buddhism and as of the date of writing this, is touted as the birthplace of the religion by many.

There are tunnels within the temple. Most are only seen by those who work there. The entire sequence surrounding the massive stupa at the top was concocted by me. While there may be something inside one of the stupas, I am not aware of a way in or out.

The Tiger's Nest monastery is located in one of the most beautiful places in the world. Bhutan could be one of Asia's best-kept secrets in the travel industry. The dramatic mountain views, lush forests, and natural beauty are all worth visiting. The monastery itself is open to visits and on the other side of the bridge is a cafeteria and visitor's area.

There is, to my knowledge, no secret tunnel leading into the mountain, although I'm sure the monks would be happy to talk to you about it.

Susa in Iran is considered to be the burial location for the prophet, Daniel. It is visited frequently by travelers but getting into the country can be tricky, especially for Americans.

Relations between the U.S. and Iran have been poor for decades and it doesn't seem there is any end of that in sight, which is unfortunate. Iran is a beautiful country and Tehran's location is unique and breathtaking.

As far as technology and encryption decoding goes, Tara and Alex use a fictional piece of technology I call a hyper quantum algorithmic processing or, HQAP.

The world of quantum computing is not fictional, it is very real and developing at a rapid pace.

With HQAP, people would have the ability to run billions of sequences, codes, and possibilities in a fraction of the time as a normal processor. If you're wondering whether or not the government is working on this sort of thing, that is anybody's guess. In my stories, however, the Tommy's finances enabled him to build computers that could effectively break down highly encrypted databases in a short amount of time.

This goes against the Snowden report. Or does the Snowden report go against HQAP?

I hope this answers some of the questions you may have had for the story. If you'd like to know more, you can always contact me through my website ernestdempsey.net or through Facebook or Twitter.

Table of Contents

ISBN: 978-0-9963122-4-0

Made in the USA
Coppell, TX
03 June 2021

56804726R00222